ENEMY
CALLING
DESCENT

ERIK BILICKI

Outskirts Press, Inc.
Denver, Colorado

Outskirts Press
http://www.outskirtspress.com

ISBN-10: 1-59800-394-1
ISBN-13: 978-1-59800-394-9

Outskirts Press and the "OP" logo are trademarks belonging to
Outskirts Press, Inc.

Printed in the United States of America

For Jennifer, Grace, and Noah,
around whom my universe revolves.

ACKNOWLEDGMENTS

Thanks to Bryan for introducing me to the world of RPGs when we were young, from which grew my fascination with fantasy worlds and the possibilities they presented. Many thanks to my friends and family, each of whom have influenced my life in one way or another and unknowingly guided me on the path to writing this book. Thank you to my parents, who introduced me to science fiction at a young age, and to my brother Scott who helped to stimulate my imagination as we grew up. And last, but not least, a special thank you to my wife, Jennifer, without whom this book wouldn't exist. Your willingness to read and edit my work, as well as the creative input you provided, helped make this come to life. Your encouragement kept me going during the times I wanted to give up on the whole process. Thank you.

PROLOGUE

Lorker Citadel, Je-Fin, Fe-Ruq System, 1500 Local Time

Sergeant Aedge Faerre stood ramrod straight, feet spread shoulder width apart and legs locked at the knees. He held his beam rifle tight across his chest, butt end closer to his right thigh, with the weapon placed diagonally upwards so the business end of the weapon was near the left side of his jaw. All around him, humanoid male and female soldiers of various species all mirrored the same stance. Each faced the same direction in their crimson military uniforms, with polished black boots rising just below the knee where it met black piping that went up each side of the pant legs. The trim continued to the torso as it melded into similar piping that rode up the sides of each soldier's military jacket. For Sergeant Faerre, it was a beautiful sight to behold.

A light rain was beginning to fall on the parade ground, and the generally gray overcast skies had begun to thicken and blacken in the distance. Many of the soldiers in his squad had commented how they should bring their field sack and wear their weather gear instead of their dress reds. It was not an unusual sentiment, taking the planet's weather patterns into consideration. The senior officers were hoping for merely a dry overcast day, but nature was working against them.

The layer of breathable air enveloping the planet of Je-Fin had long been a haven for strong atmospheric disturbances, from constant squalls and months of rain, to ferocious storms that battered coastal areas with intense lightning strikes. Sunny days weren't necessarily a rare occurrence on Je-Fin; just so unpredictable that it was difficult to plan for events outdoors without the fear of getting wet. Because of this, many of the outdoor activities were planned for with rain in mind.

The group of senior officers on the dais far ahead of Sergeant Faerre took turns speaking to the assembled soldiers, trying to turn the opening ceremonies of the military exercise into a rally. The one currently speaking was rambling on about the Shalothans, and their religious beliefs, and how great it was to be a part of the Fe-Ruq system, where the truth was evident. There was no god, the senior officer preached. Only evolution. And therefore, the only ones who could protect their planets, their lifestyles, each of their families from the scourges of the galaxy such as the Shalothans would be the soldiers themselves. The speaker was pointing and waving his arms at the assembled group in an animated way, making a feeble attempt to electrify the crowd. Sergeant Faerre heard, but didn't listen. He knew in his heart there were no such creatures as gods or goddesses, one omnipotent being, one maker of the universe. Logically, if not scientifically, it didn't make sense. He had known nothing else, so this thought process, this certainty of knowing, was second nature to him, as it was to all of those assembled in the stadium. And it all changed in an instant.

The rambling senior officer was in midsentence when a bright light suddenly filled the sky, blinding all who were present. Sergeant Faerre dropped to the ground, instantly positioning himself in a protective stance, pulling his weapon into firing position. He heard the other soldiers around him dropping to the ground as well, and murmurs rose from whispers to questions as the light continued. He squinted against the searing brightness, trying to see the source of the light. He could feel warmth on his skin, and heard other soldiers asking if anyone else could feel the heat. He began to wonder if it was some new weapon variant. Suddenly a voice boomed across the parade ground:

Behold the Son of God!

CHAPTER I

Commander Tennison looked up at the star-filled night, and then checked his personal locator device. If the PLD crew had gotten the orbital sensor packets dropped in time, the PLD satellites should have settled into their orbits by now. Which meant the PLD should be working, yet all that Marshall saw on his was the little flashing symbol that showed it was trying to pick up the signal from one of the orbiting satellites.

"Lieutenant, check the PLD on the *Spirit* and see if that one can pick up anything. Anyone else have a signal yet?"

A diminutive man hunched over a data tablet slightly turned his face towards Marshall and gave a slight frown. "Commander, it should have been active before we even crashed. They're not coming." He turned back to his data tablet and let his fingers continue gliding over the controls.

Marshall let his gaze linger over the man for a moment before abruptly turning and walking over to the entry platform of the *Alaurian Spirit*. Looking up at the side of the ship, he could see the gaping hole created by the weapon that finally penetrated the shield array. Carbon scoring from the suborbital battle partially blacked out the name of the ship, *Alaurian Spirit*. Smoke still poured out of the damaged vessel as the Emergency Response Crew (ERC) robots circled the ship, dousing it in fire retardants. Letting his gaze wander to the left, he could see more ERC droids processing the human remains of those that hadn't survived the battle, including the clone of the commander himself. That loss alone was enough to render Marshall suicidal. After all, once a soldier had lost his clone body, his chances of surviving life-threatening injuries decreased greatly. With no body to harvest blood, tissue, or limbs from, the medical droids would have no means to repair major damage or internal injuries.

"Commander, we have to make a decision. What's it going to be?" Marshall broke his gaze to turn and face the man standing behind him. He couldn't remember if this was the clone of Ensign Theore or the original himself. He'd have to review the casualty log later. Right now, the only task he needed to do was answer the question.

"Pull the information on this hemisphere from the mapping probes and do a quadrant search for any sizable mountains. The message indicated a sizable mountain, so we know where he's at, and we're going after him."

"Sir, you can't be serious." Marshall cut him off with a wave of his hand.

"Ensign Theore, either follow orders or report to the security droid. Either way, you better move out of my way now!"

"Sir, you're chasing the Son of God!"

Marshall glared into the eyes of the man before him, waited a few seconds and breathed, "I know". Commander Marshall Tennison then spun on his heel to gather his gear before beginning the chase for his prey.

Two weeks earlier:

United Space Federation (USF) Naval Headquarters, 1017 Local Time

"Captain Pollard, welcome, and please, have a seat." The man waved his hand towards one of the visitor chairs in the well-appointed office. The walls, rather, the few that weren't windows, were colored dark beige. The furniture was modern, and a luxuriant Egaran-green carpet covered the floor. The walls contained plaques and certificates of various types, while the smaller wall featured a door, with a starship diagram framed and hung neatly in the center of the available space.

Captain Angelina Pollard nodded and sat down to the right of the desk. Pollard was a veteran military starship captain, and her experience was well known to the man who called this room his office. The captain, in her midforties, was physically fit (as required by the United Navy), but was otherwise unremarkable in appearance. Her hair was shoulder-length, but she wore it up in a more efficient manner. Her naturally auburn hair had started graying, with a particularly thick streak just to the left of the center of her head. Her face was squarish with severe lines, and featured a flattened nose resulting from various operational skirmishes during her time in the fleet that had left her nose broken and scarred. Her pale skin could be attributed to either her skin tones or the fact that she had spent all of thirty days off her command ship in the past two years. She was above average in height for a human female, measured by their species at standing just over five foot eight. The stockiness of her body and her no-nonsense demeanor caused her subordinates to sometimes refer to her as "the brickhouse bitch". Unfortunately for them, Angelina found it a source of pride that her crew would think of her that way. It was certainly better than being a captain who was everyone's best friend. It was just as well, because it made her job easier when a crew member would die, either through accident or battle. She hated having to write communications to the family.

Vice Admiral Glenn Caturorglimi sat back in his chair behind the desk and shuffled some papers before speaking. In his late fifties, the man looked much older, and sported a bald head and bushy eyebrows. His neck was short and thick, making his round head look like a ball perched on a tee. He looked over at the captain and offered a slight smile, and then launched into his speech with a deep baritone voice.

"As I'm sure you're wondering why you're here, and knowing that your time is precious, let me cut to the chase. Are you aware of the events that happened on Je-Fin in the Fe-Ruq system forty-eight standard hours ago?"

Captain Pollard shook her head and waited for the Admiral's description of events. He leaned forward and pushed a folder across the desk at Angelina.

"Read it."

Unmarked on the outside, the contents of the thick folder were neatly arranged and sorted using tabs to separate different groups of papers. Angelina began reading the first page, a high-level overview of the situation specifics contained in the folder. The document stated that a contact stationed on Je-Fin with the codename Nova Chaser was a covert observer of the Fe-Ruq government's joint military exercise. The document went on to state that prior to the exercise, within the stadium used for opening ceremonies, a bright white light filled the sky, and a voice boomed through the sky, *Behold the Son of God.* The document ended by stating that several means of recording, as well as multiple personal accounts, corroborated that this happened.

Angelina glanced up at the Admiral and raised an eyebrow. He nodded and motioned with his hand for her to keep going. The second set of documents were transcripts of communications between ground troops at the stadium and orbital defense stations. Just from reading some of the communications, it was obvious the light and the voice, whatever it was or where it originated from, created immediate chaos and panic. Each of the orbital defense stations had experienced a similar event, as well as other nonparticipating military craft in the area.

The following set of documents contained a personal statement from Nova Chaser about the event. Nova Chaser confirmed the light and voice, and additional details revealed information not given out on the com channel. Large numbers of soldiers congregated in the stadium suffered sunburn-like symptoms. Nova Chaser's monitoring equipment was recording at the stadium as well, and analysis revealed that the booming voice could not be heard on any of the recording instruments, nor was the flash of light captured on the image recorder.

Pinching the bridge of her nose between her left forefinger and thumb, she flipped to the last grouping of papers. These were intelligence reports about the responses from different civilizations to the reporting of the event on Je-Fin. Not surprising, there was some sentiment from the Fe-Ruqians that the entire event had been staged by one of their enemies as part of a psych-ops strategy. A military spokesperson even went as far as to dismiss the event as a mass-hallucination, denying any claim of success by the enemy.

The response from the Republic of Shalotha was much more harsh and critical. The majority of the worlds in the Shalotha System were forced into Christianity centuries ago, and the news of what appeared to be the beginning of the Second Coming was met with skepticism and disbelief. The skepticism existed because the distrust between the two systems was deep. The governments of Shalotha and Fe-Ruq had just come to a reluctant peace accord within the past decade, and the tension was cause for an uneasy peace. The disbelief stemmed from the fact that the deeply Christian Shalothans couldn't accept the possibility that the return of The Savior would happen *on their enemy's home planet.*

"Admiral, I assume that at some point my crew and I are being assigned a mission, otherwise you would not have brought me here to show me these documents. What is it that you need us to do?" Captain Pollard closed the folder and placed the package on the corner of the desk, just out of reach of the Admiral.

The directness of Captain Pollard pleased Caturorglimi, however it did not surprise him. He had worked with Pollard on previous missions; even participated on a Special Operations mission with her back when they were both junior officers. It had been a few years since the two of them had met face-to-face, and seeing her reminded him of why she had made Captain so quickly. She was all business.

"The Senate Defense Council has asked the Fleet to immediately dispatch a ship and crew to the Fe-Ruq system for a mission with dual objectives. The first objective is to monitor the situation in the system based on the information that you've just been briefed on. In the best interests of all involved, you will be reassigned to a smaller scout ship, the *Alaurian Spirit*. When you leave this office, you will be given a package containing the crew assignments and further detailed commands as to your secondary mission objective. Both objectives are classified Top Secret at this time, and as such you will have a smaller crew made up entirely of officers. Technical specifications on the *Alaurian Spirit* will be included in your package. Time is of the essence Captain. The Senate fears the Shalothan Imperium may be planning to raid Je-Fin on the belief that the subject has already appeared and is either being held captive or has chosen to align with the planets in the Fe-Ruq system. Protocol for reporting transmissions is detailed in your operational spec packet." The Admiral paused for a moment, searching for any change in the face of the woman sitting across from him. *Not even a change in her posture or breathing when I mentioned she'd be switching commands. She'd be interesting at our poker table*, he thought.

"Admiral, if I may." The Admiral nodded for Captain Pollard to continue. "What is *our* position on what happened at Je-Fin?"

"In summation, the official response from the System Senate is that if this is indeed truly the Son of God, then we welcome Him with open arms and await the return of the King. Behind the official diplomatic facade, most Senators are thinking in the same vein as the Fe-Ruq military – a psych-ops tactic as a pre-emptive strike to a new round in an inter-sector war. Unfortunately, most of our esteemed Senators are politicians only. They can't accept the fact that any advantage gained from that type of attack would have been lost within hours, and would now be worthless since there hasn't been any military or domestic terror operations since the incident.

"And my crew? Who is being assigned as Captain of *The Seraphim*?

"Captain Dante Nicolai from *The Eccentric* has been transferred to your former command, effective today. In fact, we are having a courier pack your personal belongings from the stateroom and take them to your new command. You will report directly to your new command to expedite your departure."

Formalities ensued, with Captain Pollard dismissed in short time. Striding out of the office, an assistant to the Admiral called out from Angelina's left and presented her with a data tablet card and authorization encryption codes. Nodding as a receipt, she took the package and stuffed it into her briefcase as she walked towards the hover-lift terminals. She stated "Shuttle Deck" and the lift smoothly dropped to the correct level.

Stepping out of the lift, she was immersed in a sea of activity, as personnel of all types swarmed past her in the travel aisles and on the flight decks. The shuttle deck itself wasn't a deck at all, but a vast hanger designated for use by transfer shuttles to the orbital stations and other ground bases on the planet. It was also the preferred hangar for visiting dignitaries, and as such was heavily armed with United Space Marines stationed throughout the area. To the left of the lift terminals was a series of glass enclosed meeting rooms with central access and scrolling holonews updates projected on the back wall of each the room. To the right, further down the flight deck was the central Flight Command Center, also known as FCOM. This was the gateway to the base, and all flights arriving or departing had to be cleared through this building. This was her destination, as she needed to get information on which orbital station the *Alaurian Spirit* was docked at, and then take the requisite shuttle up to the dock.

The whine of the antigravity engines powering the shuttles in and out of the bay was just short of deafening, and as such it wasn't recommended that anyone be exposed on the deck for long periods of time. Striding down to FCOM, she put her hands over her ears to blunt the impact of the noise. The crews that worked on the deck regularly had their protective suits and headgear on to protect against the noise, but even then they were rotated out regularly to protect their hearing.

Walking into the FCOM, there were data screens suspended from the ceiling to her right and left showing the orbital station names, with the flight info for arriving and departing shuttles. Since the stations were so vast, it wasn't uncommon to have three or four shuttles listed as arriving and another three to four as departing, all within the same hour. Because of the small capacity of the shuttles, each ship could only transport eight people at a time, not including the pilot.

Angelina went past the screens to a data terminal and pulled up the name of the ship she was looking for. Finding it on the first screen alphabetically, she glanced to the left of the name of the ship to see which orbital station it was berthed at. The station listed was currently flashing a flight backlog of forty minutes, meaning it would give her some time before a shuttle would be available. Tentatively, shuttle USF-187 was assigned to the next departure flight.

Angelina realized she hadn't eaten or drank anything all day, so she asked a nearby officer if there was a mess hall in the FCOM, to which she was directed down to an adjoining hallway. She grabbed a hot chocolate and piece of fruit, and then headed back to the deck to use the down time to analyze her data card.

Stepping into one of the glass walled rooms, she touched a small square outline near the doorway, which immediately tinted every pane of glass in the room to nontransparent black. She laid down a paper napkin she had taken from the mess hall on the table in the center of the room and set her fruit and drink on it. Sliding her briefcase strap off her shoulder, she took out the data card given to her from the Admiral's assistant and glanced at it. It was one of the newer cards that didn't need a reader. One side of the card had a touch screen keypad imprinted on the face, and then other side of the card was a black face that could be activated by entering the proper encryption sequence on the keypad side. Once activated, the user only had to set it on a flat surface, blank side up, and the built in nano holoprojector would display the materials and information in three-dimensional format roughly a foot above the card. The user of the card could then use a bare hand to manipulate through the data by "touching" some of the data keys that were being projected. Since the projector constantly scanned fingerprint signatures, it only responded to movements of authorized prints on the hologram keyboard just as a computer receiving commands from a physical terminal would.

Angelina pulled up the information on the *Alaurian Spirit* first. A technical drawing of the ship came up, rotating slowly in space. Operating specifications were shown to the left of the drawing. The information indicated the ship was originally an Odysseus-class long-range frigate, but had recently been modified and reclassified as a USF Protector-class long-range scout ship. Angelina touched the modifications line and certain parts of the ship diagram started blinking red. She touched one of the blinking items and watched as that part enlarged and rotated up above the ship for three hundred and sixty degree viewing. She cycled through various weapons additions and defensive upgrades. Among the most impressive was a full installation of an MCAC multitarget missile system and a MERL device. The ship also had full military-grade physical shield arrays installed near all view-ports, access ports, and the entire bridge, as well as a minimal energy shield array. Within the two hundred meter long ship, over half of all the crew functions had been automated, either through enhancements or additional Navigation droids. As an unautomated frigate vessel, the crew compliment had been approximately 40 people. With the enhancements and additions of droids, the new headcount requirement for the crew was only eighteen; quite small for a ship of that size. The ship was originally designed in three sections, with the front section being a rounded orb-type structure that originally housed all the crew. This section connected to the middle one by a narrower 'neck' that contained emergency bulkhead doors and air locks. The lower deck on the front section of the ship had been converted into the housing for the MERL device. The equipment housing the sensor instruments and military upgrade shield generation equipment were housed in the deck above that. The vessel's general operations stations were located on the deck above that, with the bridge being the top deck. This forward module connected to the middle section of the ship, which had previously been the cargo hold of the frigate. This area was compartmentalized into several different "cells", each with different functions. The two forward cells were dedicated to the MCAC system, including operations stations, munitions supplies, and infrastructure upgrades required to run the system. The aft cells were dedicated to engineering, with the aft-most cell containing the fusion generator and antigravity components required for both orbital and suborbital flight. The engines and thrusters were in the last section of the ship, making up almost a third of the ship's length.

Angelina studied the technical specifications, trying to absorb as much information as possible. Using a zoom function within the map of the ship's decks, she quickly found where her stateroom would be in the forward section, along with the other officers nearby. She continued her virtual tour through the ship, noting one of the strengths of the craft. The vessel boasted a state-of-the-art sensor package that would allow the ship to be used effectively as a long-range reconnaissance ship, thus limiting the opportunity for detection by standard commercial and low-level military craft. This feature alone was enough to make Captain Pollard wonder just how sensitive her mission would be.

Catching herself losing track of time, she glanced at her wrist krono and decided she needed to start working her way towards the shuttle. She touched a virtual-key within the projection, shutting it down, and gathered the data card off the table and stuffed it back into her brief case. Standing and touching the glass wall again, she returned the translucency back to normal and walked towards the shuttle that would take her to her new command.

CHAPTER II

Radael Asalor watched the reports of the event on Je-Fin once again in his personal Reflection Chamber. Certain he had missed something, the being that held the title Shalotha Primary thoughtfully rubbed the black keratin ridges that ran along the backs of his fingers. Most of his advisors had immediately dismissed the strange reports as a shrewd warfare strategy that bordered on the edge of blasphemy.

Two arguments had come to the forefront of the majority of his advisors and the General of the Armies, the supreme commander of the warrior castes. The first was that the alleged event never occurred, and that it was a ploy by the Fe-Ruqians to reengage in a military confrontation. The Fe-Ruq military had been stepping up its exercises and mock war games for months. They were getting ready for something, and the faction that supported the notion of falsehood assumed that their military readiness was aimed at an invasion of Shalotha. The theory made sense. The momentum in the war had begun to turn in the Fe-Ruqians favor as the truce had been negotiated through a third party. The Fe-Ruqians were about to gain a major territorial advantage over the Shalothans when representatives from the USF negotiated the truce. The agreement ended an offensive that many Fe-Ruqians felt could have delivered the fatal blow to the primary world of the Shalotha sector. Even now, the Primary felt, the desire and opportunity to finish the war on their own terms may be too much for the Fe-Ruqians to withstand. Using a religious event such as the one the Fe-Ruqians reported to lure their enemies into their own territory would be a brilliant tactical maneuver. If successful, the Shalothans would be going into their enemies' heavily defended system with a warrior caste greatly reduced in numbers, and possibly blinded by the religious overtones of the event. In Radael's eyes, it appeared to be a recipe for disaster.

The second faction favored the argument that it actually was the Son of God, sent down from Heaven to return His faithful to their rightful place of glory in His Kingdom. His return in the godless sector of Fe-Ruq, on a planet known for being faithless and hedonistic, was viewed as a sign the Shalothans were righteous in their belief that they were the better species. Extremists within the faction took it so far as to infer that this was a sign the Shalothans should continue their cleansing campaign against the neighboring sectors. After all, how could they not succeed with the Son of God aiding them in their crusade against the heathens? At a minimum, many of the extremists felt the warrior caste should join the Savior as loyal disciples as He meted out His judgment against the Fe-Ruq populations.

Radael Asalor wasn't convinced that either was the correct theory. Despite his advisors' suspicions, he couldn't bring himself to accept the notion that the Fe-Ruq military would be that deceitful and blasphemous. For them to use a part of their enemy's sacred religion against them as a means to lure them into a trap would be considered dishonorable at best. He also wasn't convinced that the return of the Son had indeed happened on Je-Fin, and felt that sending the warrior caste to Je-Fin as a welcoming escort for the Son of God was an invitation to be attacked. Sovereign entities simply couldn't send their warriors to other systems uninvited and expect open arms and a warm welcome. Despite some of the advisors' assurances that the arrival of the warriors would be met with both the blessing and the protection of the Savior, it was a risky proposition. The departure of any large contingent from the Shalothan system could very well be met with excessive resistance, not only from the Fe-Ruq military, but also their allies in the Aormy and Otine sectors. With the devastating effects of the inter-sector war still fresh in everyone's minds, any slight buildup or movement by the Shalothan warrior caste would be destined to begin the war anew.

Primary Asalor stood up in his chamber to stretch. He had been sitting too long, and the keratin-sheathed muscles on his long frame ached from being idle. The Shalothans were a bipedal species, and typically stood two meters in height. Their height was accentuated by the ridges of keratin that ran along the measures of the body. Overall the body of a Shalothan was mostly covered in keratin of one density of another. Sections of keratin grew around the muscles of the arms and legs of the body, as well as around the upper torso area and shoulders. A sheath of thin keratin covered the long skulls of the species, with many sporting natural ridge growths that ran along the cranium from the top of the forehead to the base of the skull. The Shalothans featured luminous deep-set eyes, with long sharp teeth, and a long, wide nose that had three horizontal breathing ridges along the bridge. The typical skull was long, much like the body, and usually had a severe jaw line. The three-fingered hands of the Shalothans were covered in a leathery film of keratin, flexible as human skin, yet more durable than many protective gloves. Members of the warrior caste were selected from birth based on genetic tests to find out if their bodies would develop the telling horns and spikes among certain parts of the body that separated the warrior caste from other castes of the species. Warrior caste Shalothans almost always developed two-to-three centimeter horns or spikes on the shoulders, as well as the knee joints, elbow joints, along the ridges of their hands and fingers, and increased claw length. The species itself was resilient, with the keratin acting as a naturally regenerating covering that enabled warriors to absorb more blows and injuries than typical species.

Over the course of dozens of millennia, the species had developed and heightened their unique ability of pyrokinesis – the control of fire. The priest caste had developed the strongest abilities, but all individuals within the species had some control, although with varying levels of strength. For some, it was the ability to make the tip of their finger glow red with heat. For others, it was the ability to self-immolate on command, creating a walking torch. The natural keratin coating protected them from short-term damage, although long-term use of pyrokinesis to this extent had left many priests deformed and permanently scarred. The ability had lessened in importance as the Shalothans developed into a more sophisticated society. The extent of the ability now was for visual effect, particularly during hand-to-hand combat. It was then that the two-meter tall Shalothan warriors would summon flames to cover their bodies as they approached their enemies. Much of the effect was psychological, although there was no doubt the flame itself would do damage to an enemy should he, she, or it become exposed to the fire.

As a result of their ability, and the continuing practice of it, Shalothans had a unique smell about their species – that of burned keratin. The more a Shalothan practiced this ability, the more it burned their keratin skin, thus generating the odor and further blackening the keratin. The benefit was the keratin always grew back thicker and stronger, unless the being was sick or infected. This smell, mixed with the incense that the priest caste members were constantly burning, created sickening odors for other species, which added to the repulsion that many felt for the Shalothans.

Realizing that it was nearing the end of his standard wake period, Radael walked over to his solution bath and pressed a combination of buttons on the console to start the process for mixing the calcium-based bath. The bath wasn't a necessity, but aided the body in regenerating any damaged keratin sections and promoted growth of new ridges. The bath lasted the entire sleep period, with the user wearing a breathing apparatus while sleeping in order to fully immerse one self into the bath. Radael told himself he would think through the reports as he lie in his bath, but as soon as he settled in, darkness quickly took hold as he was overcome with sleep.

The various species within the primary system of the Fe-Ruq sector were one of the most diverse systems within the known universe. With its empire stretching over twenty-two systems, the Fe-Ruqians were encapsulated by various species indigenous to the multitude of planets within the systems that comprised the sector. In the primary system of Fe-Ruq, there was Je-Fin; originally settled as an early human colony, it had grown throughout the millennia to become one of the galaxy's largest planet-bases. The human population that had accompanied the colony establishment on early Je-Fin had ballooned throughout the centuries to become the largest human population within any system.

Beyond Je-Fin, there were other unique worlds that had added to the diversity of the primary system of the Fe-Ruq sector. The species on Feu-Jegt were advanced in their intellect, and had been a highly integral part of the development of the military. They had been the first species to exhibit any sign of interdimensional manipulation. It was their breakthrough in this technology that laid the foundation for the first versions of the early full-ship cloaking device. The species themselves were humanoid in form, with large black eyes, with exceptionally thin, frail bodies. Their grayish skin tone was a hallmark of the species, and their overall body type had become the face of aliens on the planet Earth.

Another species that had assisted with developing the system was the Crawf, from the planet Egara. These beings were smaller in stature than human beings, but what they lacked in height they made up for in technological skill. It was a Crawf droid that became the first to use its artificial intelligence to successfully command a sentient being battalion. It was said the droid's ability to translate and speak in any language, as well as its technical warfare solutions software, provided it the means to succeed. After that initial breakthrough, Crawf droids became heavily relied upon as warfare technical operations specialists and were permanent fixtures on every Fe-Ruq military class starship.

The Fe-Ruq military commanders huddled in their war operations facility, reviewing all the information they had access to. The event that had occurred at the parade ground was disturbing, and no scientific basis for explanation had come to light as of yet. General Ardos Odine had ordered his security staff to elevate all the in-system planets to highest alert, wary that this entire event may have been a precursor to some sort of attack by the Shalothans. Odine didn't see it as an overreaction when he decided to heighten the alert level. He knew all too well what the Shalothans were capable of, and would not have been surprised to learn that this was a preemptive strike against the morale of his troops.

The troops that had been at the parade ground that day had all been taken to a remote base on Je-Fin, debriefed, and then reassigned off planet to various units. The purpose of the exercise was to ensure that pockets of his soldiers would not be unduly affected by any such attack. If they were, taking them off-world and reassigning them so each were in different units would help defuse any potential uprising or breakdown of command through a mutinous action. The risk involved was that each soldier now had access to an entirely new group that had not been present, and would be able to relay the story. The debriefing was supposed to prevent that type of activity from occurring, but Odine was willing to bet his rank that at least one soldier would tell his story. It was only a matter of time before the rumors began floating around.

To complicate matters, Odine knew that the United Space Federation had spies in-system, if not on Je-Fin itself. He could only assume that they were aware of the event, and would be sending an observation unit to watch for any activity that could be deemed threatening. He also assumed that some form of an intelligence unit from the Shalotha system had been in-system during the event. With the truce being tenuous at best, it would have been foolhardy for the Shalothans to not have some type of reconnaissance unit within the system.

Ardos sat back in his chair and laced his fingers together, bringing his index fingers to together to form a point. He absent-mindedly tapped the two fingers against his chin while he thought through the possible chain of reactions resulting from the event.

As his intelligence staff saw it, the most logical view was to assume the Shalothans were behind it. It was a Christian themed attack, and the deeply Christian Shalothans were keenly aware that most of the species within the borders of the Fe-Ruq sector were atheist. Also, the Fe-Ruq military outlawed practicing faith for any enlisted individual or officer of the military.

Some of his personal advisors had another point of view. One suggested the USF had possibly initiated the event in hopes that it would push the Fe-Ruqians into an assault on the Shalothans, thereby violating the truce agreement. With the violation, the USF forces could launch 'peace' campaigns against the Fe-Ruq sector, all in the name of protecting the greater good of the galaxy. Many members of the Fe-Ruq Parliament felt that the USF had stood to gain the most out of the truce, and may be waiting for an opportunity to seize more worlds and assets from the Fe-Ruq system. Trade sanctions were already in place for several of the outlying systems, and the economic impact had slowly crept to the core of the system, draining the life out of the once-wealthy sector.

To Ardos, the USF forces were no better than the Shalothans. The Christian Shalothans waged war based on religious faith; the USF waged war based on self-righteous beliefs that they were the protectors of the galaxy and all systems within it. The Fe-Ruq system would benefit greatly to have both of these entities wiped out of the galaxy.

He looked out the window of his office across the sprawling complex and beyond. He could see the tiny dots of aircraft against the roiling black clouds of an impending storm. Several patrol squadrons were flying routes around the area in an attempt to keep sentry against any enemy intrusion. He could make out the deadly forms of the new Fe-Ruq variable wing suborbital fighter, code-named Devilspear. Beyond the clouds he knew that several orbital battle stations were on alert for craft entering on hyperspace threads or through dimensional drops. Past those orbiting stations, three fleets complete with support vessels had been recalled to Je-Fin. They were summoned to the planet partly to take on the reassigned soldiers, but also as hastily prepared stopgap support against any impending invasion forces.

General Odine swiveled his chair around to face his data tablet. Something was gnawing at the back of his mind, but he couldn't quite figure out what was bothering him. He tapped the screen a few times to cycle through an identification screen, then logged onto part of the intelligence network. He pulled up the surveillance videos from the day of the event, scanning the initial moments frame by frame.

He almost clicked past the part showing the

beginning of the bright light when he caught a glimpse of something on one of the camera shots. He digitally enhanced the photo, then switched through the other cameras to see if they had picked up the same angle. Frustrated that only one camera captured what he was looking at, he tapped a button on the secure communication console on his desk and ordered his intelligence staff to his office immediately. Within ten minutes, several of the staff were inside his office, and several others were on their way from other parts of the base.

"I want each of you to take a look at this," he ordered. He pointed to a digitally enhanced picture that had been magnified several hundred times. The picture was of what appeared to be light glinting off something metallic or glass. He tapped the screen to reduce the magnification, which revealed that the location of the glint was within a tree cluster that bordered the pavilion outside the parade grounds.

"Have any of you reviewed this and determined what this was?" He looked around questioningly at each of the officers there. One officer stepped forward and saluted.

"Sir, I have reviewed that section of film, and I felt that it was insignificant in the context of the event. There was no projection light coming from that direction, nor were there any individuals there, based on the thermal scans of the area prior to the event and immediately after.

General Odine sucked in on his cheeks and narrowed his eyes at the officer.

"Insignificant you say?" Odine asked. He looked around the room at each of the officers, then let his gaze return to the officer that had spoken.

"What is your name, soldier?"

"Lieutenant Aemel Wolfus, sir," the officer replied.

Without saying a word, the general pushed a button located beneath his desk, revealing a small hand blaster. He quickly pulled the weapon from beneath the desk and shot the officer in the center of his forehead.

"Officer Wolfus, I believe I just made your life insignificant." He pointed to two junior officers who stood to the side with shock written on their faces. "You two, get this carcass out of here. As for the rest of you, I want a thorough search of this tree cluster immediately, with a report back on my desk in six hours. And, in case anyone here is not clear on the matter, *nothing* is insignificant when it comes to the safety and sovereignty of the Fe-Ruq sector. I want to know what caused that glint. Dismissed."

The officers all saluted and quickly retreated out of the room. Within minutes, a cleaning droid arrived to clean the mess up off the wall and floor. General Odine looked back out the window, where the first drops of the storm were starting to collect on the window. *Insignificant*, he thought. *What a poor choice of words.*

Captain Pollard found the assigned landing area for her shuttle and briskly walked over to the waiting area. The shuttle had already landed and was releasing various pressurized gases out of the rear exhaust ports. The shuttlecrafts were not particularly sleek machines, built more for function than form. Almost rectangular, the shuttle featured a hatch on both the port and starboard sides of the craft for more flexible docking connections in space. The front of the vessel was mostly covered with outdated heat shield plates to protect the nose of the craft from the heat generated by the numerous atmospheric re-entries each day. A small strip of a transparent alloy used for the viewshield bisected the face of the craft, and wrapped around the corners of each side, allowing the pilot to have limited visuals to both sides of the craft. The engines were quite small, having only suborbital and limited spaceflight ability. The antigravity unit was the smallest available from AeroFlight Corp, allowing more space for the passengers and crew. The passengers themselves had individual chairs with data ports for contacting awaiting ships or contacting individuals waiting on orbital stations.

Above the cacophony of the flight deck, a new sound rang out from a box near the painted outlines of the landing dock, warning individuals to back away from the vessel until the shuttle doors were completely open. A bottom lip unfolded from just above the bottom of the craft, and then the rest of the door swung upwards on hydraulics, creating a slight hissing noise.

Two other officers arrived in the waiting area near Captain Pollard as the door touched the deck, and she returned the salutes of both junior officers. A green light just to the right of the door blinked on, indicating it was safe to approach. Seeing the light, Captain Pollard walked forward, stepping on the ramp and into the craft in a few steps.

After a slight delay in boarding, the shuttle lifted off uneventfully, rising above the deck on its antigrav engines, and swinging slowly outwards until it was clear of the immense hangar. Facing the forward viewshield, Captain Pollard watched as the entire expanse of the United Space Federation's Navy headquarters complex migrated into her viewing area. The flight hangar itself was larger than four training arenas sitting next to one another, and the surrounding support complexes sprawled for miles. Above the flight hangar was the office spire that she had had her meeting in earlier that day. Beyond the support complexes were several other large modern buildings containing more offices and living quarters for the officers stationed at the base. Low-lying clouds prohibited her from seeing beyond that, but she knew from previous visits that the entire base covered more square miles than many large cities on the planet. Between living quarters for the families of the officers and crews, dry docks for fleet vessels, weapons manufacturing plants, fuel refineries, a sister base for Marines, and various governmental agency buildings, the city-base contained more than three million people.

Picking up speed, the ship engaged its orbital engines and rocketed towards a flight pattern in low orbit. The clouds dropped away from the shuttle, and the bright blue sky turned to dark blue, and finally to black as the ship broke through the atmosphere. Angelina watched as the multitude of stars quickly gave way to the enormous orbital station that crept into the viewshield. The orbital station itself was over three kilometers long, and featured over fifty docking berths, not counting the reserve docks for the shuttle. As she watched, docked ships crept into view as others slid underneath the station as it rolled in place. She leaned forward in her seat, trying to pick out the *Alaurian Spirit* among the docked ships. The ships were attached at various points along the station, resembling lampreys attached to their host. Dock numbers were stenciled in large military block by each hatchway, and the viewshield heads-up display switched on automatically once the ship came within a few kilometers of the station. The HUD listed the dock numbers and ship identifications in an overlay that matched the view from the pilot's seat. Ship-to-surface shuttles were assigned to reserve docks, and Angelina could see the cluster of like shuttles gathered at one end of the station's spindly docking arms. The pilot locked onto the assigned arrival dock and switched to autocontrol to guide the ship into the port. Within minutes Angelina was slightly jarred in her seat as the craft attached itself to the mouth of the dock. The dock receptacle formed a seal around the flat side of the shuttle, and allowed the shuttle to open its door in an air lock. The pilot waited until the pressure sensor on the door control switched to green and the ping indicating a secure seal chimed.

The ramp swung down as the hatch swung up, and Angelina stepped out of the craft with the other officers, walking to their respective destinations. She stepped out of the air lock passageway and into the bustling corridor. Throngs of people walked by in either direction, heading to various spots in the station. This particular corridor ran the length of the station, and supplied access to all of the docks on this side of the station. In either direction down the corridor, air lock lights located above the pressure doors were yellow, green or red, depending upon the status of the dock. Green meant the ship was docked, air lock and doors open. Yellow meant the ship was either still pressurizing after having just attached to the air lock seal, or depressurizing to separate from the station. Red meant the dock was empty, and the air lock was closed and locked. Many of the shuttles in the reserve docks were just arriving from various points on the planet. As a result, the multitude of lights in the reserve docks were quickly shifting from an equal division of red and green to a majority of the latter.

Hoping to beat the rush of incoming passengers, Angelina stepped up her pace and headed towards the central access corridor that would take her deeper into the station. She stopped at an information kiosk and pulled up the information on the berth of the *Alaurian Spirit*. The latest update showed that it was docked in B-41 on the other side of the station. Taking a mental note of the station schematic that popped up on the screen and showed her the route to the B dock corridor, she canceled her request on the kiosk screen and started out towards B dock.

CHAPTER III

Refreshed from a pleasant sleep period, Radael Asalor felt healthy and invigorated, and decided to start his day with some exercise. He walked across his chamber and put on a combat tunic and sandals, then walked to the chamber entry and touched a combination of keys on the panel imprint on the wall. The door slid open, and two of his personal guards stood at attention, awaiting his command.

"Summon Commander Apxlus, and have him meet me in the training arena in the annex. I'll be awaiting his arrival."

Radael dismissed the one guard so he could summon Apxlus. He motioned towards the other to indicate he wanted an escort downstairs. As they walked down the white marble spiral staircase, Radael took in the view. His chamber was at the top of an atrium within the Primary Palace. The spiral staircase was the only way up to or down from the chamber. The staircase spiraled up from a lush courtyard, which had several tiered sections that provided isolated spots for private conversations among the many visitors to the palace. The atrium itself was covered with a transparent metallic alloy that provided a clear view of the sky and surrounding trees, while protecting the courtyard from the dangerous storms that could develop on Shalotha.

The Primary Palace was much more than just the residence of the most powerful being in the System Republic of Shalotha. The Palace was also the residence of several other key government officers, as well as the central meeting location for members of the Imperium, the planetary government on Shalotha. Because of its high visibility and accessibility, hundreds of members of the warrior caste were permanently stationed at the Palace as a garrison. Warriors could be seen in almost every conceivable location within the palace, whether it was the cookery, or the outer vestibule leading into his office, or the training arena locker rooms in which the Primary was a regular visitor. The only place the Primary was permitted out of sight of a warrior was in his personal chamber.

As the Primary, Radael Asalor held dual roles. His main role was as the leader of the Shalotha system; a twelve-planet system with governmental headquarters based on one of the largest and most populated habitable planets, Shalotha. In this function he represented the entire sector when working with neighboring sectors such as the Fe-Ruq, Otine, and Aormy.

His secondary role, yet just important, was as a spiritual guide for his people. Following the ancient teachings, the Shalothans believed in God and all that He represented. They believed that He had sent His only Son to the universe some time ago, and they believed that He would soon announce His return. The guidance the Primary provided was akin to a high priest in other religions. Holding this position was a convenience for the Primary, as it allowed him to give directives to his fellow Shalothans under the premise of being a religious act when the governmental rule seemed to be inappropriate.

The event on Je-Fin was an example of when it was a blessing to hold both positions. As the spiritual Primary, he would decide for his congregations whether to believe the Son of God had indeed returned. It was his voice, his guidance, which they all would follow.

As the governmental Primary, he would be the one to decide when or if the warrior caste needed to be deployed in the name of God. It was his decisions that kept the System Republic from another Civil War, and his decisions that had propelled his constituents into the interstellar war.

In short, he could either lead them to salvation from his religious position, or lead them to damnation with his government position. He preferred the former to the latter, if only because he himself was a very strong believer.

Radael and his guard arrived at the arena, and the Primary ordered his guard to stay outside the entrance. He walked through the training doors and surveyed the arena. Several tiers of seats circled the round training field. Entrances to a medical room and locker rooms were off to the right. Wall mounts holding the various training weapons were fastened to a section of wall on his left. He glanced around to see if Apxlus had arrived yet; he had not. The Primary walked over to the training weapons and selected a long staff. Adjusting his tunic, he walked to the center of the arena and turned to face the entrance.

In short time, the door opened, and a large Shalothan entered through the door. Battle scarred keratin armor covered the body of the warrior, and the red and black bandolier that he sported signified that he was a commander within the warrior caste. The warrior stopped just inside the door and scanned the interior of the building. He quickly saw his foe standing in the center of the arena.

"Reaz Apxlus, son of Patharhu, select your weapon and advance." Radael stood still as he spoke, forcing his voice into a deeper tone. He watched Apxlus, and thought he saw him smile slightly.

Apxlus walked over to the training weapons wall, never taking his eyes off his opponent. He reached for a small shield and took it off the wall. Holding it with one hand, he flung it across the arena floor towards his opponent.

"Take the shield, Primary. You shall need it today!" Apxlus ran across the arena floor at full tilt. Radael was caught off guard by the thrown shield. He hesitated for a moment, deciding whether he should stand and defend himself with just the staff, or use the shield that Apxlus had thrown at him. Before he could decide, Apxlus was upon him, only a few meters away. Radael threw his staff up in self-defense as his opponent neared, causing Apxlus to slow to a halt. He twirled the staff slowly in front of him with both hands, never taking his eyes off the commander. He started to circle to his left slowly, trying to maneuver his opponent out of position. Apxlus rotated to his left as well, keeping the same distance between the Primary and himself. As he neared the shield on the ground, he took a slight step back, putting himself in line with the shield as he continued to circle with his opponent. Just as it appeared he would step past the shield, in one deft motion he stomped on the upturned curved edge of the shield, flipping it up into the air, then caught it with his left hand and flung it overhand at his opponent. Radael had not expected this, and narrowly deflected the shield with the staff. The shield had barely touched his staff when Radael realized he had just made a costly mistake. Apxlus was already in close quarters, grabbing the staff with his left hand and pulling it towards him. At the same time he thrust the heel of his right hand into the jaw of Radael, knocking him away from the staff and causing Radael to stagger backwards. The Primary had barely caught his balance before the staff in Apxlus' hands swung down in an arc and into the back of his knees, knocking him to the ground. Radael quickly rolled to his right, and jumped up, only to receive an open hand smack into his throat, grabbing hold at the same time. Instinctively his hands reached for the arm attached to the hand seemingly attached to his throat. Before his grip could be secured, a leg snaked around Radael's leg and the hand around his throat forced him backwards, causing him to fall over his opponent's leg. The viselike grip did not ease as he landed on his back with a thud. Instead, the smiling visage of Reaz Apxlus came into view, lips curled back showing sharp teeth.

"You would be receiving your Judgment from God, should you have been a real foe Primary," Apxlus snarled. He released his grip on the Primary's throat and offered a hand to help him up.

"Good morning Apxlus," Radael said smiling. He rubbed his throat slightly, still feeling the blood circulating near the hand imprint. Apxlus gathered the shield as Radael went to pick up the staff. "I am close to a decision about the situation on Je-Fin. I wanted your counsel before I make the final decision." Radael waited until the commander had turned his back towards him, and then darted towards Apxlus with the shield out in front of him. Apxlus reacted instantly. In one fluid motion he twirled to his left with his stiffened left arm outstretched to block a blow from Radael, while the kinetic energy from his movement carried the rest of his body around behind his attacker. The block shifted Radael's weight to his right, unsettling his balance. Apxlus's dropped to a crouch and initiated a leg sweep, knocking Radael to the ground again.

"You are louder than a thundering herd of jettalons, Primary. It is good for your health that you are a politician, and not a warrior." Apxlus towered over the Primary, waiting for any sign of attack. Seeing none coming, Apxlus again offered his hand to help the Primary to his feet. Radael took his hand and pulled himself up. He took the shield from the ground and reached for the staff from the commander. Taking the weapons back to where he had taken them from, the Primary motioned for the warrior to walk with him.

"Apxlus, the Republic has come to a crossroads in our existence. We have hurt ourselves with civil war, and further damaged our standing across the galaxy with the wars that we've waged. And for what gain? Many of our cities still lie in ruin. Our warrior clans are decimated. Our enemies hate us even more now than they did a century ago. We have no allies at this time in history. Everything that has happened to us, we have brought upon ourselves. Yet, our faith has persevered through all of these troubles. Like the ancients of old, we've held onto our faith, knowing that one day our Savior would return." Radael paused as he placed the weapons back into their spots on the wall. He turned to face Apxlus, who continued to listen silently.

"Apxlus, as my most trusted commander, I need your absolute best assessment on what I'm about to suggest. Pay no heed to concerns about political issues. Listen as a Christian, not as a warrior." Radael paused again to see if the Shalothan standing in front of him had anything to say.

"The event at Je-Fin can be interpreted one of several ways. The most common is that it's a strategy with the goal of enticing us back into the Fe-Ruq system for an ambush. The other is that this is indeed the first of many signs of the return of our Savior. Do you agree with this assessment?" Apxlus nodded agreement, but said nothing.

"Apxlus, my personal belief, based on the intelligence that we have today, is that this is not a military tactic. With that said, I do not think that having our Savior on the world of Je-Fin is the best situation possible for all involved. He has returned for His thousand-year rule. To believe in Christ is to believe that we are His army. Could this sign be His attempt to call His army to Him? What if Je-Fin is the world that He in all His wisdom has decided to return on? How would the Fe-Ruqians react? I don't believe that they will be welcoming Him with open arms, do you? But more importantly, if word of this event were to spread through our system, what effect would it have on our people? If He were to skip over our planet, and appear at a sworn enemy, an enemy opposed to Christianity, wouldn't at least some of our people begin doubting their faith? The solution to all of these problems brought me to the decision that I want your assessment on. I need you to bring the Savior to our planet when He arrives, wherever He arrives, and do it under concealment. His arrival needs to be announced as if it were originally on Shalotha, for the good of our people for their faith will be strengthened. His arrival needs to be announced on Shalotha because His arrival anywhere else strengthens the views of our foes that we are too self-righteous. And lastly, His arrival needs to be announced as being on Shalotha so that all in the galaxy will understand that we are His chosen warriors, the army of God that will cleanse the universe and pave the way for Christ's one thousand year rule. Apxlus, tell me your thoughts on what I have just said."

Apxlus looked at his Primary for a moment, lost in thought about what he had just been told. In Shalothan philosophy there was always an absolute right and wrong. This situation presented neither, as each potential solution, including the Primary's, had significant drawbacks.

"Primary, your wisdom in this manner is beyond any reproach. I agree with your decision, although I caution that the other advisors will not come to agreement with you on this. They could leak information to the masses, exposing what actually happened, to further certain individual beliefs that you should not be the Primary any longer. They could warn the Fe-Ruqians, allowing them to forestall any attempt to enter their system and assist the Son of God off the planet. Worse, they could release information to the galaxy revealing your plans to kidnap the Son of God. Christian based faith or not, other systems would not look at us favorably in light of the information. We have everything to gain from your decision, yet I caution that we have everything to lose. Your excellency, I will do thy bidding as you command." Apxlus bent down to one knee before the Primary. His use of the word 'excellency' signified that he was recognizing Radael as his high priest in this manner, not his political chief.

"Apxlus, you will gather a small force, number to be determined by you. I need not tell you what qualities they must have. You will plan entry into the system, plan for assisting Him offworld, and plan an exit strategy out of the sector, all before the time He arrives. I doubt it will be much longer, so time is truly of the essence in this manner. All of your current duties will be reassigned to other warriors under the auspices that you have fallen ill. You have access to all of the information that you need. Inform me of the starship that you wish to use, and I will see that it is fully operational and conveniently loaded for the mission when you are ready. My efforts and involvement will be minimal and secretive, as they must. If this plan is discovered, you and your men will be acting as a rogue bunch, without direction from any higher authority. Even upon successful completion, details of this mission must never be leaked. You will need to do whatever is necessary with your men to ensure that the details are not slipped during conversation, or even handed down in generational stories. The people of Shalotha, the system, and the galaxy can never know of our tactics. Do you understand the implications of that statement?" Apxlus certainly understood. For all but himself, this would be the final mission for these warriors. Without their knowledge, he would make them martyrs for the cause, either directly or indirectly. The absolute in this decision was that Apxlus was responsible for ensuring that these warriors could never speak about the mission again. It was a task he did not want, but understood it was needed for the greater good. He would have to choose his group wisely.

Radael turned on his heel and left the training arena, motioning for his guard as he walked out of the door.

Apxlus waited for a few moments, and then followed the same exit path out of the arena. He looked up at the sky and took in the warmth emitting from the bright sun, and then headed for the building his chamber was in.

It had been five hours and fifty-six minutes since General Odine had ended the life of Officer Wolfus and sent his intelligence team out on a mission for answers. It had been a long six hours for the General. He continued to review the events, searching for other clues that could lead him to a more scientific answer to what happened. After all, according the event to a theological origin would be akin to forfeiting his life. He would not last the day in office were he ever to suggest that the event was truly the supernatural announcement of some deity.

The communication device on his console beeped, and General Odine accepted the call.

"General, Major Tunrak reporting with results from our search. Sir, it appears that we were being spied on." The general sat back slightly, interested to hear of this development.

"Sir, the reflection that we saw on the video is from the lens of a recording device that had been planted in one of the trees within the cluster. The unit appears to be controlled remotely, and self-destructed when one of my men attempted to examine it at a closer distance. A forensics team is on location now, and will be removing the remaining pieces for investigation and review. Awaiting further orders, sir." Thunder boomed in the background as the officer was reporting.

"Assemble teams to search every tree and bush within the area surrounding the grounds. We need to find out just how many of these units there are, and how many are currently operational. Report after the entire area has been searched." With that the general clicked off the communication console, and sat back in his chair. This would not look good for his career. His headquarters under surveillance by an opposing force, probably the very force that they had been at war with. Too many questions were unanswered. How long had it been there? Was it operational at the time of the event? Who was receiving the information? Was that person or persons on-world to receive, or did the unit transmit back to a surface based deep-space relay unit that sent the information out of the system? He would need to find these answers quickly, before any information obtained from the device could be used against them.

McDonald's had been Christian Franklin's first choice at employment when he turned sixteen. Many of the people he had come to call friends worked there, and it was a decent paying job considering the job market. More than minimum wage, it was enough money for him to save for dates or the latest Playstation games, and still have some left over to fix his car when it failed.

He really enjoyed the crew he worked with. Some were friends from high school; others were teammates on his high school baseball team. Others, such as Katie, were from a different high school, but still part of the group of people he considered his friends. But if there was one person that he looked forward to seeing each day at work, it was Katie Anderson. A year older than Christian, Katie was mature for her age. Short and petite, with shoulder-length blond hair and brown eyes, she was considered one of the better looking females at her school, let alone the smaller group that worked at McDonald's. At the restaurant, she was a goddess; the one who earned the stares of the truckers coming in for coffee, and the husbands who stole lustful gazes between mouthfuls of fries.

She was going to graduate at the end of this year, but didn't have the grades to go onto a big university. She'd already made it known around the kitchen that she was looking to stay in the area and attend the local community college.

He'd only been with McDonald's since October, but already Christian was feeling like a veteran only two months in. He really looked forward to coming to work on the weekends. He even wore his logo-branded shirt with pride. He had aspirations of becoming a crew-trainer at the restaurant. His manager was very encouraging, and had suggested the opportunity to him several times over the past few weeks. Becoming a trainer meant a slight raise, but anything would help.

The *Alaurian Spirit* was originally built as a peacetime long-range frigate. The vessel was designed to carry forty people comfortably, but had been modified to support eighteen bio-forms for up to six months without docking. With everything that had happened within the past two years, the ship had been pressed into service as a scout ship with the USF , and was retrofitted with military grade shield-arrays, MCAC multitargeting missiles, and an MERL device.

The Multiple Contact Auto Control was an intelligent weapon system designed to defeat standardized shields. The MCAC would fire multiple missiles within milliseconds of one another, targeted at the same point on a ship's shields. The first hit would weaken the field as the shield energy dispersed from the impact. The second missile would hit the weakened impact site and break through, striking the actual hull of the ship. It was most effective for long-range attacks, as the target ship would need to be moving fairly slow for the missiles to track and compensate for ship movement and still hit the same points on the shield. Engaged in a dogfight, the MCAC weapons system was merely an ordinary missile array; capable of fast-firing missiles and hoping that one would get through a weakened or damaged shield.

The MERL, or Multiple Energy Radiation Level, device worked as a variable power energy weapon. The weapon's energy beam could be refracted to a wide beam at weaker power for a broader range of impact, or condensed into a tight beam with extremely high levels of power for a more pronounced effect. A widely accepted practice was to use the broad range capacity in a battle to weaken other ships' energy fields. The vessel with the MERL would station itself away from the battle and selectively target ships with the beam. The broad range beam would direct constant energy at the target ship's shields, thereby draining the power from the shields. Other ships in the area would then have free range of their weapons systems, or could board the ship if desired. The tight range beam was widely used for attacking communications vessels and the accoutrements that were located on those ships. Once the communication systems of a battle group were knocked out, the battleships were essentially flying blind when their shields were up. Thus, ships such as the *Alaurian Spirit* became essential partners in large-scale battles.

The new commander of the ship, Marshall Tennison, was in the middle of his career. Brought up in a military family since birth, he had gone to the Military Space Command Academy with his sights on getting a space command of his own. He had always desired a large command such as the *Salient Justice*, a Dreadnaught-class battle cruiser that was famous in earlier battles. But time and maturity changed his heart. As he finished his first command on the refueling ship *Everlast,* he began to realize that the captains of the bigger vessels were merely puppeteers of big, brutish machines that worked best when stationed across from their foe. The captains of those ships didn't worry about where to aim their MERL, or which angle of attack would give them an advantage over their prey. No, they worried about how fast they could fire their weapons systems, and hope that their shields outlasted those of their foes. It was essentially two heavyweight prizefighters slugging it out without any pretense of avoidance or defense.

With that realization came the desire to be the captain of a smaller, far more nimble ship. He wanted to be able to scout and recon without having a flotilla under his command. He needed a ship that needed his command, not just as a figurehead. A ship that had a small crew with talent to be discovered, not a ship filled with battle droids and military clones. In the end, it was the *Alaurian Spirit* that found him, not the other way around.

CHAPTER IV

Commander Tennison reviewed the data tablet on the workspace table in his quarters. He couldn't understand what had happened to his command. One moment, he was mentioned as possibly the next captain of the *Eccentric*, a USF Infiltrator class starship, and the next he was receiving orders to report to a Protector class scout ship with a rank of Commander, not Captain. He felt his career careening into a bulkhead. His desire to be captain of a scout ship certainly caught his superior by surprise during their last meeting. He had even explained his desire to captain a smaller ship so he wasn't commanding a ship full of clones and droids. Yet, here he was, assigned to a scout ship with an abundance of battle droids, a crew roster that listed five clones among the eighteen officers, and he wasn't even the ranking officer of the ship. It was not what he had been expecting when it was time for his next command.

The clones listed on the roster were being used for various purposes. In the military, clones were typically kept on board as harvest bodies – bodies that medical droids could harvest body parts from in the event of catastrophic injuries to the original. Intelligence divisions used clones as backup databases, assimilating highly technical and specialized information from the original into the host, also in case of incapacitation or death. Outside the military, clones were used for various purposes. General labor, medical studies, and test crews for experimental starships, among other things. Wealthier citizens had the luxury of ordering a clone for themselves to help prolong their life by harvesting organs, skin, and even healthy brain tissue from the clone. The harvest clone was kept in a liquid stasis container in a suspended state in order to preserve the living organisms, as well as limiting the amount of escapes. For those clones that weren't harvest clones, but merely labor or test crews, they held onto the bottom rung of the social status ladder in class hierarchy. Clones weren't allowed to vote, weren't allowed to assume officer status in the military, and were forbidden to procreate.

Like many officers in the military, Marshall had elected to keep his clone on the planet Earth, leaving it there to develop naturally in the environment. Marshall had elected to have the clone for harvesting purposes, and saw no need to keep the clone on hand until he was older. All of his assignments had been safer than most, and the difficulty level in plucking a clone off-world was much easier than one would expect. Most clone acquisitions went reported as strange disappearances and unexplained phenomena; subjects the natives of Earth strangely found acceptable when rationalizing why someone disappeared. Marshall was wagering with his life, but he gambled that any injuries he suffered could be stabilized for a few days as a team acquired the clone and brought it to the medical facility. Once on board, the clone would be kept in a hibernation chamber, and then harvested to repair any life threatening injuries.

At least, that was his theory until he came across

the section in his orders that directed the *Alaurian Spirit* to pick up the clones for Captain Pollard, Lieutenant Andrew Parsons, Lieutenant Louis Daniels, Ensign Kevin Theore, and himself. Not knowing the mission specs for the ship, he assumed the top four ranking officers were directed to have their clones available because they were being sent into harm's way. As for the clone of this Ensign Theore, he would have to look up exactly what this officer did. He guessed something of a technical nature, but wouldn't know for certain until he reviewed the crew dossiers that were being uploaded in a few hours. Glancing back at the roster, he saw the five clones were part of the crew of eighteen that made up the full crewing complement of the ship. Almost a third of the ship would be clones. Marshall frowned at the thought and looked out the window at the other ships docked at the station. He hated clones.

Captain Pollard reached the B dock after a lengthy trip through the orbital station. She stopped once to grab a hot chocolate, and drank it on the way. Other than the stop, the walk had been uneventful.

To her the B dock seemed exceptionally busy. Remembering the delay for the shuttle, she wasn't surprised by the volume. Many of the individuals walking in the B dock terminal were military of some form or another. Others appeared to be crewmembers coming back or going to shore leave. Others were officers like her, taking the time to enjoy the environment before boarding their ships for the next few months. Almost all of the individuals in this particular dock were human, with one notable exception. Off to the side of the B-12 dock, there was a cluster of Shalothans using an information kiosk.

The physical makeup of the species itself was enough to give many of the humans pause as they passed. Averaging two meters in height, with flesh tones ranging from medium gray to black, the species naturally stood out against the humans. The white tunics that they wore set off their skin tones even more, and the red gothic crosses embroidered on their tunics would have drawn attention to them even if they had been human. Seeing the crosses, Pollard assumed they were clergy visiting from outside the system. She watched for a moment as they finished using the kiosk and then as a group walked back towards the central part of the station. As they passed, one of them caught her eye and held her gaze for a moment. He then bowed his head and continued down the corridor.

Pollard stepped into a doorway and turned to watch the group. The one who had bowed his head continued looking around, as if searching for someone. She counted seven individuals in the group, but they seemed to be sub-divided into groups of three and four. At a corridor split, three of them went to the left, and the rest headed straight. The captain wondered for a moment about what she had just seen. Was there something to it, or was she on edge because of everything she had just learned? She made a mental note of the group, just in case the information proved useful in the future, and then continued down to B-41.

She reached the dock within ten minutes, and stopped to take another look down the dock corridor. Seeing no sign of the Shalothans she had caught sight of earlier, she stepped into the air lock vestibule and entered the access code onto the entry panel to her right. The ship was secured when docked, as was protocol for all military ships. The panel immediately beeped back at her, and a small plastic pad slid out from the panel. It had an outline of a right hand in red striping, with several dots uniformly spaced across the hand. She placed her right hand on the pad, palm down, and waited. Within a few seconds, she felt her hand pinpricked in several places, then a cool sensation as the pad emitted a gel that sanitized and sealed the pinpricks. The DNA sample was processed and verified, and the access door to the ship's air lock slid open.

Entering the ship, she felt very alone. There was no guard stationed inside the ship's air lock, and she saw no foot traffic on the deck that she had entered on. Remembering the deck map that she had reviewed, she sought out the turbo-lift to the bridge. The lights within the ship's hallways were dimmed, with motion sensors lighting the section she was in, and the one she was walking into. The entire effect was eerie, and she felt very uncomfortable. *The entire ship is running as if it's been in hibernation for a while*, she thought. She found the turbo-lift and stepped inside. Pressing the button for the bridge, she readied herself to officially take command. The lift stopped, and she stepped out, prepared to announce her arrival. The lift door opened, and she stepped onto the bridge of the *Alaurian Spirit*. The bridge consoles were arranged in a V-shape, with the point of the V aiming towards the bow of the ship. The point of the 'V' was the pilot's station, with the secondary pilot stationed just to the right. The weapons console was stationed just to the left of the pilot's seat. Various system consoles were placed along both inside edges of the 'V'. The captain's chair was situated in the center of the formation, equal-distance from the point and the ends of each console bank. It was flanked by a visitor chair and the second-in-command's chair. The forward physical shield array was retracted, allowing Captain Pollard to see out of the view-shield. The bridge lights were also dimmed, and many of the station consoles were darkened, admitting that they were powerless.

Captain Pollard stepped behind the captain's chair and rested her hands on the headrest. She looked out the view-shield at the other ships docked with the station. Looking beyond the ships, she caught sight of a familiar looking ship coming around the planet in orbit. She leaned forward a little closer, hoping to catch a better view. It was the *Seraphim*, still stationed in the same orbit as when she had left almost a full day ago. The running lights were on, and the lights on the outside of the bridge lit up the ship's name. Several shuttles were approaching her former command, carrying replenishments and crew. Captain Pollard looked around at her new, darkened command, and silently swore to herself. *Good luck, Captain Nicolai. You lucky bastard.*

Captain Pollard sought out her new quarters, and was surprised to find that her personal effects had already been transferred off the *Seraphim*, and were neatly stacked in containers at the foot of her bed. She slipped her briefcase off and dropped it next to her data-table. She surveyed the room, taking note of how much smaller this room was compared with her quarters on the *Seraphim*.

The viewport was tiny, as was the bunk crammed in a corner of the room. The data-table was brand-new, probably part of the extensive upgrades that Tech Ops had to do to complete the ship's transformation to a Protector-class ship. She sat down at her data-table and pulled up the crew roster. Surprisingly, the system indicated that someone else had already checked in. She wasn't the only one in the ship. She looked at the name and said it out loud: Commander Marshall Tennison.

She pulled up the deck map on the data screen and found Tennison's quarters. His was located on the main deck containing the officer's quarters. She touched the map drawing of his quarters, outlining the room in a flashing line. She pushed the communication button and leaned in to speak.

"Commander Marshall Tennison, this is Captain Pollard. Please report to the bridge." There was a pause, and then a voice came back over the speaker.

"Aye aye, Captain. I wasn't aware that you had boarded." The captain didn't respond to the statement; rather, she walked out of her quarters and back on to the bridge. She arrived before Commander Tennison, who would need to take the lift up to the bridge. She would have to remind the young commander that extraneous comments, such as the one he just voiced, were not going to be tolerated. She wanted a tightly run ship, and it had to start with her second in command.

Looking up at the sky, the low lying clouds gathered the luminescence of the city lights from below, creating a glowing effect above and to the south. The mist that accompanied the clouds settled onto his windbreaker as Christian walked towards his car. An older model minivan with rust slowly eating away the doors, the vehicle was not exactly the epitome of what a teenager would want as his first car, but it was free, and it was his alone. His parents had given him the car as a birthday gift when he turned sixteen. He'd had his share of problems with the car already; bad brakes, two blown tires, a cracked windshield, and a passenger side door that didn't close quite right. In the winter, it was the door that irked him the most. He would come out of the house after a fresh snowfall only to find a small snowdrift on the passenger seat, with ice lining the inside of the window. Tonight, however, none of that mattered. With only a mist in the unseasonably warm December air, the seat would be dry, and his date would be sitting in it.

Katie had actually been the one to suggest the date. The conversation had started as a pity party, with the both of them complaining how each had been stood up the week before. Katie by her longtime crush, and Christian by one of the girls from his biology class. They compared notes as to whom was the bigger jerk, and Christian conceded that Katie's crush was the winner. Katie suggested that as a consolation prize the two of the them should go out and get over their misery. Christian had been only too happy to agree.

He had been planning the date for two days, and could only hope that everything would go as planned. Hopping into the driver seat, he glanced around the floorboards to make sure there wasn't any missed garbage or soda bottles. He had spent all afternoon cleaning and washing the interior, and it now smelled faintly of Armor All mingled with the New Car Scent air-freshener he had place under his seat. Satisfied that everything looked acceptable, he pushed the shifter into gear and headed out of his parent's driveway.

The house that Katie lived in wasn't far from Christian's parents, but the anxiety of this date made it seem as if every car in front of him was doing the minimum speed, and every light turned red as he approached. Passing a florist shop that had the interior lights still on, Christian pulled into the next available entryway and jumped out. The lights from the shop spilled out onto the wet parking lot, giving the asphalt a sheen that made it look new. Silently complimenting himself on remembering to pick up a flower, he pulled open the door and went inside.

Minutes later, having paid for the flower, he made his way back to his vehicle and pulled out onto the road. He reached her street within half a minute, and pulled into the driveway of her house, being careful not to drive stupidly in case her parents were watching.

He grabbed the flower and walked up to the front door. The door was already open, but the only lights from inside were from a television that was playing on the far side of the front room. He heard a woman call him by name and tell him to come in. Entering, he saw a woman seated on a couch in the corner, and a man seated in a recliner across from the TV.

"Hi Christian," a voice came from behind him before he could speak. Christian turned to see Katie coming from the darkened kitchen. She was wearing a pair of jeans, a tight halter-top, and a leather jacket. He couldn't see if she had any makeup on, then again, he didn't feel she ever needed any.

"Mom, Dad, this is Christian. He's one of the guys I work with. We're going to hang out tonight, so I'll be home a bit later." Katie looked over at Christian and smiled.

A light next to the couch flicked on, and Christian

squinted against the sudden brightness. Katie's mother and father smiled at him and exchanged introductions with Christian. After the greetings were finished, Katie's father turned to her and reminded her to be home by midnight, her curfew. Katie said her goodbyes, gave her dad a hug, and led Christian back out into the night.

CHAPTER V

Captain Pollard waited patiently for Commander Tennison to reach the bridge. Within minutes her second in command arrived, looking every bit the officer. She guessed he stood about six foot three or four, and appeared to be athletic. His jet-black hair was close-cropped, as was typical with fleet officers. He had well-defined facial features, centered around the long nose that was prominent on his face. His blue eyes scanned the room as he entered. His skin was tan, surprising Angelina somewhat. He must have recently returned from shore leave, she thought. The only differentiating mark that she could see was a small scar that ran just along the top of his left eyebrow.

He came to a stop in front of her and saluted.

"Commander Marshall Tennison reporting for duty, ma'am," Commander Tennison stated. His salute was crisp, but Angelina received the impression that for some reason he was a bit disappointed to be here. Perhaps it was the way his eyes faded when he saw who his new commanding officer was; she couldn't be sure. Something about the look on his face betrayed his attempt at hiding his disappointment. She was sure it was there, but she wasn't sure why.

"At ease Commander. Please, sit." Angelina motioned towards one of the station chairs as she sat down in the console chair next to him. She stayed silent for a moment to allow the Commander time to gather his thoughts.

"Commander Tennison," Angelina said thoughtfully. "I've heard that name before, haven't I?"

He looked at her with indifference, not offering a possible explanation. She tapped the console with two fingers while she thought about it.

"Yes, yes, I have heard of you. You were up for the *Eccentric* captainship, weren't you," she asked. She knew he had been, but wanted to see how he handled the question. She guessed that he might be a bit put off by having to report to a scout ship instead of getting his own command. She needed to get any resentment or frustration out in the open if they were to work well together.

Marshall hesitated a moment before answering.

"Yes Captain, I was one of the officers being considered for promotion. I'd heard the *Eccentric* mentioned, however my previous commanding officer had indicated that there were several ships that might be up for a new captain.

"Commander, do you have any idea why you were assigned to this particular mission?"

Pollard wanted to see what he knew about the mission. To the best of her knowledge, he had been briefed and given detailed orders regarding the first half of the mission, but she doubted he had as much detailed information as she currently held in her possession.

"Captain, the orders that I received indicated that I was to report to the *Alaurian Spirit* as a Commander, detailed the crew roster, and indicated that we would need to add five clones to our crew – the clones of four officers and an ensign. Other than that, I wasn't privy to the mission specs." Marshall was a little irritated at being interrogated about what he knew, and he hoped the irritation wasn't showing on his face.

"Commander Tennison, you, as well as the rest of the crew, will know the full mission details within twenty-four hours, after we break dock. However, I want you to understand *why* you were selected for this mission." She waited for a moment, watching his reaction to see if he had any idea why he was selected.

"The information I have on you indicates that you have had a successful career as an officer, most recently as a commander on another ship. It also indicates that you had, at one time or another, expressed certain desires about your career. Desires that could be interpreted as not having the proper ambition or mental makeup for someone the USF brass had hoped would command one of the larger battle cruisers someday. The mission that we are going on is one that is crucial to the safety of our sector, and yet, they have chosen not to send a fleet of battle cruisers. Why do you think that is? It's because of the simple fact that sometimes smaller is better. I assume you'll agree, based on the past conversations you've had with your previous commanding officer. Commander, just because you've been assigned to this mission on a 'lesser' ship, don't for one moment think that this mission is not as critical as any battle that you may have run into as a captain on the *Eccentric*. This mission has far more importance than the sentry duty that the *Eccentric* is currently assigned to within our sector. You are on this mission because you are needed here. It's not a demotion or slight, and I would venture a guess and say that any successes that you have here will translate into future successes in your career as a captain. You are being closely monitored, Commander, and you need to know that. Everything you do on this mission will be evaluated, broken down, and evaluated again. I'm not entirely sure what else you've done to warrant this type of scrutiny, but let there be no mistaking the facts – you are being given a chance to prove yourself on this ship."

Pollard paused for a moment to let the Commander think about what she had just said. She waited a few moments, and then stood up. Before Commander Tennison could stand, she motioned for him to remain seating.

"Commander, part of our crew will be the clones, as you mentioned. We will be departing tomorrow for Earth, and will be picking up the clones for you, Lieutenant Parsons, and myself from that planet. As I understand it, your clone is just a teenager, by Earth standards. You are almost double his age, if my information is correct. He won't be much of a benefit in terms of harvesting limbs, but his organs should be in excellent shape. You may want to consider logging a directive with the medical droids should they need to amputate one of your limbs during the course of our mission. Without a directive issuing clearance to use cybernetic replacements, you would wake up without a limb. I'm not sure if you were aware of that." She glanced over to Tennison as he shook his head to indicate that he was not aware of that critical piece of information.

"Once we have the clones, we will take a thread to our mission theatre. You and the rest of the crew will attend a briefing overview tomorrow. I need to plan out the details of the clone acquisitions for tomorrow.   Standard protocol regarding detection, interaction, and acquisition will be followed, so please keep that in mind when planning the action out. Unless you have further questions, you are dismissed.

Commander Tennison indicated he had no further questions, stood and saluted, then turned to leave the bridge.

"Oh, Commander, one more thing," Angelina Pollard called out behind Marshall as an afterthought. He turned to face his captain. "I was the captain for the *Seraphim* prior to my assignment on this ship. We've all made sacrifices to be here. Please remember that when you're dealing with the crew."

Marshall's eyebrows raised slightly in surprise. He had known Pollard was captain of an Infiltrator class starship, but he hadn't realized it was the *Seraphim*, sister ship of the *Eccentric*. He nodded to her and continued his departure from the bridge. What was she doing here? If things had been slightly different, they would be the captains of sister ships right now. If only things had been different.

Apxlus sat in his chamber, reviewing the histories of the elite warriors throughout Shalothan history. He carefully analyzed the known makeup, philosophies, and characteristics that each warrior possessed, as well as the type of situations that they had succeeded and failed in. He felt the history of each warrior was a vital tool in selecting his group of warriors for this mission. After all, if successful, they would have a mission with more importance than all the Shalothan histories combined. To seek knowledge and learn from the past warriors not only paid homage to their greatness, but helped Apxlus narrow his search through quick elimination of fatal flaws that he found in otherwise excellent warriors.

He was in his third straight wake period since his mandate from the Primary. He spent his first wake period trying to develop a plan to escort the Son of God off Je-Fin. The wake period was almost over when he realized the plan would never be perfect – he needed to have warriors that could be flexible enough to react to the situation as it occurred. Spending all of his time developing a plan to infiltrate one of the Je-Fin military garrisons would be wasteful if their Savior was moved off world. There were too many contingencies to plan for in a short amount of time. Instead, he decided to focus on selecting the best talent that would fit the ideal of a supremely flexible squad.

All told, he had reviewed hundreds of histories, and eliminated thousands of prospective warriors. He started to fear that he would not have enough warriors with the characteristics needed for his plan. Through his research, he had created a list of all the traits he sought for his warrior group; excellent strategists, cunning warriors, proven successes against seemingly insurmountable odds, loyalty, and proven leadership abilities. He had narrowed his list to warriors that possessed all of these characteristics, and then added one more that he felt was important to the success of the mission. He eliminated those warriors who did not have a strong knowledge of their religion, as well as those whose faith was not as deep as it should be. He could ill afford to have warriors who did not believe in their mission.

Apxlus found eighteen warriors who possessed all the traits that he was seeking. He was nearing another sleep period, but decided he would forestall sleep until he had reviewed the list once more and ensured that he had not overlooked anything. He knew that he would continually review the list in the coming days, and that his determination in selecting the best possible warriors would provide him with many more uncomfortable sleep periods.

He broke his list down into three sections. The first section contained six warriors who appeared to have the best leadership abilities and had proven themselves to be natural strategists. Four of the six had seen extensive off-world combat against the Fe-Ruqian military, and had lead successful ground campaigns on many of the Fe-Ruq sector planets. One in particular, Umahael Moak, had led the highly successful Je-Fin campaign. His knowledge of Fe-Ruqian military tactics stood unmatched by any in the pool of the chosen, and his loyalty was beyond reproach. These six would be the chosen leaders of the three grouplets that would make up the entire group. The others that Apxlus included in this group were Olasit Metocaniel, Zenaztalon Secael, Sozateson Sasnalre, Itunexm Sapttam, and Todzopsu Naron.

The next six warriors were those that had proven to be survivors. It was not surprising, Apxlus thought, that these were also the six that seemed most entrenched in the faith. The most unbelievable history of survival had been that of Rrapam Naoh. One of the oldest of the chosen warriors, Naoh was just a young warrior in the ranks of the planetary troops when the bloodiest battle of the Shalothan Civil War had occurred. He had escaped the Battle of Pasrasier unscathed, one of the few warriors from his clan to return home. In later years he had participated in the Siege of Adedim 2 in the Aormy sector, a seven-year siege that had killed millions of Aormians, and hundreds of thousands of Shalothan warriors. It was during this siege that he had twice survived being overrun while stationed at one of the forward bases on the planet surface, once as the lone survivor of the unit. He had a knack for surviving that Apxlus could not ignore, and hoped that it would serve Naoh and his chosen brethren well in the weeks ahead. Patcon Alkraz, Huzhataep Leas, Daraseuzhot Asael, Zpikasat Uphael, and Mahatsehael Hahot also fell into this category.

The last group of warriors contained the six that possessed all the characteristics that Apxlus had been searching for, yet were not as distinguished as the other twelve. All were younger warriors, but had seen their share of battle. Many had even served under the other twelve in some capacity or another. One in particular, Mahrpar Anacen, was part of the same lineage as the Primary. That particular lineage had produced not only Anacen and the Primary, but also several other highly honored warriors. Apxlus thought about how the Primary would react if he ever learned that one of the members of his lineage had been selected to go. Sadly, even if gloriously martyred, Anacen's involvement could never be revealed.

Completing his review of the roster, he secured all the information and prepared himself for his much needed sleep period. Tomorrow he would begin assembling his group and introduce the mission.

Christian opened the car door for Katie and helped her in. He was acutely aware that her parents were watching out the window of the house, and he wanted to make a good impression. He waited until she settled into the seat, then closed the door and headed to the driver side. He wanted this night to go perfectly for the both of them. He slid into the driver seat, glanced over at Katie and smiled. She smiled back, and then turned to look up at the window of the house and gave a slight wave of her hand. With that, Christian backed the minivan down the driveway and out onto the road.

"Sooo, where are we going," Katie asked with smile. She fidgeted with the radio while he drove. The misting rain had stopped, leaving just damp roads.

"I got us reservations at this restaurant in downtown Pontiac called Pike Street. It's supposed to be really nice. My brother went there with his girlfriend for their Winter Formal this year, and he said it had fantastic dinners. I guess they have pretty standard food; nothing exotic or anything."

"That's good, 'cuz I'm kind of hungry!" Katie finally found a song on the radio that she liked and sat back. "You didn't have to get me a flower. That was really nice of you. Thanks."

Christian smiled and looked at her out of the corner of his eyes. "You're welcome" was all he could think of to say.

They drove the rest of the way engaged in small conversation about work. Katie's topic of conversation was typical of a teenager; gossiping about people at work and wondering which of her co-workers liked the new cashier. Christian didn't mind the gossip, and found some of it amusing, especially when it pertained to his friends. When they arrived at the restaurant, Christian jumped out to open the door for her. Walking up to the restaurant, Katie grabbed his hand and held it in hers. Christian didn't know what to say, so he looked over at her and smiled.

They arrived early for their reservation, so they sat in the waiting room and continued talking about work. Rather, Katie did most of the talking as Christian marveled at how he hadn't known about half of the things going on at work. The conversation was lighthearted, with both of them laughing at what Katie was saying.

Ten minutes after the original reservation time the host took them to their seats. They spent a few moments making jokes about all the food on the menu while they waited for someone to come to the table. Many of the meals were listed in French with the English explanations typed below. Christian kept looking at the cost of the meal each time he read through the description. He had started out wanting steak, but had talked himself down to a basic chicken dinner. He secretly hoped that Katie didn't have the appetite that she boasted of during the ride here.

They were enjoying their meal, each commenting on how nice the restaurant was, and how good each of their dinners tasted. Katie had decided on a chicken dish also, but it was one of the pricier ones. Christian silently added up how much he had in his wallet, trying to calculate in a tip and money for later. He hoped she didn't want dessert too. It wouldn't leave much for the rest of the date.

They were almost finished with dinner, and had seemingly exhausted every topic imaginable about work. Katie decided to ask if he had read any books lately. Surprisingly, Christian seemed to perk up with the topic.

"Yeah, I just finished reading this sci-fi trilogy. It's kind of a rip–off on Star Wars at first, but I really got into it. The villain isn't actually the villain, and ends up being a good guy. It's weird though. During the book this guy keeps having visions about killing the only woman he would ever love, and he couldn't understand how or why. He even warns her that she will die by his hands, but she blows him off, thinking his visions are wrong. Anyway, there is this big galactic war, and then it looks like the long lost prince is going to die. Then the villain, who is a good guy now, goes to the prince's rescue, along with the woman he's in love with. They rescue the prince from this dude, but during the fight the woman gets poisoned with some weapon that will make her go crazy and become evil. She ends up asking the guy that loves her to kill her to spare her the torture of becoming this evil person that the poison would create. So, in the end, the prince is safe and goes on to rule the galaxy, but the guy ends up killing the girl to save her from going mad and possibly becoming an enemy to the prince. He goes into exile because he's lost his one true love. It's kind of weird at first, but it gets really good."

"Sounds romantic, in a weird spacey kind of way," Katie said. She didn't read science fiction all that much, and had no idea what book Christian was talking about.

"Maybe you can let me borrow it sometime so I can read it," she offered. She smiled and looked at Christian, who had gotten slightly animated when talking about the book. He realized she was watching his animated motions and suddenly felt sheepish.

"Have you read anything lately," he asked her, trying to get her attention off him. He started to feel a little embarrassed talking about science fiction with Katie. She seemed amused by his enthusiasm for the subject.

"I just finished reading the *Odyssey* for one of my classes. It's a shorter version than the original, I think. It was still long though; probably a hundred pages or so. You'll probably have to read it next year for one of your classes.

"Yeah, we read that this year too. We read it early in the fall. What did you think of it?" Christian was hoping that she liked it.

"It was kind of boring at first. I really liked how he came back to his home after being away so long and his dog recognized him. That was cool, same with when he had to win against all of the guys hitting on his wife. I don't think I would have waited around for someone to come back after all that time."

"She loved her husband though. You don't think you would wait for the one you love to return?"

"Not if everyone thought he was dead. Twenty years is quite a long time to wait. Think about that. If I got married to someone when I'm twenty-five, and he disappears, I'm not waiting around until I'm forty-five wondering if he's still alive. Anyway, in that story, didn't he end up shacking up with some girl for seven of the years that he was gone?" Katie was laughing as she said it, but Christian thought he detected a slight defensive tone in her voice, as if she didn't want Marshall to think of her as a lesser person for admitting that she wouldn't wait.

"Yeah, he did. He also battled monsters and held his eyes open with toothpicks. Not exactly true-to-life stuff, ya know? I know what you're saying though. I probably wouldn't wait around either. Especially not if she had a sister I could shack up with!" He laughed as he said it, and Katie feigned a disgusted look before throwing her napkin over at him. He caught it, and both laughed a bit longer before they caught the stares of the people at the tables around them.

"Come on Sci-Fi boy, I think it's time to leave." With that, Christian flagged down their waiter and took care of the bill. He silently thanked Katie for not getting dessert. At least they would have some cash for later in the night.

They walked out of the restaurant hand in hand, and discovered that it had started raining again. It was a steady rain, but with the temperature dropping, Christian guessed that it could turn into freezing rain later that night.

CHAPTER VI

General Odine was sleeping soundly when the console next to his bed went off. Bleary-eyed, he rolled over to shut off the incessant beeping. Touching a button to silence the noise, he swung his legs out of bed and walked over to the desk against the door-wall. He tapped a security code into the communication unit, and upon verification, it projected a small hologram of an officer standing patiently in a rainstorm.

"Soldier, this had better be an attack, or you will be washing the inside of a garbage scow before the night is out." Odine rubbed his eyes with the heel of his hand as he awaited the soldier's response.

"Begging your pardon General, but this is important. You asked our intelligence group to notify you if we found anything significant. Sir, take a look at this." The soldier pointed to his left, and the hologram view switched to a picture of what appeared to be a human male standing in the center of the main parade ground. In most cases, spotting a man standing in the middle of the parade ground during a midnight rainstorm would be difficult, but in this case, the General could see the person very clearly. He was glowing.

"What the hell is that, soldier?" General Odine was confused, still wondering if he were awake yet. He took a closer look at the picture, and saw a man with his arms outstretched before him.

"General, we had a squadron of our men surround him, and all he would say was 'behold the King'. He won't answer any of our questions. One of the men in the squad tried to get closer, but it began raining so hard that he swears he was brought to his knees by the torrent of water that fell from the sky. The others in the squad corroborated his story. The odd part is that it only rained harder *on him*. We didn't feel any change up here from our view point."

"How did he get past all of our security? How long has he been there?"

"No one saw him enter the parade grounds. We noticed him about thirty minutes ago. He hasn't moved since. Sir, we've called in support vehicles to surround him.

"I want him taken into captivity immediately. Seal off the parade grounds, and have someone find out how he got in there without any of you seeing him. Also, make sure he doesn't have others with him. He may be a suicide droid, so be cautious when apprehending him.

"Yes sir," the soldier replied, saluting the general. The hologram flickered out, and General Odine rushed to dress and get down to his command center.

Twenty-five minutes later, Odine arrived at his command center, only to find it buzzing with activity. Several dozen soldiers stood stationed outside the center, and several triads of Devilspears flew overhead, slicing through the pouring rain. As he exited his hovering staff vehicle, one of his aides rushed up to him.

"General, the subject arrived about five minutes ago. We just received a report indicating that no orbital craft or atmospheric vehicles were found nearby. It appears he must be traveling on foot or with a ground vehicle. He still hasn't spoken since they apprehended him. Apparently the glow faded away and the rain let up just after you were called. He stood motionless as some soldiers approached, and they took him without incident. He's currently in a maximum-security detention cell. We have every available interrogator on their way in for a crack at this guy, sir."

General Odine nodded as he walked into the building. The aide stayed in step with him, giving more detailed information about the captive. Odine glanced around and looked at the soldiers. Many of them had a look that betrayed their fear. This was cause for concern to Odine, as he took it to mean that they were beginning to doubt everything they had been taught. *There is no God*, all Fe-Ruqians believed. After being taught that for an entire lifetime, witnessing something along the lines of this could easily shake their belief system. Whoever, whatever this person was, they needed to get it off planet and out of the system as soon as possible. The longer it was here, the more destructive it became, just by the knowledge of it existing. Odine had to give the Shalothans credit; they knew what would be effective against his troops. He would see to it that they were repaid in full for the attack on his troops. That was exactly what he considered this appearance by the man claiming to be Christ - an attack on the morale of his troops. It supported the theory that his intelligence units had come up with when the first event happened not so long ago. They had no evidence, no proof at the time to make a claim against the Shalothans. Now, with the capture of their agent, he could show the galaxy the treachery the Shalothans were capable of doing.

Marshall Tennison slept fitfully during his first night on the *Alaurian Spirit*. He awoke well before he needed to, and decided to head back into the orbital station to get some coffee before they left for their mission. He dressed quickly, throwing on his ship uniform instead of the dress blue uniform that he had worn during his travels to the station. He stepped out of his quarters into the deck corridor, and felt a cool breeze brush past his face. All of the corridor lights were on now, opposite of when he had arrived. The ship was venting all the stale air and pumping in fresh oxygen, an indication the post-hibernation process was in full swing. He made his way down to the air lock and exited the ship.

Stepping out of the air lock into the orbital station vestibule, he walked out into the main corridor and merged with the flow of people traveling to the various docks. After passing a few docks, he stepped out of the flow and over to a small food station where several people queued up for service. He fumbled around in his pocket for his currency card.

"Commander, let me get it," a voice to his left said. Marshall quickly glanced over to see Captain Pollard standing next to him. She held a data card reader in her hand, and her currency card in the other.

"Good morning Captain. You're up early," Marshall said. He was surprised to see her down here. More than that, he wondered if she had followed him down here, or if it was just a coincidence.

"I came down about an hour ago to get something for breakfast. The galley wasn't up and running by the time I woke up. The ship still has a few hours before all the secondary systems are online. That's the only drawback to these ships – the hibernation period takes so long to wake up from that you could charter another ship and be finished with your mission before all the systems come back online."

"Captain, do you know why the *Spirit* was in hibernation?"

Captain Pollard held up a finger and nodded towards the service counter. "I'll have a hot chocolate and," she glanced over at Marshall for his choice.

"Coffee, black," he finished the sentence. She swiped her card in the reader and the droid passed the drinks across the counter within a few seconds. Angelina handed Marshall his drink as they stepped away from the service counter.

"I read up on the history of the ship last night. It was originally a long-range frigate, built about twenty years ago. About two and a half years ago a USF patrol stopped the ship as it was attempting to smuggle weapons into the Fe-Ruq sector. After being captured and taken to the closest orbital base for processing, the ship was sent to the Aormy dry-docks for storage. About six months after that, the USF began converting the ship to a scout ship, having lost an abundance of scout ships in recent battles. Here's the interesting part though – the ship retrofit project was completed within six months, but the vessel was never sent out on a mission. It sat awaiting a command for six months before someone at headquarters decided the ship was better off in hibernation than staffed with a skeleton crew. A year later, here we are."

Captain Pollard sipped her hot chocolate and took a look around the orbital station's B-dock corridor. The corridor featured a high ceiling, with large transparent sections of hull that provided impressive views of the planet, the moon, and several large starships that had come to port while she and her crew had slept. The walls and bulkheads looked like polished titanium, and the deck floors were a slate gray, with the crests for each of the planets within the sector stenciled on the floor in bright colors. Information kiosks were located at the vestibule of each dock, and at every fifth dock there was a small area that contained several food stations to serve the crews of the docked ships, as well as any visitors. Security droids stood silently in various locations against the bulkheads, and custodial droids constantly roamed about the corridor, polishing and cleaning everything. Dozens of people milled about the corridor, some going to their respective ship, and others coming out for various reasons. Angelina and Marshall watched in silence for a few moments before Marshall spoke up.

"Captain, do you know if the rest of the crew is aboard yet?"

She took another sip of her hot chocolate and nodded.

"Of the fifteen that are supposed to board before we depart, twelve of us are here. Ensign Kevin Theore and his clone are in transit. Lieutenant Ernestine Soloman is in-station, but there was a delay in the transfer of her command. Her current ship is down in the C dock, so she should be along shortly."

"Ensign Theore travels with his clone?" Marshall was curious to know why an officer traveled with his clone. For that matter, he wanted to know why a junior officer had a clone when more senior ones on the ship weren't going to have one.

"Ensign Theore is our MERL specialist. Because of the highly technical nature of the device, his clone is a backup knowledge base for the weapon. All MERL specialists now have their clones with them as part of their assignment requirements. It's a fairly new protocol for the USF, but it makes sense. If you're on a ship that depends heavily on the MERL for defense and support, such as our ship, then losing your MERL tech would be devastating."

Marshall nodded in understanding. He hadn't had much experience with the MERL device, other than the few simulations in his advanced training sessions. He wondered if the MERL specialist clone would also sit in on the officer meetings since they were designated as knowledge base backups.

"Are you going to head back to the ship, Captain?" Marshall asked, trying to make small talk. He downed the last bit of his coffee and scanned the corridor for a trash bin.

"No, I'm going to stay down here for a bit longer. I've been on a ship for all but two of the days of the past standard year, so I think I'm going to stretch my legs a bit and walk around. I'll be back on board by oh-six hundred ship time."

Marshall glanced at his wrist krono and saw it was only oh-five thirty ship time. He looked up at one of the various monitors hanging near the food station and saw the orbital dock time was almost twelve hours ahead. *The station must be tied to headquarters local time*, he thought.

"I'll see you back aboard, Captain," Marshall said, saluting her. She saluted back and smiled. He quickly turned and made his way back towards the B-41 dock vestibule.

Four hours later, Commander Marshall Tennison sat in his chair on the bridge of the *Alaurian Spirit*, working with the crew to run through final system checks before departure.

Upon arriving back on the ship after his venture out into the dock corridor, he spent another hour in his quarters and then made his way up to the bridge to begin checking off all preflight systems. Over the course of the next hour, several members of the crew reported for duty to the bridge. Commander Tennison greeted each of them and informed them of their assigned duty on the bridge. During the first few hours, Marshall met both pilots, Ensigns Claude Roach and Duncan Cummings. Recalling the information he had received, he knew that Roach had more battle experience than Cummings, but Cummings had piloted a wider variety of ships during his short career.

Lieutenants Louis Daniels and Andrew Parsons also reported to the bridge. Both had experience on larger starships and battle cruisers as weapons officers, but for this mission Lieutenant Parsons would work that station, while Daniels would work at the systems control console.

Several of the other crewmembers were in various parts of the ship, running diagnostics on specific control functions. The MCAC weapons array was being loaded with its missiles. As the ship's MCAC specialists, Ensigns Jason House, Omer Douglass Kramer, and Aileen Sears were coordinating the entire process. One observed from a station within the firing control center, monitoring the system to warn the others against any malfunction. Another was stationed in a life-support suit outside the ship's hull, keeping watch as the ordnance droids loaded the missiles through a hatch near the reserve chamber. The last of the crew was inside the reserve chamber itself, running safety checks and logging information as each missile was loaded and locked into place.

On the deck containing the MERL device, Ensign Kevin Theore and his clone Kevin Theorre were putting the control system through a series of tests to bring the system online. Several of the non-clone crewmembers had looked at the pair strangely when they boarded the ship together. Typically, clones were thought of as second-class citizens, and most officers would have his or her clone shipped in well after they arrived to a new ship. To many of the crewmembers, this particular officer and his clone actually seemed to be friendly with each other.

Captain Pollard met with the remainder of the crew in various parts of the ship. Lieutenant JGs Barry Guy and Buck Dalton were being briefed on the communication protocols of the mission. Because of the nature of the mission, standard communication protocol wouldn't be used once they were in the Fe-Ruq sector. Once they had finished their meeting, the two junior officers headed to their quarters to unpack their gear and report up to the bridge for their systems' checkoffs.

Lieutenant Ernestine Soloman had arrived shortly after Commander Tennison went back aboard the ship. She was escorted aboard by the Captain herself, and given a quick tour of the ship. Soloman was introduced to the commander once she and the captain had finished the tour. Marshall quickly learned that the Lieutenant had previously served aboard the *Seraphim* with the Captain, and her during her last four months she had been an attaché with Admiral Caturorglimi's office. Of all the officers on board the *Alaurian Spirit*, it was Lieutenant Soloman that impressed Marshall the most. She carried an air of confidence and authority about her that made Marshall forget that he was her senior officer on this mission.

Ensign Roach approached and saluted the Commander, breaking him away from his thoughts. Claude Roach was a smaller man, but thickly built. He had a shaved head, and the lights on the bridge reflected off the deep brown skin on his head. His file contained information about his piloting skills that Tennison had found fascinating. He had originally been a suborbital fighter jock for the USF on one of its interstellar carrier class ships. He had sixteen verified kills before the truce had been negotiated between the systems. Once his six-month tour on the frontlines was up, he rotated back to an orbital defense station and began learning to fly larger starships and frigates, such as the *Spirit*. He had been volunteered for this mission by his commanding officer on the orbital defense station; not so much because he was an exceptional pilot, but more because Roach had become unhappy away from the frontlines. He had become an adrenaline junkie, and was going through withdrawals. Rather than attempt to 'rehabilitate' him through mindless simulations and boring patrols, his CO felt that this challenge would be the best way to utilize his talents, as well as help the young officer continue to grow.

"Commander, flight operations system check is complete. We are green for departure."

Commander Tennison nodded, clicked the communication button on his armrest, and leaned over slightly to speak.

"Captain Pollard, flight operations are a go for departure."

"Thank you Commander," the voice came back from speaker. "Please begin the departure procedures."

Commander Tennison was a little surprised the Captain was not taking on the responsibility for the process. It was more common for the ship's captain to be the one to lead the departure procedures. Not wanting to dwell on it, Tennison flicked on the all-ship communication button.

"Prepare for departure sequence. Flight operations, are we a go for departure?"

"Flight operations is a go."

"MERL command is a go."

"MCAC command is a go."

"Engineering is a go." The last response came across the speaker as the voice of one of the engineering droids. Tennison still couldn't adjust to the idea the ship would be run by a crew with more than half of the operating crew comprised of droids. The medical facility had a med-droid running day and night. The ship's security was being managed by an upgraded security MP analog droid, with the rest of the security group roles filled by standard sentry droids. The only major functions that weren't automated through the use of droids or system upgrades were navigation and weapons control.

The remainder of the lesser functions continued to report 'go for departure' in their computerized voices. Once all systems reported in, Commander Tennison clicked his comm button to contact the dockmaster on the orbital station.

"The is the *Alaurian Spirit*, requesting permission for dock departure." Commander Tennison looked around at his crew on the bridge, and suddenly felt a surge of confidence and exhilaration at beginning the mission.

"*Alaurian Spirit*, this is the dockmaster. Stand by as we seal the dock air lock and vestibule." There was a slight pause from the dock while they sent the commands to seal off the entry point to the orbital station. "Stand by for magnetic clamp deactivation." There was a loud clunk as the large electroplates that were holding the ship to the hull of the orbital dock demagnetized and retracted flush with the orbital dock's hull, breaking the hold on the *Alaurian Spirit*. The ship slowly drifted apart from the hull of the orbital dock. "*Spirit*, you are clear to engage docking thrusters." Ensign Cummings looked back at Commander Tennison for the signal to engage the thrusters.

"Engage thrusters," Tennison commanded, smiling as he watched through the viewshield. A slight hiss sounded throughout the ship as the thrusters engaged. Tennison and the rest of the crew on the bridge watched as their ship rotated away from the orbital dock until it was almost perpendicular to the hull. The ship began to move slowly forward as it began its path out of the orbital shipyard. Tennison felt a little tense as they maneuvered through the orbital dock traffic. Several large ships were inbound, and numerous ships that were too big to physically dock with the station floated in clusters around the orbital dock, a few kilometers away. This was one of the most crucial points of the mission, as ship accidents were most common in congested spaces such as this.

Twenty minutes later, the ship had cleared all of the orbital dock traffic and was on a deep system vector away from the planet. Tennison ordered the pilots to continue at their current speed, and then radioed Captain Pollard that they were underway.

Commander Reaz Apxlus woke from his sleep period with a feeling of consternation. The previous two wake periods had been very busy, and he felt that he might have missed something. In the morning two periods ago, Primary Radael had contacted him to inform him that he and his team needed to depart for Je-Fin within the next two wake periods. In his brief message he stated there was activity detected on Je-Fin that indicated the Fe-Ruqian military was conducting an extensive search operation, and had possibly captured a person of interest. No other details were given, but Apxlus was not surprised by the lack of information. He had immediately sent orders out to all of his chosen warriors, informing them that they were to report to a specific berthing location in one of the outer palace garrison centers. This wake period was the time that they were all due to arrive.

Apxlus quickly dressed in his standard uniform, but had planned to bring several other outfits for various situations. In his orders to the chosen warriors, he indicated that they were to do the same. He opened his weapons closet and began selecting the items that he would bring. He chose his Krangth staff, made of hardened wood from the legendary Krangth tree. Stronger than many metals, it was lighter than many wood and metal alloys. It was standard issue to all warriors once they went through the Devotion ritual. He had modified his, first by adding small barbs in a four-centimeter strip around each end, and then by burning his clan name into the center of the handle. He also selected his forearm blaster, which was worn as a sheath on the forearm of the warrior's firing hand. To use the weapon, the warrior would slap the top of the sheath with his opposite hand, or as other warriors had discovered, against any hard surface. This percussive force triggered the weapon to slide up from the underside of the warrior's forearm into his grasp. Unlike the typical single-barrel blaster made by the humans, this weapon had two thinner barrels, connected by a handle with a pressure sensitive grip that allowed the user to fire in single shots or squeeze harder for faster stutter fire. The weapon was not terribly accurate, but was useful in close quarters or for covering fire.

Apxlus finished packing up his gear and headed down to a berthing station, where he loaded his gear up in his personal hover transport. Basically an air sled, it was big enough for two warriors with full gear, and could travel for hundreds of kilometers on the same power cell.

The trip wouldn't normally take long, but he took a circuitous route to avoid any curious onlookers viewing him making a direct approach to the berthing station at a garrison outpost.

Upon arriving, Apxlus was pleased to see that all of his chosen warriors were waiting for him. They were standing around in a few separate groups, apparently discussing why they thought they were there. He also saw a Fe-Ruqian military cargo ship that had been captured during the war was berthed in the station that he had directed his warriors to. On the side of the ship, just below the forward cockpit, was the name stenciled in Fe-Ruqian military block: *Nowrimo's Revenge.*

The ship wasn't exceptionally large or sleek, which

was just what Apxlus had wanted. Looking under the belly of the ship, he noticed the addition that he had requested; the flattened barrel of a particle beam weapon protruded from a weapons package that had recently been added to the ship. In the same package he could see the tips of four snub-nose missiles protruding from a launcher. He assumed there were more within the cargo hold, but he would have one of his warriors check, nonetheless.

"Warriors," Apxlus called out as he stopped his transport, "board the ship immediately. Stow your gear in the cargo hold, and situate yourselves for immediate departure." Apxlus unstrapped his gear from the vehicle, and briskly walked towards the boarding ramp of the *Revenge*. Walking up to the ship, he realized it was longer than he had expected, reaching almost fifty meters in length. Most of the ship was empty cargo space, but there was a decent sized crew pod attached to the forward portion of the ship, under the cockpit.

The warriors all reacted immediately to his command, filing up the boarding ramp into the belly of the crew pod. Apxlus was the last aboard, closing the ramp with a slap to the control pad with his hand. Having memorized the skills of his warriors, he began issuing assignments.

"Warrior Anacen, Warrior Athes, and Warrior Moak – you will go to the cockpit and begin the startup sequence for liftoff. Warrior Caxon, you will go find the weapons package control system and bring it to stand-by readiness. The rest of you prepare for immediate departure."

Apxlus ventured up into the cockpit, where the three warriors had already found seats and had begun the startup sequence for the ship. Apxlus took one of the rear seats and strapped himself in. He noticed that Athes had taken the command seat, with Anacen and Moak in the pilot and copilot seats.

The three warriors brought the ship's systems online and switched the antigravity unit on, lifting the ship off the ground. It rotated slowly as it lifted above the berthing station, providing an excellent view of the palace in the distance. Once sufficiently above the ground, Moak switched the atmospheric thrusters on as Anacen directed the ship up at a steep ascent. Minutes later, the darkness of space enveloped the ship and its inhabitants, with the cockpit illuminated only by the glow of the instrument panels.

Sufficiently satisfied the departure went well, Apxlus directed Athes to plot a course to the moon of Jethl, in the Fe-Ruq system within the sector of the same name. Receiving Athes' acknowledgment, Apxlus descended out of the cockpit and went to meet with the other warriors.

CHAPTER VII

Approximately an hour after the ship cleared the orbital dock and planet, Captain Pollard called for her senior officers to convene in her quarters. She brought in enough chairs for everyone to sit on, and had the galley droids bring up coffee.

Commander Tennison handed off control of the bridge to Lieutenant Junior Grade Buck Dalton and made his way down to the captain's quarters. Lieutenants Daniels, Parsons, and Soloman were already seated. Seeing the others with coffee, he grabbed a cup for himself and took his seat. After he was comfortable, Captain Pollard began to speak.

"As I'm sure all of you have been waiting, we are now going to review the mission objectives. Please feel free to ask questions during the presentation. I want this to be as informal as possible." She looked at each of her officers, and seeing no questioning looks, continued.

"A contact on Je-Fin reported in with some unusual information recently. The report contained information about an event that occurred during a military presentation on their parade grounds on Je-Fin. The contact stated that during opening ceremonies for a joint military exercise, a bright light filled the sky, and a voice was heard across the area. The voice allegedly said 'Behold the Son of God'." Captain Pollard paused and looked at each of her officers. Tennison raised an eyebrow, and Parson's eyes widened a bit.

"Naturally, the event upset the Fe-Ruq military, as the entire system is atheist, and the military is very anti-religion. The initial reaction from the Fe-Ruqians was that it was a Shalothan attack. Likewise, when higher ups in the Shalothan government learned about the event, they suspected the Fe-Ruqians were staging the event to lure the Shalothans back into the war. Tensions were high on both sides, however, the Shalothans kept the information secret within their system. Reports have since filtered into the system from traders and so on, but they're being taken as rumors only. Our mission, in short, is to go into the Fe-Ruq system and observe what's going on. We want to prevent any escalation of hostilities, so we're going to be the first point of contact should we see any escalation or buildup of forces. The USF intelligence agents suspect it will be the Fe-Ruqians to make the first move, as the Shalothans are still licking their wounds from the last few battles." Pollard paused again to take a sip of hot chocolate, which she had requested for herself instead of coffee.

"The mission is difficult enough considering the tensions on both sides, and the lack of trust the Fe-Ruqians have for the USF. Recent events have changed our role. This morning, just prior to our departure, I received an urgent message from Admiral Caturorglimi. Last night our contact reported that military forces on Je-Fin had captured someone claiming to be Christ. It wouldn't have been so remarkable except for the fact that this person was glowing, and somehow caused rain to fall in torrents on specific field units. As you can imagine, this new event will almost certainly cause a response from one or both sides. A contact on Shalotha reported that a small cargo ship hastily departed from a garrison port shortly after we received our information. It appeared to be a Fe-Ruq transport, based on markings and ship design."

"They're using it as a disguise to get into the system," Tennison offered. Pollard nodded her head towards him in agreement.

"Based on the outbound trajectory, the ship is on its way to the Fe-Ruq system, but we don't know with whom or what on it. The Shalothans obviously can't send a fleet in to rescue the man claiming to be Christ. My guess is that it's a small force that will attempt to infiltrate Je-Fin and extricate the individual. But if we know, then you can bet that the Fe-Ruq military have information about the ship as well."

"How does that affect our original mission objective, Captain?" It was Lieutenant Soloman who asked.

"We are now reassigned to find this cargo ship, believed to be called *Nowrimo's Revenge*, and track and observe. We are not to engage or contact it under any circumstances. The Admiral just wants us to track the ship so they can project a sector entry point and move forces to that area to prevent them from violating the boundaries of the Fe-Ruq sector. With the change, we'll be increasing our speed to reach Earth and extricate the clones. Unfortunately, it will most likely be a rough extraction, since we'll be short on time. We will be forgoing the standard observation and isolation times."

Captain Pollard paused and looked around at each of her officers to gauge their reaction to the last statement. Not having an observation time to survey the targets would be risky, and a few of the officers raised their eyebrows at her last statement.

"One other thing. For reasons I cannot divulge at this time, the five of us are not, I repeat, not to reveal this change in the mission. The name of the ship is not to come up at any time with the junior officers. To them, we are still on an observation mission only. I will let you know when you can provide more detail to them. Is that understood?"

All of them verbalized their understanding. Tennison shot a quick glance over to Pollard and slightly raised an eyebrow at her. She caught the look, but didn't acknowledge it. She stood and dismissed the group, but as they were filing out, she asked Commander Tennison to stay for a moment. Waiting for the rest of the officers to move down the hallway, she closed and locked her door and asked Tennison to sit.

"Commander, before we get to any questions you may have, let me take a minute and add to the information that you're allowed to know. The Admiral does not want to have the entire crew be aware of the purpose of our updated mission for two basic reasons. The first is for security purposes. There is always an outside chance that we could be taken prisoner by the Fe-Ruqian military as we approach their primary system. They will certainly be on edge because of this, and not knowing what exactly what the Shalothans plan on doing, they could detain us as a precautionary measure. If we're detained, we don't want any of the junior officers to be able to reveal information about our updated mission under duress. To the Fe-Ruq brass, an observation mission is much easier to accept when offering up diplomatic apologies for capturing a USF ship. If they were to discover that we are planning on tracking the Shalothan ship with a scout ship armed with an MCAC system and MERL device, it would appear to them that we were doing more than observing. Perhaps even appear that *we are assisting*."

Captain Pollard put an emphasis on the last three words, causing Commander Tennison to tilt his head slightly in question.

"Captain, are you saying that we may end up assisting the Shalothans?" The tone used in Commander Tennison's question was dubious. He certainly couldn't believe the USF council would ever approve a mission to assist in a kidnapping by a system that they had been at war with recently.

"Commander Tennison, I can only tell you what you just heard. I trust in your ability to read into the meaning of it," Pollard replied, showing a slight smile. She brushed her hair back with both hands, and then took another sip of hot chocolate.

"And the second reason?"

"Also for security, but more so for our own. Suppose we tell the entire crew the true nature of our mission. Then, during the mission, let's say one of our MCAC operators or MERL techs suddenly gets overcome with a feeling of anger over some perceived unfair deed that God did to him or his family. Perhaps the death of a young child, the loss of a parent, anything that could be considered 'unfair'. Then this disgruntled officer discovers that we are within visual range of a ship potentially carrying the Son of God. I would be concerned with letting that person near any firing control console. Who's to say that they don't act out in anger for past grievances against God, and decide to fire upon the ship that may be carrying the Son of God, blowing it into subatomic particles. At the very least, the

Shalothans would be angered over an unprovoked attack on one of their ships, which may result in retaliation against us or another USF vessel in the system. More so, if the ship truly was carrying the Son of God, then what would we have just done? We've killed humanity's savior? The person that trillions of people have been waiting and praying for centuries to arrive? We would, in effect, have signed our own death sentence. Personally, I don't want to spend the rest of my life hiding in some hole in an asteroid, afraid to show my face, all because an angry crewmember of mine decided to try to get even with God."

Marshall nodded in understanding, fully comprehending the breadth of the mission, and the risks that were inherent in it. He sat back in his chair and let out a long, slow breath. He thought about what he would do if faced with the fact that the ship they were tracking was carrying the Son of God. Would repressed angers well up inside of him? Could he fire on the ship if it started to fire on the *Alaurian Spirit*? His thought process stopped as he thought about the ship. He played with the ship's name in his mind, trying to pull apart the name and think about what it meant.

"Captain, who came up with the name of this ship?" Marshall leaned forward a bit, hanging on Angelina's words.

Captain Pollard pursed her lips together, and bored her eyes in the commander.

"Are you familiar with the planet Alaura?" Marshall shook his head to indicate that he did not. "Alaura was a planet densely populated by early human colonists. They became ultra religious, to the point of being fanatics. The entire population believed that their planet, Alaura, was the arrival planet for the second coming of Christ. So profound was this belief that many of their leaders, already zealots of unheard proportions, declared that the Alaurians were actually creatures of God, sent to protect His Son when he arrived on Alaura. The masses were overjoyed to hear this, elevating themselves on a pedestal as better than everyone else in the galaxy. Their leaders saw this religious furor, and the power it contained. They spread a message to the population that would doom Alaura forever."

Captain Pollard paused to take another sip of hot chocolate. Commander Tennison found himself leaning forward in his chair, arms resting on his knees.

"The leaders spread word that Christ was coming, and that the Son of God needed His guardians to protect Him. The caveat was that it was the spirits of the Alaurians that held the power to protect Christ. So, in order to get to a spiritual plain, what do you suppose they did?" Captain Pollard waited for Tennison's answer.

He shrugged, searching for an answer. "Mass suicide?"

"No, for they believed suicide was the tool of the devil, not of God. Suicide would condemn them to hell for eternity. The leaders of Alaura realized this, and created their message to capitalize on this problem. They announced that in order to become the guardian spirits, each person would need to die a glorious death in the name of Christ. Thus, the Alaurian Crusades began."

"I remember something about that back from one of my classes at the university!"

"Probably a very short review on the subject. It

wasn't a long crusade. The Alaurians massed onto their ships, bent on purging the galaxy of sinners. Within days they reached the nearest planet that they, in their mind, felt was populated by sinners. This planet was a planet deep in history and culture, built on similar Christian beliefs. But they weren't human beings, and the Alaurians knew in their hearts that only the human soul could be the guardian of Christ. So they attacked the planet en masse, but were repelled and thoroughly defeated. But that wasn't the worst for the supposed guardians of Christ. The beings they attacked launched a massive counterattack against their planet, wiping out almost all of the planet's population within days. History says the attackers came at Alaura like a swarm of locusts, arriving in such force that all of Alaura's planetary defenses were overwhelmed within hours. The Alaurian Crusade lasted exactly two weeks – from the day it was launched, until the day the last city on Alaura succumbed to the counterattack.

"Sounds like an impressive military force, especially considering how long ago that was. What planet did the Alaurians attack? Is that species still around? To wipe out an entire planet within days…" Commander Tennison shook his head wistfully, trying to picture the ruthlessness that went into the elimination of an entire population within days.

Captain Pollard nodded slowly in silent agreement with Marshall's unfinished thought.

"The species is still around, Commander. In fact, the planet that was attacked by the Alaurians is now the government seat of that entire sector. Based on your experiences in the USF, I suspect that you know the species very well. It was Shalotha that the Alaurians attacked.

Commander Tennison's eyes grew wide in understanding at what his Captain had just said. This revelation could mean a few different things. Was their ship actually on another mission that even he didn't know about, sent to attack the Shalothans in the spirit of the long dead Alaurian zealots? And if so, did that mean that someone intended for them to all die in order to reach the spiritual state that the Alaurians felt was necessary to attain to fully offer their service of protection to Christ? Was the ship named as such to imply that they weren't merely observers, but sent to be the protectors of the man that was claiming to be the Son of God? And if the Shalothans decimated the Alaurians so long ago, wouldn't a ship with the name *Alaurian Spirit* attract the attention of the Shalothans? The questions raced through Marshall's mind faster than he could begin to think of answering any of them.

Seeing this, Pollard spoke up and interrupted his thoughts.

"Commander, you're reading too much into this. It's the name of a ship. I've had the same inner battle over what this could mean. It's the name of the ship, that's all. We're still here to do our job, which is to observe and track that Fe-Ruqian ship full of Shalothans. We're not waging another crusade to do it." She looked into the eyes of Commander Tennison, willing him to understand with her stare. *Don't lose it on me, Tennison,* she thought.

The communication board on her data table beeped, shaking her out of her stare, and Lieutenant Soloman's voice came over the speaker.

"Captain, I don't mean to disturb you, but the nav system has finished computing the thread information.

We'll be on the thread within five minutes, and to Earth within twelve hours. Any further orders Captain?"

"Carry on Lieutenant. Thank you." Captain Pollard reached over and clicked the communication board off. She looked back at Tennison, who had taken the unexpected break to compose himself and sit upright in the chair.

"Commander, we'll be in an Earth orbit within twelve hours. I expect that we will locate our targets and complete the extraction within six hours of arrival. I want you to coordinate the crew. You'll be using the atmospheric pod, so plan accordingly. Restraint cells have been set up in the medical center so they can be monitored continuously. Because of our time constraints, stealth is not a necessity in this operation. Please submit your plan to me before we enter orbit. Let's be efficient about this, Commander. Any questions?"

Commander Tennison declined to ask any questions, and Pollard quickly dismissed him. Captain Pollard waited until the door had closed after Tennison, and then walked over to her briefcase. Pulling a personal communicator out, she clicked it on.

"Ernie, I need you to come up when you can sneak away." She clicked it off and stashed it away. *Tennison could be a problem*, she thought.

Apxlus entered the cargo hold and let his gaze fall over each of the warriors. Several were speaking in a small group, and a few others were off to the side sitting against the cargo hold wall. Upon seeing Apxlus enter, each warrior straightened his posture, and those sitting quickly stood up.

"Glorious warriors of Shalotha, please gather so I

may brief you on the mission." Apxlus sat down with the group, and he spent the next hour reviewing the mission details, the objective, and the updated information that had launched the mission. None of the warriors spoke during the information period, and few had questions when the chance was offered for them to ask. All had shown surprise when informed whom it was that they were going after on Je-Fin. Many had bowed their heads and silently offered up a prayer of thanks for being given the opportunity to assist Christ in His return to the galaxy.

After briefing the warriors in the cargo hold, Apxlus assigned four warriors to relieve the three in the cockpit and the one at the weapons station, and then repeated all of the same information to them.

After finishing with those four, Apxlus went into the crew pod to search for a suitable room he could convert to a command center. He found a room just below and behind the cockpit, probably an office for the former captain of the ship. It was large enough to accommodate several people, and had a data table and chair in a corner of the room. Apxlus decided to use the room, and then sent word for Moak, Metocaniel, Secael, Sasnalre, Sapttam, and Naron.

In short time they arrived in the room. Apxlus had them make themselves as comfortable as possible, given the space constraints. He then launched into a detailed breakdown of the team assignments, and their responsibilities.

Lieutenant Ernestine Pauline Soloman excused herself from the bridge when the cochlear implant in her ear beeped. The faint voice of the captain could be heard deep in her ear canal, but it was faint enough that even someone whispering in her ear would not have heard the transmission.

Hearing the request, she walked posthaste to the captain's quarters, knocking lightly to announce her arrival. The door slid open, and Soloman stepped into the room swiftly.

"Captain?" Soloman asked, standing in front of the data table. Captain Pollard motioned for her to sit down. She brought her own cup of hot chocolate to the table, and poured a cup of coffee for the officer.

Ernestine Soloman thanked the captain for the coffee, and wrapped her fingers around the cup. Her head was completely bald, and the light in the room glistened off the crown of her head. She was thinly built, but tall, with well-defined facial features. Her black eyes sat in stark contrast to the fair skin that she had. Afflicted with a rare disorder, her body was unable to grow hair, and as such she grew up not having real hair or eyebrows. It wasn't until she joined the ranks of the USF that she felt comfortable enough to leave her quarters without the synth-hair on her head. Despite her affliction, or because of it, Lieutenant Soloman was exceptionally driven to succeed.

"Ernie, what's your take on the Commander?"

Soloman rubbed the top of her head with her hand, pausing to frame her words.

"Seems to be disappointed he's not captain. Other than that, I haven't spoken with him enough to get a good feel."

"I need you to shadow him. I'm going to request that he take you with him on the extractions, if he doesn't add you himself. After that, I want you on the bridge at the same time. I'll put the two of you on the same bridge rotation."

"What's wrong, Captain? He have a shaky history?" Soloman chugged down the rest of the coffee.

"No, no, nothing like that. Just my own instincts. I don't know if he's realized the true nature of our mission or not. He's knows less than we know, but enough to make his own conclusions. Hopefully they're not the wrong ones." Pollard stood up and stretched.

"Captain, do you want me to pre-empt him if he starts behaving erratically?" She narrowed her eyes at the captain, waiting for the answer.

Captain Pollard looked down at Soloman, stone-faced.

"Absolutely."

CHAPTER VIII

Christian sat on the couch, beer in hand. Katie sat next to him, laughing at the guys holding the freshman up in the air, doing a keg stand. The two of them had spent the last two nights together on dates, and this would make the third. They had gone bowling the previous night, after the expensive date at the restaurant the night before. Katie had told him about a party that one of her friends had heard about. One of the guys that had graduated last spring was going into the Marines, so his friends were having one last party for him. Unfortunately for Christian, the party was in Romeo, a long drive from his house. He figured he'd have a beer or two, and then hang out until Katie was ready to go. Katie's parents were out of town for the evening, so he hoped that Katie would want to leave the party early and go back to her house.

The party continued on, with the soon-to-be Marine and his friends getting very drunk. Katie and Christian both had consumed a few beers as well, but they seemed to affect her more than Christian. About two hours after they had arrived, she stood up and pulled him off the couch.

"Let's go outside. I need to get some air. And another beer," she smiled at him. He didn't resist, and happily went outside with her. He hadn't gotten a buzz from the two beers he had downed, and contemplated getting another one.

They walked out into the garage through the door in the kitchen, and proceeded to go through another door into the backyard. The yard was open, with only a few smaller trees. The land opened out into a farmer's field, barren now during the colder months. Christian hadn't realized how cold it had gotten, and immediately wished he had brought his jacket. He looked up at the sky, rubbing his hands together to keep warm. Katie had grabbed another beer on the way out, and was sipping on the plastic cup.

"So, what time do you want to leave?" Christian asked, hoping she would want to go after her beer. He looked up at the stars, waiting for her answer.

"Leave? Why? It's free beer, and I don't really have a lot of money to do anything. Do you? Was there somewhere you wanted to go?"

Christian's heart sank. This was the side of Katie that he feared he would see tonight. He had heard all the stories about how she partied, and with beer flowing freely, and no parents at home, he quickly grasped that she had no intention of leaving so soon. He watched the stars twinkling in the sky, and wondered which satellite it was that he saw moving way up above.

"I just thought maybe you might want to go back to your house and watch a movie or something. We can stay here though. I just can't drink anymore."

"Oh, you're a big boy. You can have another beer or two. We'll stay until midnight and then take off, how's that? Four beers won't kill you." She tipped the plastic cup up and chugged down the rest of the beer. Christian was still looking up into the sky, and realized the satellite he saw was getting brighter.

"Hey, do you see that," he said as he pointed

towards the dot of light getting brighter. She squinted a bit, then shrugged.

"Probably a plane coming towards us. What, afraid it's an alien ship coming to take us and do anal probes on us?" She laughed as she said it, hoping to get him to cheer up a bit. She could tell immediately that he was disappointed that she didn't want to leave yet. She looked back up, and now noticed the light was getting brighter. And was growing in size quickly.

"Uh, if that's a plane, it's coming straight for this house." Christian started to feel a bit nervous about the light, as it continued to grow. He couldn't hear any engines from the plane, but he figured that didn't mean much if it was coming straight at them.

As the two of them watched, the light grew until it was just about over the house. Both Christian and Katie stood watching in fear. Whatever it was, the object hovered thirty feet off the ground, the only sound a soft whine from the bottom of the object.

Paralyzed by fear for a few seconds, Christian finally got the nerve to push Katie towards the house.

"Go," he said softly at first. "Go!" he yelled. She stumbled and fell as she tried to turn and run. The bottom of the object opened, and a white beam of light shot down to the ground. Within seconds, a tall being with dark eyes and no hair stood at the bottom of the beam of light. Fear engulfed Christian, causing him to lose his voice. Katie was whimpering on the ground next to him. Where were all the people in the house? Couldn't they see this?

"Come with me," the being said. Christian couldn't move, but noticed the being stepped out of the light towards them. He couldn't make out all the details once the being stepped into the darkness of the late evening, but it appeared be to gray skinned or wearing gray clothing. It was humanoid, from what he could see, and the voice sounded warm.

"Come with me," the being said, a bit harsher now. Katie screamed next to him, and Christian looked over at her to see her finding her way to her feet.

"Come on Christian," Katie yelled, dragging him by his arm. The being walked closer, now only about ten feet from them. Christian stumbled over his feet, Katie still pulling him towards the house.

"They're running," the being said. It lunged towards Christian, grabbing the back of his shirt and pulling him backwards. He instinctively flung his arms around to fight. The being was as tall as he was, but by being so close, he could see it was a human who had a hold of his shirt.

A bright, thin beam lanced out from the front part of the hovering object, striking Christian in the chest. He felt a brief flash of pain, and then blacked out. As he crumpled to the ground, Katie screamed for Christian to get up, and then turned to run back towards the house. Another beam shot out from the object, hitting her in the back, causing her to fall forward unconscious. The being was already bent over the still body of Christian, strapping something onto it, before Katie even hit the ground.

"Commander, I have the antigrav lifts strapped onto his body. Stand by to receive," Lieutenant Soloman said into her communicator. She pushed tabs on each of the four sheaths that she had placed on his four limbs – one on each arm and leg. The body started levitating off the ground as soon as she pushed the button, and the atmospheric pod floated forward on its own antigravity engine to position itself over the floating body of the young man.

"Soloman, sensors indicate that some of the people in the dwelling are coming out. Get out of there." It was Commander Tennison's voice that she heard.

The lights on the ship flashed out, leaving the pod floating in the pitch-black sky. Soloman hit the buttons on her own antigrav sheaths, and floated up towards the opening in the bottom of the pod. She had just pulled her body in the hatch when Ensign Roach pushed forward on the thrusters, sending the ship hurtling over the farmland past the house. As soon as the hatch seal light lit up, he piloted the pod towards a higher altitude, on a vector towards their next clone destination.

Soloman dragged the limp body of the young clone of Marshall Tennison towards the back of the pod. She placed him into one of the restraining harnesses they had brought with them.

"He doesn't look like you," Soloman said in jest. Commander Tennison grunted but didn't say anything. "I guess they never do," she continued. Having finished securing the clone, she strapped herself back into one of the forward seats.

The entire extraction process took just under five hours. Other than the close call when extracting the Marshall Tennison clone, the mission went smoothly. Commander Tennison, Lieutenant Soloman, and Ensign Roach clambered out of the atmospheric pod, giving way to the medical droids. The droids would be working with the clones to review their health and ensure there was no chance of infection from native diseases. The typical isolation period had been skipped, leaving the three of them at risk should one of the clones be a carrier. Before leaving the cargo bay, the droids would also scan the officers to ensure that they hadn't picked up any bacterial organisms. Earth was infamous for making non-natives sick.

Two smaller droids hovered off the ground, and dragged the bodies of the clones out of the side hatch. A sentry droid was present to secure them as they were transported through the ship to the medical station. Quickly scanned for any potential hazards, the three officers were given the 'all clear' from the medical droids, and proceeded out of the cargo bay back towards the bridge.

Commander Tennison had just stepped onto the bridge when Lieutenant Dalton approached him.

"Captain Pollard requested that you and Lieutenant Soloman report to her quarters as soon as you arrived. I've got the bridge." Both Tennison and Soloman turned to go back to the Captain's quarters. Dalton called out behind them. "Commander, how did it go?"

Marshall turned halfway, smirked, and nodded. "It went well. I'm sure there are more alien sighting reports on Earth this morning. We may have been seen by one group, but based on initial analysis of the clone, it appears the entire group may have been inebriated. The legend lives on."

The legend Marshall spoke of contended that aliens were constantly abducting people from Earth, only to do scientific experiments or other diabolic things to the humans. Each new report was usually the witnessing of a clone extraction that didn't go exactly perfect. It was unfortunate, but if the Earthlings ever developed interstellar space travel again, it would be an interesting revelation once the two civilizations met up.

It took just a few minutes to get to the captain's quarters from the bridge, walking at a leisurely pace.

Soloman had tried to make conversation with Tennison, but he seemed withdrawn and distant. She quickly gave up and settled for silence on the rest of the walk.

Upon arriving, Captain Pollard greeted both and asked them to sit. Offering coffee to each, she sat at her data-table and pulled out a data card. Sliding it into the reader on her desk, she motioned both of them to look at the information presented on the display.

"What you're seeing is surveillance footage from a deep-space probe just outside the Shalothan sector." The video had a basic telescopic video recorder that was triggered when its sensors detected something within range. The video of whatever object triggered the unit was then sent back to the USF intelligence division for analysis. In this particular footage, a nondescript cargo frigate flying well outside of the normal shipping lanes was the culprit.

"This surveillance is from seven hours ago. The object that triggered the recorder was a frigate that matched the description of the ship that left Shalotha. The trajectory of this ship, based on the information available, indicates that this particular ship is on a direct course towards the edge of the Fe-Ruq primary system, near the outer planet of Jethl." Captain Pollard touched the screen near the time stamp, and switched to a different screen.

"This is a report from a contact that goes by the moniker Nova Chaser. This came in three hours ago, direct from the Admiral. The report states that two of the Fe-Ruqian fleets were dispatched towards points unknown near deep space between the Fe-Ruq and Shalotha sectors. It's unknown whether this was in response to information about the rogue ship from Shalotha, or if it's just a coincidence. Either way, the fleets should reach the outer edges of the sector about the same time the other ship reaches Jethl."

Marshall raised a finger on his hand to indicate he wanted to ask a question.

"Any chance that we get to the system edge before this ship and the fleets?"

"Unfortunately, no. Using the best thread possible, at maximum speed, we'd probably reach the edge after the ship passes through, but just as the Fe-Ruqian fleets are arriving.

Lieutenant Soloman leaned slightly forward, looking at Tennison and then Pollard.

"Captain, it sounds as if we're already late to the party. Any assistance available from other USF ships in the area?

"Good question Lieutenant. I asked the same question, and the answer I received was a definite no. There are no other USF ships in the area, and we would most likely be the closest resource at this point. Intelligence is going to monitor the situation on Je-Fin through Nova Chaser, but other than that single source, we'll have to observe from outside the sector. The Fe-Ruq military announced that effective immediately, all system trade routes and open sector borders were being closed until further notice. They don't want anyone in or out, including any USF vessels.

Captain Pollard waited for either of the officers to speak. Both officers sat silently for a moment as each digested the information they had just received. Soloman bent her head in thought, then raised it to speak.

"Isn't it a bit odd the Fe-Ruq military has reacted so strongly to this event, especially since I'm assuming this is an unpublicized report of a single ship heading towards the general direction of their borders?"

Captain Pollard nodded and smiled slightly. "I can only assume the Fe-Ruq intelligence groups have just as much information as we do, if not more, on the incoming ship. Even if they don't, I have to agree with you. They have to know that this ship is being sent to retrieve the supposed Son of God. And if they do indeed suspect that, standard practice would be to raise the alert level and prepare to defend against the intrusion. Sending two entire fleets to defend the border against one ship seems to be overkill, wouldn't you agree? I suspect that they have something other than a standard defensive tactic planned. In any event, we should be around to see what happens."

Commander Tennison listened intently to his captain, following the trail of thought. He took it a bit further in his mind, envisioning the *Alaurian Spirit's* role in any altercation. Would they defend the Shalothan vessel, or sit quietly off to the side as the massive fleet vessels of the Fe-Ruq military captured or destroyed the single Shalothan ship? Their mission, as he understood it, was still only observation. Any intervention between the two sovereign bodies would most likely be unwelcome at best, possibly provocative at worst. Putting himself in the captain's role, he realized he would most likely decide to assist the Shalothan vessel. He tried to convince himself that politically it was a poor strategy for the Shalothans to take, but for the good of the galaxy, at least in Marshall Tennison's eyes, it was the most noble thing to do. He disliked the Fe-Ruqians as much as the next person, and he knew, no matter what the intelligence reports may suggest, the Fe-Ruq military would never let the Son of God come to power in this galaxy without a fight. And it was that mentality that swayed his thoughts to a defensive posture in support of the Shalothans. *I need my own command*, he thought.

"Commander Tennison?" Captain Pollard's voice interrupted Marshall's thoughts, bringing him back into the present. He glanced over at Soloman, and then back to the captain. "Do you have anything else to add?"

"No captain. Sorry captain. Just thinking through the scenario."

"Anything you care to share?" Captain Pollard furtively glanced at Soloman, and then back to Tennison. Looking at the floor, he shook his head, then swung his head back up.

"Dismissed then. I'll see you both on the bridge."

The *Nowrimo's Revenge* quietly sped through deep space towards its destination point. All but three of the warriors encapsulated by the hull of the flying machine were resting in their sleep periods. The three that had volunteered for the sleep period watch were stationed in the cockpit of the frigate, silently monitoring the various system controls for the ship's functions.

Their mission commander, Reaz Apxlus, had briefed them on the basics of the mission objectives during the last wake period. The warrior currently sitting in the commander's chair, Ronoson Athes, contemplated the glorious opportunity for honor given to him. To serve their Lord in any capacity was humbling and glorious, but to be given the opportunity to lay his own life on the line for Christ the King was beyond any honor ever bestowed upon him.

Sitting in the commander's chair, he fingered the ridges on the back of his hand, a twinge of guilt playing on his mind. He wondered if the Son of God would shame him when he first saw Him? Would He pass judgment on him immediately for all the millions of beings that Athes' bloodline had terminated? Or, being the all-knowing and loving God that he knew from the ancient teachings, would He grant forgiveness to him and his clan? Athes thought about the rich history of his clan, and the price that he may have to pay in short time. The life that God granted him was used to take away the very same gift of life from other beings. It had been the same for centuries, since the most glorious of his clan, Troras Athes, lead the initial devastating assault on the heathen world of Alaura. Troras himself had been responsible for the decision to take away the gift of life from millions of sentient beings. It was his hand that had operated the controls that dropped the first wave of ordnance against the largest community on Alaura. And it was his decision to ignore the pleadings for surrender from the remaining leaders on Alaura, instead choosing to slaughter everything in his path. His unyielding passion to defend his home planet had stoked a rage within that blinded him to the basics of the ancient teachings.

Yet, it was Troras Athes that many held in the highest regard. His quick decision-making, his fearlessness, his loyalty to his planet and brethren; all of those traits had been built up into almost mythical proportions through the ages. But there were other traits that history had forgotten about. The ruthlessness. The treachery. The excessive violence. The torture. The Athes clan knew the truth though. They knew about the hatred the great warrior had used to feed his rage. They hid away the dark truth about the deaths of his clan members, and the inexplicable deaths of friends and comrades when in Troras' presence. Through the centuries, denial about the sinful deeds of their forefather was passed on generation after generation. Ronoson Athes feared the dark history of the patriarch of his clan was heavily weighted against he and his descendants. He could not change the past. He could only ask forgiveness for his own sins, committed under the auspices of the Shalothan creed to defend their Lord and their religion at any cost.

Athes studied the navigation computer above his head. The chrono indicated there were still over fifteen standard hours left before they reached the edge of the Fe-Ruq system and converted to a cloaked status. Apxlus had surprised all the warriors when he revealed that the ship they traveled on contained an Inter-Dimensional Manipulation Device, typically referred to as an IDMD. The IDMD created a gap in the threads of the dimensional layer that they normally existed in, and allowed them to travel in a 'bubble' of space between layers. The IDMD allowed ships to leave the current dimensional plane, and travel from one point to another in their original dimensional universe without ever being discovered. The ship was able to travel direct from one point to another while using the IDMD. Traveling between the threads of the dimension differed from the typical thread travel, as a ship traveling in a thread, or wormhole, in the dimension fabric could still be detected, and was still susceptible to outside forces within that dimension. Traveling between the threads, or 'gap travel' as it was known, allowed the ship to traverse space impervious to the physical forces within the originating dimension. Using IDMDs effectively negated enemy sensors and tracking devices, and effectively 'cloaked' the ship from anyone else within their dimensional universe. IDMDs weren't recommended for long trips or an unknown route, as interdimensional travel was fairly new, and many of the outside forces between dimensions had not been discovered, let along understood. The dangers inherent in using the IDMD for prolonged periods of time presented a higher risk than if a ship had stayed within the dimensional universe.

Almost all IDMDs resided within Egaran space in the Fe-Ruq system, so to have a rogue starship outfitted with one was extremely unusual. Athes considered the fact that the ship they were on was Fe-Ruqian in origination, and assumed the captured frigate had had the device as a means to evade capture when smuggling goods. The ship would activate the IDMD just outside the system, and stay interdimensional until arriving at Je-Fin. The trip was particularly lengthy, considering that all the travel would occur with the IDMD. Athes wondered if any ship had successfully traveled for such a long distance continuously interdimensional. With such limited knowledge of the possible dangers, any misstep outside of the dimensional universe stood the chance of prematurely ending the mission.

CHAPTER IX

Marshall Tennison awoke with a start, sweat pouring from his body, soaking his sleeping garments. He quickly looked over at the chronometer on the data table near his bed. He had been asleep fewer than four hours.

Swinging his legs over the side of the bunk, he reached for his uniform pants in the darkness. The dream was already fading from memory, but the realness of it permeated through his mind. He hadn't had a nightmare in a long time, and the surprise at having one now, during this mission, disturbed him. The last time he had had one like this, one of such random death and destruction, he found himself in his first large-scale battle within a week. Several of his friends had not survived that battle; several of his own errors contributed to some of their deaths. He had doubted himself then, and it had cost lives. He could not afford to make the same mistakes again.

He finished pulling his uniform back together, and wiped the sleep out of his eyes. Walking across his quarters in the darkness, he slapped the control that opened the door and squinted as the light from the hall bled through the newly opened doorway.

The ship was still traversing towards the Fe-Ruq system, and only a few of the crew were stationed on this shift. He thought about heading to the bridge, but stopped himself and headed towards the galley. Since he was up, he might as well get something to eat.

The low hum of the engines seeped through the floor and walls, indicating to Marshall that they were operating near maximum power. It was the first time during the mission that he had noticed the noise. He hoped the strain on the engines wouldn't be too much, especially considering the entire ship had recently been sitting in hibernation. It wasn't exactly a new ship, and thoughts materialized in his head; visions of the engines shutting down, setting the ship adrift in the vastness of space, unable to reach their destination in time. *Would it really matter if we didn't make it?*

Stopping in front of a door, he looked around to get his bearings. To his chagrin, he found himself in front of the medical bay door. His clone, as well as the other clones, would be in medical restraints on the other side of this door. He pushed the pad to open the door, hesitated for a moment, and then stepped through.

Various banks of portable monitoring stations had been positioned in a semi-circle around several medical isolation capsules. The capsules were lined on end against the far wall, a few feet separating each from the rest. Rising to almost the height of the ceiling, the capsules were about a meter and a half in diameter. Several controller boxes were mounted on the sides of each, providing information crucial to the sustainability of the organisms inside each. The base of each capsule consisted of a small platform where the clear sides of the capsule began, and displayed several indicator lights along the edge.

Two medical droids silently moved about, performing what appeared to be routine tasks in other parts of the room. Marshall slid through a space between two of the monitoring stations, and quietly stepped towards the capsule banks. As he neared the large containers, he could see the human outlines of the beings inside. Searching the outer edges of the capsules, Marshall could not find nameplates or some indicator as to which clone was in which capsule. In the dim lights, and behind glass that was reflecting the ambient light in the room, it was difficult to make out specific features.

"Which one are you," Marshall said out loud. One of the med-droids, the one nearest him, whirred over near his position.

"Please repeat the question, sir," the droid stated. It waited patiently for the commander to be repeat the question. Marshall looked at the droid for a moment, wrestling internally about whether he should ask or not.

"Which of these is the clone for Commander Tennison," he finally managed, suddenly feeling nervous. The droid activated a control panel on one of the monitoring stations, and pushed several buttons. Looking back towards the capsules, Marshall watched as one of the capsules lit up from lights embedded in the platform. The light shining upward cast an eerily glow to the body inside the capsule. He stepped over to the unit and peered in at his clone.

"So you're my DNA match, eh," he said softly to the still form in the capsule. He surveyed the facial features, wondering if at any point in his adolescent years he had resembled this human at all. His memory failed him, and he could not bring up a vision of what he looked like at that age. He guessed that this clone was in his mid- to late-teens. The human appeared to be sleeping, but Marshall understood that the continual sedative piped in from tiny spouts in the ceiling of the chamber was inducing a state of hibernation in the human. He would sleep, and sleep well until the clone was removed from the chamber for its medical destiny.

The clone had been with another human being at the gathering they descended upon, and Marshall wondered what they had been doing. Was the young woman that was with him a family member, or a love interest? What had the group been celebrating that was cause for inebriation? Was there even a reason? Was this human intelligent? Was he a waste of life? He wondered what this clone's life had been like prior to the extraction.

Almost all clones had a life prior to selection for harvesting, but rarely were the human master copies privy to the details of the life of their clone. Psychologists throughout the galaxy had warned against learning too much about one's own clone. Only learn about the health of the subject, they would say. Nothing else matters once the clone is harvested, they would argue. Marshall wondered if this clone had ever even thought about the possibility that the entire reason for his existence was for the medical benefit of another human being.

Marshall touched a hand on the capsule, feeling the surface cool to the touch from the gas inside. He hoped that he would never need his clone. It happened quite often during missions; a clone is harvested, and restrained in a medical capsule. The mission is completed, and the officer never needs to utilize the clone. Many officers had elected in the past to return the clone back to Earth, spurring on the 'abduction theory' that was so popular among the natives. He could only imagine the wild story that his clone would have should it be lucky enough to avoid losing body parts to medical harvesting.

He stepped backwards, away from the capsule. Looking at the human form inside, he almost felt a hint of jealousy creep into his mind. *You don't even realize everything that happens in this universe*, he thought. The entire planet that upon which his clone was raised seemed stuck on sending out small probes rather than redeveloping interstellar travel. Until they could demonstrate their ability to traverse the galaxy, they would be in the dark about the political upheaval in the galaxy, devastating wars, and their own space-faring history. He smiled inwardly, thinking about how unaware of everything this civilization truly was.

"Huh," Marshall grunted aloud. "Your one true purpose in life is to serve other human beings in a capacity you probably can't even fathom. And yet, you and your people are the most valuable to us when you're not even conscious. How pathetic is that?" Condemnation crept into Marshall's voice, and he waved off the med-droid that started to approach him again about his statement. He stared into the face of his clone, searching for any sign or indication that he had heard him. Marshall knew it wasn't possible, not while in a hibernation state inside a medical capsule. He marveled at how two beings with the same DNA could have such varied value to the galaxy. One, a respected commander leading men and women to success in battle, the other a worthless clone who couldn't even operate the most basic data pad.

"Have a nice night, clone," Marshall sneered, adding emphasis to the last word. He patted the face of the capsule and turned to walk away. *I hate clones*, he thought.

Apxlus knelt in a corner of the room that he had converted to a reflection chamber. Only two hours away from Fe-Ruq space, Apxlus and the others were eager to reach the insertion point into the sector. Flying directly towards the sector edge invited hostilities, and he wondered how many deep-space probes had been triggered by their travel. He half expected to learn that the Fe-Ruqians had a fleet waiting for them just outside the primary system's edge. To make the entire trip undetected between systems would have been fortunate, but highly unlikely. It was more reasonable to expect some semblance of a defensive force awaiting their arrival.

With time drawing near, Apxlus needed to pray and ask for a cleansing of his sins. He would not have another opportunity once they were in-system, and he felt he needed to prepare himself before meeting with the Son of God. Many of the other warriors were spiritually preparing themselves as well. Apxlus had expected it, and ensured that each warrior had some semblance of privacy in the waning hours before reaching the Fe-Ruq sector.

The voice of Naoh jarred Apxlus from his prayer. He was slightly shaking Apxlus' shoulder. Mentally returning to the room, Apxlus slowly stood and faced the warrior.

"Commander, forgive my intrusion. We are minutes from engaging the IDMD. Do you wish to be in the cockpit for the event?" Naoh was soft-spoken, respectful of his commander's prayer time.

Apxlus nodded, and clapped Naoh on the shoulder. "In minutes we begin the journey to serve our Lord. Are you ready?" Apxlus bore his eyes into the warrior before him. Without question, he felt that all of his warriors were ready. Nonetheless, he felt obliged to ensure that they felt ready. Naoh clapped his hand over Apxlus', and confirmed he was ready.

Making the journey back to the cockpit, the two of them detoured to the cargo deck to let the others know that they were about to engage the IDMD. Several of the warriors had never even seen a ship use an IDMD, contributing to the level of apprehension in the room. Although all of them were seasoned warriors, not knowing exactly what was going to happen, or what was supposed to happen, made them ill at ease. Out of the nineteen warriors on board, only Apxlus, Naoh, and Sasnalre had ever experienced a ship using the IDMD during a mission. Naoh by far was the most knowledgeable about the unit, having learned the inner workings and theories behind it when he had spent time with a Fe-Ruq citizen who was a Shalothan sympathizer. The scientist who imparted his knowledge to Naoh had intended for his treason to help balance the war. Naoh had spent months learning about not only the IDMD, but also other highly classified weapons systems and developmental starships that the Fe-Ruq military were currently testing at the time. The knowledge gleaned by Naoh would be put to the test on this mission.

Working their way back to the cockpit from the hold, Apxlus stopped by the weapons package console to check on the warrior staffing the station. He found Osisrazao Caxon at the station, placing all weapons systems on standby as he conversed with the cockpit crew about the impending activation. Apxlus stopped to glance over the controls, seeing for himself that all the ready lights were appropriately lit, and that none of the system controls were showing any signs of distress. Satisfied, he crawled up the ladder that took him to the cockpit level.

Seeing the commander step into the cockpit area, Mahatsenael Hahot swiveled in the command chair to face his leader.

"Commander Apxlus, we are on a one minute countdown to activation," he said, standing up and moving away from the command chair.

"Hahot, return to your seat. I have come to observe only. Proceed with the process." Apxlus waved him down into the seat, then stepped off to the side of the command chair, looking out of the forward viewshield. The outer ring planet of Ru-Nula shown brightly in the distance, appearing larger than a distant star, but still small enough that none of the warriors could distinguish any details of the planet's surface features. Besides the distant planet, the system sun could be seen, as well as various suns that belonged to other systems, all appearing as twinkling stars.

"Ten seconds to engagement," Zpikasat Upahel announced. Naoh had returned to the other seat in the cockpit, and began to feverishly push buttons on his control panel. Within seconds he was the only person moving in the cockpit as the other warriors awaited his activation of the IDMD.

"IDMD, engaged," Naoh called out. He turned slightly to look out the side viewshield. The outside hull of the ship glowed a faint blue, and the immediate vacuum of space around the ship turned a different shade of black. The distant suns and planet disappeared from view for a moment, as the hum of the unit echoed through the ship. Within seconds, there was nothing visible outside the viewshield, just pitch-blackness.

Apxlus glanced furtively at Naoh, and then swung his gaze back forward. After what seemed to be an eternity, the distant stars and the planet slowly faded back into view. The starlight emissions seemed to be dulled, as if seen through a fog. The planet itself appeared to be discolored, as if faded from years of too much sunlight.

"IDMD activation is a success," Naoh said, a hint of relief in his voice. He turned to face the other pilot, and instructed him to enter the coordinates for Je-Fin. "The trip will be shorter than normal. We can avoid any gravitic anomalies or planet masses when moving in this mode, so we can plot a straight path. Use coordinates that would have us drop back into the universe in an orbit around Je-Fin. Once we deactivate the device, the ship will immediately reappear on every sensor within range. We'll have minutes to get to the surface before every patrol in the area is converging on our location.

"Naoh, how long will this trip take?" Apxlus asked, curious about how much time would be saved. Naoh turned to face his controls once more, then looked back up at Apxlus.

"Assuming no interruptions, we should drop back into dimensional space within seventeen hours." Apxlus nodded at the information, then turned and left the cockpit. He headed back towards the office that he had converted into a chamber, and began to review his plans for their mission. If all went well, he hoped to be standing before the Son of God within twenty hours.

The remainder of the trip went surprisingly well. Apxlus had assumed the worst for this portion of the mission. Not having any precedent on how long a ship could safely travel with the IDMD engaged, he prepared himself for damage to the ship, loss of life, or detection by the Fe-Ruq military. Strangely none of these possibilities occurred.

The commander was summoned to the bridge two hours into the flight after a Fe-Ruq fleet could be seen in the near distance. Apxlus had been concerned about the fleet, which he immediately assumed were coming after them. But as they approached, the proximity warnings didn't even beep. Still not feeling comfortable around an entire fleet, Apxlus ordered the ship to alter its vector to steer clear of the fleet. He found it disconcerting to be able to see the fleet without aid of sensors, yet they were oblivious to how close one of their enemies were passing. At the same time, he had wished that they knew more about the technology, and what the consequences would be if he were to fire his weapons on the ship while still traveling with the IDMD engaged. Naoh had cautioned against it, arguing that unless the missile or beam itself was equipped with an IDMD, the exercise would be a waste in weaponry. The missile or beam would continue traveling on the same plane as the *Nowrimo's Revenge*, which meant that the missile could even appear to hit the enemy ship, but wouldn't cause any damage. It would pass right through, because those particular coordinates on the missile's plane of existence were empty.

After that seemingly close encounter, the *Nowrimo's Revenge* continued on the rest of the trip without incident. With half an hour left before reaching Je-Fin, Apxlus summoned all of the warriors except Naoh to the cargo hold to address them.

The warriors were in various positions of recline throughout the cargo hold. Some stood silently waiting for Apxlus to speak. A few sat on the ground, preparing their weapons and going through last minute checks. The rest were kneeling on one or two knees, spread throughout the hold, but close enough to listen to Apxlus without moving. He slowly looked across the hold. Letting his gaze fall on each of the warriors.

"Fellow warriors, you were selected because you are the very best that Shalotha has to offer. Today we go into battle as brothers in arms, united for Shalotha, united for God. All of you know the importance of the mission; the importance of the man that we have risked our lives to come rescue. The Son of God, Christ Himself, is on that planet. We will risk all to bring Him back to Shalotha, for that is His rightful place. Many of you will not return from Je-Fin. For our Savior's safety, we cannot travel as one group. Six of you will be chosen to be left behind and provide us safe exit from the system. You will do everything you can to sabotage any attempts at capturing the Savior, while bringing as many sinners to judgment as possible. I cannot guarantee that you will ever be extricated from the planet by us, or any future forces. Naoh, you will not travel with us to the surface. You will engage the IDMD as soon as we have departed the ship, and wait for our return. For the other eleven of you, six of you will launch a forward attack on the center that is holding our Savior. Myself and the other five of you will infiltrate the detention center through another side. The six that are staying behind to provide cover will also join the forward attack, but will separate and go to their pre-designated target assignments to create the diversions. You will receive glory and honor for the ages for your sacrifices today. Your names will be remembered as the ones who gave their life for not only Shalotha, but for Christ himself. You will be martyrs!"

Apxlus' voice rose with the last statement, and several of the warriors cracked their staffs against the cargo hold floor or bulkhead wall.

"Who will be the ones to be glorified today? Who of you desire to serve your Christ and rescue Him from the heathens and sinners that infest this planet?" Apxlus was not surprised to see every warrior before him step forward or raise his staff. "Right now, right at this moment, we are merely warriors of Shalotha, a noble responsibility in itself. Within less than an hour's time, all of us will be warriors for our Christ. Let us go forward and display our devotion to him by sending the sinners to judgment!" The gathered warriors started hissing 'sinners' over and over again, working themselves up into a frenzy. The warriors were cracking their sticks against the bulkheads, or smashing the ends of the staffs against the floor, creating a cacophony that Apxlus drank in. He had already chosen which six warriors would serve as the rear guard defenders. He stepped forward and walked around the cargo hold, tapping the selected six warriors on the shoulder with his staff. Zpikasat Uphael, Todzopsu Naron, Mzumaras Kason, Osisrazao Caxon, Olasit Metocaniel, and Patcin Alkraz knelt as each was tapped, pledging their devotion and voicing the honor that they felt at being chosen. For these warriors, they were humbled to be chosen for this task. Each felt that they would receive their glorious reward in Heaven for their sacrifices.

Apxlus went to each of the other warriors and confirmed what their assignments would be. All pledged their devotion to Christ and promised success. Apxlus was feeling very pleased with the warriors. He had expected nothing less, but as the zero hour approached, he felt more confident on the probability of success for this mission.

The warriors spent the last ten minutes preparing themselves for the reentry into dimensional space. The plans that Apxlus had gone over with each in detail were ingrained upon their brains, and each warrior knew exactly what would happen between the reentry of the craft into dimensional space and touchdown on the Je-Fin surface.

CHAPTER X

With a minute left showing on the reentry countdown chrono, Naoh clicked the all-ship communication button to let the warriors know they were fast approaching mission time.

"Warriors, we are less than a minute away from reentry into dimensional space. Strap yourselves in if seats are available. For those that are not near any available seats, be prepared to hold on. We will engage thrusters at maximum capacity as soon as we deactivate the IDMD. It will be approximately two minutes between deactivation and atmospheric entry into Je-Fin. God protect you." Naoh clicked the button twice to signal he was observing radio silence from that point forward. The seconds on the chrono ticked away, counting down from ten. At nine seconds left, Naoh switched on the pre-burners for the thrusters. At five seconds left, he checked the safety harness strapping him into the cockpit seat. The chrono beeped, and Naoh deactivated the IDMD. The blue glow around the ship faded, and the colors of the planet below suddenly became more vibrant and real. The perceived fog that had obscured the distant stars and sun during the trip suddenly vanished, and the entire viewshield was filled with the crisp, brilliant colors of dimensional space.

"Thrusters engaged!" Athes called out. The ship shot forward as the engines roared to life. Something on one of the consoles started beeping incessantly.

"The ship has been detected. Sensor sweeps are originating from an orbital defense platform. There it is." The targeting reticule projected on the viewshield shifted to silhouette a small orbital station almost fifty kilometers away from their current location.

Apxlus leaned forward in the cockpit command chair. "Moak, target that platform and destroy the sinners." Almost before Apxlus had mouthed the last syllable, two bright streaks shot out from the underbelly of the ship, on a vector towards the platform. The ship rolled away from the trailing path of the missiles, and dove straight into the upper atmosphere. Just before the ship was engulfed in the fiery orange glow from reentry, Athes caught a glimpse of the missiles impacting on the orbital defense platform, causing two huge fireballs that quickly extinguished in the vacuum of space.

The ship shuddered under the pressures being exerted on the hull. Sensors and system controls screamed warnings at the pilots, indicating that the stresses were approaching intolerable levels. Each time it seemed the ship would break apart, the pilots made a slight adjustment to the descent angle and throttled back slightly on the thrusters to keep the ship moving on the edge of self-destruction. The glow faded away quickly, allowing those in the cockpit a beautiful view of the atmosphere on Je-Fin. Rippling clouds extended as far as they could see, and lightning danced across the tops of many of the cloud formations. The ship continued to shake violently, but it was extreme upper atmospheric turbulence from the massive planetary storms that caused the shaking, not reentry forces.

"The navigation system has acquired the

coordinates of the holding center. Adjusting flight trajectory to compensate." The pilots continued to work the controls of the ship, forcing it to adhere to their commands.

"Commander Apxlus, unidentified ship types are now in flight, on an intercept vector with us." Athes looked back at the commander, seeking his direction.

"Do not evade. Get us down on the ground so we can begin the mission. Weapons control, target and fire at will." Apxlus suddenly felt a heightened sense of urgency to get to the ground. The sensors were still not able to identify the type of ship trying to intercept them. He strained to see any sign of the ship out the viewshield, but dark gray clouds and lightning filled his view, with rain streaks racing along the viewshield surface as the wind whipped by the ship.

"Thirty seconds until destination target is reached. Standby," Athes called out. Proximity alerts started to sound off, indicating nearby ships. Just as soon as the alerts had sounded, the warrior running the weapons control fired into the clouds with the particle beam weapon. The weapon locked onto the nearest target, and the warriors in the cockpit saw a dull flash in the clouds. Just as soon as the flash had occurred, the ship shook against the shock wave of an explosion. Immediately after, a dark shape flew across the ship's flight path, startling the warriors.

"That was one of the sinner fighters,"Athes said. "One is circling around behind us. The one that we just saw was only fifty meters in front of us. It's maneuvering into a flanking position." The view from the cockpit suddenly changed as the ship broke through the clouds. The pilots pulled out of the steep descent, leveling off only thirty meters above the ground. The particle beam once again began firing at their pursuers, causing the fighters to temporarily drop back to avoid being hit by the beam weapon.

Naoh clicked the all-ship button.

"All warriors, prepare to disembark. We are ten seconds away from the drop point." Apxlus stood up and trotted down to the ship's side entry hatch. Most of the other warriors were already there, grouped in pairs of two and three. The pilot from the cockpit was following Apxlus. Naoh was the only person in the cockpit now, and one warrior was at the weapons package console.

The ship shuddered as it touched down, and Caxon pushed the control to open the door. Almost in unison, the warriors all slapped their forearm sheaths, activating their weapons. Some of the warriors preferred sheaths on both arms, allowing them to fire with dual weapons. The door of the ship slid open, and Kason and Caxon were the first out. Kason blindly began firing his weapon to lay down a covering fire, while Caxon dropped and rolled to the side of the ship, setting himself up in a position to provide additional support for the other warriors coming out. The warriors in the ship didn't wait long to disembark, jumping out in pairs and veering to the left or right of the ship. Apxlus and Athes were the last two out of the door, with Athes hitting the control button to close the door to the ship. Almost as soon as the door sealed, the warriors sprinted across the open expanse of land to find cover away from the ship. The two fighters that had been pursuing them were nowhere to be seen.

As soon as Naoh confirmed that none of the warriors were within twenty meters of the ship, he engaged the IDMD, causing the ship to fade away from view of the warriors on the ground. Apxlus watched from his cover, marveling at how quickly it had disappeared.

The landing site was enduring a rainstorm, with the ground soaked from the heavy droplets. Surveying the landing site, Apxlus could barely see two hundred meters because of the torrential downpour that obscured his vision. He looked around to get his bearings. The ship had come in almost directly upon the complex, and the landing site was actually an open area to the north of the complex that was used as a training ground for the garrison based on Je-Fin. Peering through the rain, Apxlus could make out targets that had been set up as part of a firing range. To his left there was a line of trees that offered better protection and cover than the bushes they were currently using. To his right were the various stations the Fe-Ruq soldiers would fire from. He stood still and listened. The rain pounded on the wet ground and the leaves of the bushes, creating loud *thwapping* sounds as the rain merged with puddles and pools on the uneven ground. The warriors were already soaked, and the rain ran down their heads in streams. Still, no other sounds than the rain and the distant thunder could be heard.

Apxlus leaned over to Athes and mouthed the words *Do you see anything?* Athes shook his head slightly, then nodded in the direction of the complex. Was it possible that they had caught the complex garrison off guard, or was this a trap? Whatever it was, they couldn't stay in the same spot, or they would be seen by the inevitable search craft that came out in support of the fighters. He looked back up into the sky, once again searching for any sign of the fighters. Seeing nothing but rain, he opened his mouth and made a loud clicking noise in the back of his throat, sounding like the guttural growl of any of a number of predators on Shalotha. The sound was the signal for the three groups to form up and move out towards their assignments. Two thirds of the group began running in sprints across the open area, keeping their bodies low to the ground. They alternated movement with one another, staggering their positioning and offering covering positions to the next pair that would venture forward. This continued as they made their way towards the firing stations.

Apxlus and his group headed off in another direction. Their battle tunics sagged from the rain, and the area they headed towards began to get more difficult for footing. Apxlus' destination was the tree line, where he could use the trees for cover as the group got into position for infiltrating the complex.

The warriors paired up with each other, with the three pairs rotating who rushed forward, and which ones provided cover. The six made it to the tree line in good time, and relaxed a bit once they made it to the safety of the trees. Overhead they could hear the whine of the suborbital fighters as they circled in the clouds. The rain hadn't let up yet, and the lightning seemed to be getting closer. The winds had picked up, blowing the rain into the faces of the warriors.

Apxlus couldn't understand why he hadn't heard more soldiers combing the area, looking for the ship that had blasted into the atmosphere from low orbit. Even more disconcerting was the fact that he could not detect any soldiers in the areas around the complex. It was as if the complex garrison had abandoned the idea of patrols and sentry duty.

Athes took the point position for the group, which

formed into a rough single file formation. Peering into the thickets of trees, the group of warriors tried to see past the bending trees, waving in the wind that was becoming fiercer by the moment. Something in the back of Athes' mind made him wary of venturing further. His instincts were screaming at him that they were walking into a trap.

Apxlus looked at Athes, wondering what it was he saw that caused him to pause. He too sensed that something was strange about the lack of resistance at a security complex that was holding the purported Son of God. He couldn't dismiss the feeling, yet he knew that the group would have to press on quickly if they were going to take advantage of the element of surprise. He crouch-walked towards Athes, determined to find out what he saw. Coming up behind Athes, he clicked his tongue to get his attention, and then motioned with his head towards the thickets of trees, as if to say *What do you see in there?*

Athes glanced from Apxlus to the trees and back, slightly shaking his head to signal he didn't see anything important. Apxlus waved his hand forward slightly to get the group moving again. They continued another twenty meters into the trees when Athes caught sight of movement ahead. He immediately crouched lower and waved a fist to stop the group behind him. Each of the other warriors tapped their weapons sheaths to activate the blaster, and then gripped their staffs with their other hands. Athes stared towards where he had seen the movement. The raindrops weren't falling as heavy now that they were just under the edge of the tree canopy. As his vision adjusted, he could see a Fe-Ruqian soldier in camouflage that had caught his eye, halfway up a tree. The soldier didn't appear to be looking in their direction though. He had his back to them, and his weapon trained on a target that Athes could not see.

Athes motioned for the others to come forward so they could see his instructions. Athes pointed at his eyes, then towards the area where the soldier was located. Each of the warriors nodded to indicate that they saw the soldier also. Apxlus directed Moak and Secael to flank the right, and Asael and Anacen to flank the left. He and Athes would sneak up directly behind the soldier. All of the warriors understood that they needed to be aware of other soldiers in the area; it would be unlikely that a single soldier would be out in the woods alone.

A bright flash of lightning lit the sky above, and the repeal of thunder shot through the air almost instantaneously. The warriors used the thunder to mask any sounds of their movement. The rain started to fall harder, making it more difficult to see through the trees. Athes and Apxlus were almost on their stomachs now, snaking their way through the underbrush towards the soldier in the tree. The two of them were less then ten meters behind the soldier, whose attention was focused on peering through the zoom scope that was mounted on his weapon. The soldier was sitting on a platform that was secured to the tree, with branches added to the supporting braces of the platform to add camouflage to the unit. Apxlus mouthed to Athes *Wait here*, and crept forward until he was almost directly behind the soldier at the tree base. He was about to climb the tree to grab the soldier when he heard a small beep, and then a voice talking. Looking up, it was the soldier's communicator. Apxlus strained to hear what was being said.

"All units, the rogues have landed and dispersed. We have visual sighting of a group of six attacking the forward positions of the complex. Flankers, be on the lookout for additional units coming from the side. This could be a feint. Prepare to move to the forward front if reinforcements are needed. Rear guard, close up your perimeter line and secure the hangar." In the distance, just above the sound of the raindrops hitting the leaves and branches, Apxlus could here the faint sound of blaster fire. He assumed it was the other warriors engaging in the forward assault.

He took one last look around to see if he could discern any other soldiers in the trees. Not seeing any, he slid his staff up along the trunk of the tree, lining up the barbed end with the butt of the soldier's weapon. In one fluid motion, Apxlus hooked the barbs on the end of his staff to the butt of the weapon, and pulled it away from the soldier's hand. As the soldier was swiveling in his position to see what had happened, Apxlus reversed the motion of the staff and slammed it upward, barbed end first, into the soldier's jaw, knocking him backward and off the platform. The man hit the ground with a solid *thud*, and before he could even recover and move, Apxlus was on top of him. Immediately he ran the razor sharp ridges on the back of his hand along the man's throat, slashing it wide open and causing his blood to run and pool with the rain on the ground.

Athes rushed up beside him, motioning for him to look to his left. A little more than twenty meters away, they watched Anacen snapping the neck of a soldier that he and Asael had spotted in a tree stand. Looking to the right, Moak and Secael were already moving along the ground towards them, motioning for them to look forward. Ahead of the warriors, another thirty meters or so, they could see the other edge of the tree thickets. Beyond the clearing, in the haze of the torrential downpour, they could see the lights on what they suspected was the complex. Athes surveyed the trees in front of them, and not seeing any more soldiers, indicated that they should move forward. Apxlus motioned for the two flanking pairs to move up, and he and Athes crouch-walked twenty-five meters forward, until they were just inside the edge of the thickets, still hidden from view.

The sound of the frontal battle could be heard off to their left, and occasional weapons fire could be seen through the rain. Neither Athes nor Apxlus could make out who was firing, or from where they were firing. Apxlus trusted his other warriors to make it a very fierce battle, allowing them the time to find a way into the detention center from the side.

The building itself sat before them, with security lamps all along the upper edge of the walls, illuminating the ground below. It was a squat building, but long in length. Apxlus couldn't tell from the side how wide it was, but assumed it was a basic equal sided construct. He suspected the building was likely the entrance to an underground system of bunkers and offices, designed to protect the soldiers within from air strikes. From their vantage point, it didn't appear that the building was heavily fortified. Athes counted off only ten soldiers on their side of the building, and most were grouped either to the forward corner or the rear corner. The rear of the building was attached to some sort of landing platform for smaller orbital and suborbital craft. Beyond that, the entire rear of the detention center appeared to back up to more trees and bushes. The front of the building faced an open area adjacent to a road, but Athes and Apxlus couldn't see much further past the front of the building because of the heavy rain. Athes pointed out additional weapons emplacements on the roof, but they appeared to be pointing skyward, as if they were anti-aircraft weapons. Apxlus couldn't see any break in the wall that would allow them access – no doors, windows, vents or ductwork. He stepped back into the trees and clicked loudly to bring the other four warriors in together.

"Athes, this is too easy, do you agree?" Apxlus asked as the other warriors made their way along the tree thicket edge to his location. "Three aircraft, three soldiers, and hardly any other resistance that we can see. It doesn't seem like they're trying to protect anyone here."

"The security here seems too simple for a captive such as the Son of God. Perhaps we've overestimated our enemy. Perhaps they do not want him on this planet, and are hoping that someone comes to get him. After all, they certainly don't believe in God. Having this captor here could pose more problems than if they were to just let him 'escape'. Our allies would not be so keen to know that they hold the Son of God. They would be inviting war into their system." Apxlus nodded at Athes' assessment. It was an astute observation, but one that could not be proven out just yet. They would still need to operate as if this was a maximum-security facility holding one of the most critical political prisoners that the Fe-Ruqians had ever known.

Moak and Secael crouched down next to Athes. Anacen and Asael arrived moments later. All the warriors knelt on one knee while they discussed their tactics.

"It appears the enemy has either not expected us, or they don't care enough about us to fortify their security measures. Either way, there is no access to the building from the side. We must go in through the front or the rear. I suspect our brothers are drawing the majority of the forces to the front of the building. There most likely will be a rear guard by the landing platform, but it will be the easier route for access. We will move as a group, and overwhelm any soldiers we encounter. Athes, continue on point. We will stay within the trees until we are across from the corner of the building. When we move across to rear corner, I want Moak and Anacen to secure the landing platform, and disable any ships that are docked there. After you secure the platform, position yourselves as covering fire for the rear access door. Athes, Asael, Secael, and I will gain access to the rear of the building and find our target. We will need the two of you to ensure that none of the remaining garrison attempt to trap us by re-securing the rear of the building. If you cannot hold the position, join us inside, and together we will work our way out the front and meet up with the others.

Apxlus moved into a crouch, and the other warriors followed suit. Athes snaked his way through the bushes and underbrush, careful not to move too fast and give himself away. The rain continued to pound on them, and the lightning began to intensify once again. Daylight was quickly fading, leaving the security lights as the primary source of illumination. Athes stopped across from the edge of the building, and waited for the rest of the warriors to catch up. Apxlus tapped Moak and Anacen on the shoulder, and pointed to the security lights atop the wall edge. There were two that were lighting up the areas immediately to the sides of the corner, and their coverage spread out halfway to the tree thicket. Moak nodded in acknowledgment, and he and Anacen each picked one of the lights and took careful aim. Apxlus held his hand up, then dropped it to signal them to fire. Two quick shots took out the lights, dropping the area between them and the building into dark shadows and murkiness. The six warriors sprinted out of the bushes towards the wall. Shouts could be heard above the rain, but Apxlus wasn't able to detect exactly where they were coming from. They reached the relative safety of the wall just as a group of five soldiers barreled around the corner, blaster rifles drawn. The warriors pressed themselves up against the wall as two of the soldiers edged out into the open area between the building and the trees. Secael was the closest to the soldiers, and waited until the second one had passed before he made his move. He motioned to Athes and Apxlus to cover the two that were moving forward towards the tree line, then swung around the corner and opened fire on the remaining soldiers. Anacen was right behind him, holding tight to the adjacent wall and adding additional fire. The two soldiers that had passed turned when they heard the fire, but were dropped by Apxlus and Athes before they had even brought their weapons to bear on their attackers. Secael was already checking the other three soldiers to ensure that they were dead. Moak and Anacen took a quick glance around the immediate area, searching for additional soldiers. Finding none, they took off towards the landing platform, staff in one hand, and blaster sheath activated in the other.

Shouts could still be heard above the din of the rain, but the distant sound of blaster fire added to the background noise. Looking towards the front of the building, the warriors could see blaster shots flying back and forth across the open area as their brethren attacked the front of the complex. They were gaining ground quickly on the garrison soldiers.

Apxlus, Athes, Secael, and Asael moved along the rear wall of the building, weapons drawn, and searching for additional attackers. Secael swung away from the wall and shot out another security light, dropping another portion of the rear wall into darkness. The wind had picked up, driving the rain horizontally into the both the building and the warriors. Their range of visibility was quickly diminishing in the storm and the darkness.

Blaster fire sounded from the general direction of the landing platform, and a small explosion lit up the darkening sky. Several more bursts of blaster fire followed, and then silence. The four warriors came to a door. There was a concrete path from the door to the platform stairs, and the door was marked 'Pilot Entrance', stenciled in basic military. Another security light lit the area around the door, but was quickly put out by Secael. Just as Athes was about to move to open the door, the entryway swung open, and several soldiers ran out, rifles drawn and raised as they ran towards the landing platform. Athes grabbed the door to keep it from closing and locking, and the other three warriors quickly picked off two soldiers a piece, none of which even saw the four warriors against the outer wall.

Athes swung the door open, and Apxlus sprinted in and moved to his right to cover the area just inside the entrance. Asael quickly followed, moving to the left to cover that side of the hallway. Secael waited for a second before coming in, followed by Athes. The latter held the door so that it closed quietly, and let it lock with a soft click. The hallway before the warriors was brightly lit, and had another door ten meters away. Off to the right was a pilot ready room. Apxlus ducked into the room and confirmed that it was clear. Athes moved forward, once again taking the lead. The door was solid steel, and unlike the outer door, this was an integrated sliding blast door with no handles.

"Asael, the explosives," Apxlus said as he pointed towards the door. Asael and Secael had been two of the warriors supplied with explosive gel while on the *Revenge*. Asael pulled a thin gray tube out of his battle tunic, and applied a small bead of the gel in a horizontal line from side to side, about a third of the way up from the floor. He quickly retreated from the door, and Apxlus nodded at Secael. The other three warriors turned their heads away from the door as Secael aimed at the gel bead and fired. The gel ignited and produced a flash of white light and a loud boom, and the door split into two pieces, with a large gash along the line where the gel bead had been.

Athes and Apxlus fired through to the other side of the door, trying to clear any adversaries that may have been waiting on the other side. Each ducked through the hole, and crouched off to either side to cover the other two warriors. The other side of the door opened in to a larger room, with several corridors adjacent to the central location. A guard station was the focal point of the room, with a security monitor bank on the wall just behind the station. Several of the ceiling lights near the door had been blown out during the explosion, putting half of the room into darkness. Just as Secael and Asael came through the hole in the door, a guard stood up from behind the station wall and opened fire at them. Secael and Asael both dove to the floor, face first, and

Apxlus and Athes dove on their sides. The blaster fire hit about a meter and a half up on the wall, barely missing the diving warriors. Secael flung his staff with his left arm, sending it twirling towards the guard. The guard instinctively ducked the staff, but Apxlus was up and firing on the station before the flying staff hit the ground. Athes got up and walked around the other side of the station, also firing to pin the guard down. It was Apxlus who earned the kill, finally hitting the guard in the back of the head as he cowered on the ground behind the station.

More blasts rocked the detention center, but this time it sounded as if the blasts were above the building, rather than in front of it. Apxlus motioned at Secael and Asael to cover the entrances to the room; Secael covered a corridor that was marked as an office wing, and Asael covered the door that they had just blown a hole in. Athes moved to cover the opposite corridor as Apxlus searched the guard station for information pertaining to Christ's location.

Finding none, he waved at Asael to go with Secael down one of the corridors, while Apxlus moved over near Athes so they could search the other. Apxlus took the lead, slowly walking towards another door only ten meters away. This door was marked 'Authorized Personnel Only' in red stencil, and had a hologram projector to the left of the door. It didn't matter to Apxlus what the projector was for; they would need to blow the door to get to the other side. Apxlus moved towards the door to make sure it wasn't unlocked. It didn't move when he approached, and didn't respond to his touch when he pressed on the open control button.

"Athes, we need Secael to blow this," Apxlus said,

already heading back in the direction of Secael and Asael. Athes and Apxlus had just passed the vacant guard station when several loud explosions rocked the detention center, shutting down the power system. Without any windows or natural light to illuminate, the interior of the building fell into blackness.

CHAPTER XI

"Apxlus, I'm right behind you," Athes said, placing his hand on the back of his commander. Neither could see anything in front of them. Apxlus slapped his blaster sheath to deactivate his weapon. He held up his right hand and closed his eyes, concentrating on focusing his thoughts on fire. He envisioned his hand becoming warm, then glowing red. He felt the heat on his hand, and opened his eyes to see the flicker of flame beginning to engulf his hand.

"Quickly, Athes. Let's find Secael."

Athes led the way, with Apxlus directly behind him, lighting the way with his flaming hand held up high. He held his staff in his left hand, ready to defend against any attackers.

The corridor came to a split, which left them the choice of going left or right. Athes opted to go right, further into the detention center. No sooner had he turned the corner than blaster shots flew past and stuttered against the wall. Both he and Apxlus dove to the ground, and Apxlus snuffed out the flame on his hand, pitching them back into darkness.

The blaster fire continued sporadically, with few shots coming close to the prone warriors. Apxlus crawled forward on his knees and elbows, and tapped Athes to follow him. As they worked their way down the corridor, they could hear what sounded like several different soldiers talking into personal communicators. The blaster fire appeared more concentrated just past the next corner in the hallway. Apxlus strained to make out the conversations ahead of him.

"Get the generators online! The complex has been breached. Repeat, the complex has been breached! We're falling back towards the dock."

"Colonel, we've lost contact with the rear guard. Requesting reinforcements!"

"I'm hit, I'm hit!"

"Someone get the damn lights back on before we're dead!"

"Everyone, switch on your rifle lights on my command…"

"You're crazy! They'll be able to pick us off instantly."

"Switch on your light!"

Dozens of small beams of light switched on, swiveling in the darkness as the soldiers surveyed their surroundings. Blaster fire opened up opposite of the soldiers, causing many of them to duck for cover. Directly across the hall from Apxlus, Secael and Asael suddenly created flames on their hands, lighting the hallway in front of them. Apxlus was a bit dismayed to find his warriors almost next to him, and he hadn't even realized they were there.

"Secael! Asael! Back this way," Apxlus whispered, getting their attention. Surprised to find their commander in the same hallway, both quickly crawled back down the hallway away from the soldiers. The fighting continued as the soldiers began returning fire on their unseen attackers. Apxlus was sure that it was his comrades that were engaging the enemy, but he didn't want to be one of four obstacles standing between thirty-some soldiers and the retreat to save their lives. In such a small area, he and his warriors were bound to suffer casualties.

The four warriors hastily made it back down the hallway in the darkness, and found their way to the steel door that Apxlus couldn't open. He directed Secael to blow the door open, and then moved back out of the way. Secael followed the same procedure from before, spreading a bead of gel in a horizontal line across the door about a third of the way up. Once he finished, Secael set down his staff and lit a flame on his left hand, while he aimed with his right. Firing a single shot, the gel exploded, severing the door in half. Apxlus and Athes rushed up to the hole in the door, prepared to fire on anything that moved on the other side.

The lights in the building switched back on, illuminating the corridor they were in, as well as the area on the other side of the door. Several soldiers were crouched down with their weapons trained on the hole in the door. As soon as the lights flicked on, they opened fire, causing Apxlus and Athes to dive away from the door. Athes cried out in pain, and Apxlus looked over to see a large burn hole on Athes right bicep. The still smoldering wound had evaporated a large portion of his keratin armor-skin and the flesh beneath it, revealing the bone. He slumped against the wall, slipping into shock.

The blaster fire continued to erupt through the hole they had created, and Apxlus began to fear that perhaps the most difficult part of the mission was upon them. Secael scampered over to Athes, evaluating the wound on his arm. He glanced over at Apxlus and shook his head slightly. The keratin coating of the Shalothans could protect against many injuries, and regenerated over time, but injuries as serious as this were difficult to recover from on the field of battle. Athes would be out of commission for the balance of the mission.

Asael was on the same side as Apxlus, and kept his eye on the corridor that they had just returned from, protecting against the other soldiers who were about to retreat this way. Apxlus directed Secael to move Athes over to what was left of the damaged guard station, in hopes of offering protection against enemy fire. Apxlus then waved to Asael, and pointed to the ceiling lights in the room. Asael nodded, and made quick work of the lights, pitching the room into darkness again. Light filtered in from both corridors; in one corridor, the ceiling lights lit up the floor and parts of the walls a few meters into the room. In the other, the light pouring in from the other side silhouetted the blast hole in the door.

The blaster fire stopped, and Asael rushed to the other side of the corridor, positioning himself across from Apxlus. Both of them were in the deep shadows, almost impossible to see from the other side of the door. Apxlus could see the soldiers creep forward, rifles pointed into the blackness ahead. The two Shalothans waited for all five of the soldiers to step through the hole before they moved into action. Apxlus and Asael each wrapped their arms around the last two soldiers, and quickly slid the ridges on the backs of their free hands across their throats, quietly dropping them to the ground. One of the soldiers gurgled as he bled to death, causing the other three soldiers to spin towards the sound. Asael crouched and whipped his staff towards the nearest one, connecting on the side of the soldier's left knee. The impact buckled his leg, and the soldier crumpled to the ground, weapon flailing in his hand. The staff came around and hit the soldier on the wrist of the hand that held the weapon, breaking his grip on the rifle. At the same time Asael was attacking the soldier closest to him, Apxlus moved into action against the other two. Holding his staff horizontally, he jumped behind the other soldiers, and as they turned towards the gurgling sound, he sprang from his crouch, slamming his staff upwards into both of the barrels of the soldier's rifles. Both weapon barrels were pushed upwards toward the ceiling, and one of the soldiers unintentionally fired his weapon. Apxlus swung a roundhouse kick into the side of one soldier, and brought his staff around into the head of the other. The first soldier staggered back to an upright position, but Apxlus reversed the direction of his staff, catching him in the temple and dropping him to the floor. Blaster fire rang out from his right, and he turned to see the other soldier dropping to the ground with a blaster hole in his forehead. Asael stood next to him, blaster sheath activated and searching for another target.

"Secael, get Athes situated back there and come with us," Apxlus said, stepping over the limp bodies of the soldiers on the ground. Secael propped Athes up against the back of the station wall, and moved a chair around to block the view of his legs from anyone coming down the corridor. Asael had already moved through the blast hole and into the corridor beyond. Apxlus looked back, and the stepped through the hole. Secael came up behind him within seconds.

Stepping into the light on the other side of the door, the three warriors could see that they had entered the general detention area. Several solid cell doors lined the walls of the area, and another door marked the exit about fifty meters further down. Apxlus motioned for Secael to check one side of detention area , and for Asael to check the other. Apxlus covered the door they had just come through.

It was Secael who clicked loudly for Apxlus and Asael to join him. Standing in front of a cell door with a file attached, Secael read off the information on the file cover.

"Human male, age undetermined. Arrested on charges of assaulting a soldier of the Fe-Ruq sector, attempt to incite riotous behavior, religious preaching, and psychological warfare." Secael looked at Apxlus for approval to open the door, and received a confirmation. Pounding on the door, Secael called out for anyone inside to move away from the cell door. He then spread a bead of explosive gel across the door, stepped back, and fired at the line, severing the cell door in half. The explosion echoed in the detention area, and the smoke from the explosion concentrated in the small cell. A thin human male with long brown hair sat on a bench in the corner of the room, watching the warriors.

Apxlus stepped into the room, followed by Secael and Asael. The man stood to face the warriors, each of whom lowered their weapons when they saw him. Apxlus returned the man's gaze, slightly disappointed that the prisoner did not match the visions of Christ that Apxlus held in his mind. He asked a simple question.

"What is your name," Apxlus asked softly in his native tongue. He noticed that even faced with three armed strangers, the man had a peaceful and serene look about his face.

"I am," the man replied in perfect Shalothan, to each of the warriors' surprise. He made no movement, just stood quietly and waited for Apxlus to speak again.

"Are you the Son of God," Apxlus asked the prisoner.

The man smiled and replied, "I am your King."

All three warriors knelt and bowed their heads in deference to the man who claimed to be the Son of God.

"Rise, my friends. What is it that you seek of me," the man asked quietly.

Apxlus looked the man in the eye. Rising, he motioned towards the door and the hallway beyond.

"We're here to pledge our devotion, and to offer ourselves in Your service against all of the sinners. The sinners that have imprisoned You shall be repaid in full for their deeds."

"As they should, Reaz Apxlus." The man's response caught Apxlus off guard a bit, but he ignored the feeling and motioned towards the door. "We need You to come with us. You'll be safer once You're out of here. The people of this sector would just as soon have You killed than release You to any of us that know the truth.

"And do you know the truth, Reaz Apxlus?"

Apxlus paused, not knowing what to say. He thought he had understood the ancient teachings and knew the truth that they taught. He wondered if he was about to answer falsely.

"I do, my Lord," he answered, bowing his head.

"Very good. Let us go and leave this land of sinners," the man said. Secael stepped forward to help him through the blast hole in the door. Asael was already in the hallway, providing cover from his position. Apxlus brought up the rear, thinking one last time about the conversation he had just had with the Son of God.

The group made their way back towards their originating point. Crouching and walking through the hole in the first metal door, Asael tried to see through the darkness that bathed the guard station area. Blaster fire was closer now, and the faint smell of the remnants of the explosive gel tinged the air. Errant blaster shots could be seen through the darkness across from where the guard station once was. Asael quickly slithered through the hole, and moved into a covering position. Secael came through next, followed by the rescued captive. Apxlus brought up the rear, glancing back down the corridor before making his way back through the door.

"Secael, close off both corridors, quickly," Apxlus said, clasping Secael on the shoulder. All of the warriors could sense the battle that was raging around the corner would quickly be on them. Secael pulled out the explosive gel once more, and ran beads of the gel along the walls and floor near the entrances to both hallways. Pulling the Son of God into the center of the room, Asael and Apxlus gathered to shelter him from flying debris. Secael joined them in the center of the room, and quickly fired at both beads of gel, igniting the explosives. The walls of both corridors collapsed loudly, sending out a cloud of dust that could be felt, but not seen in the darkness. Asael and Apxlus pulled Christ with them towards the entry hallway, and through the hole in the door to the other side. The lights no longer worked in this corridor either, but both warriors placed the hands along the wall to lead them towards the door they had entered the building through. Secael joined the group, and stopped Apxlus.

"Commander, what about warrior Athes," he asked. Apxlus turned his head to face Secael in the darkness. He knew the most efficient choice would be to leave any wounded warriors behind so they would not be slowed down. Just as he was about to direct Secael to do just that, his conscience reminded him that he was escorting the Son of God, and had do the right thing for the wounded warrior.

"Asael and I will take Him to the ship. Go back and check on Athes. If he is still alive, bring him with you. I will have Moak and Anacen stay back to wait for you for as long as possible."

Secael clicked in obedience, and quickly retreated into the central room. The other warriors hastily made their way towards the door. Something continued to nag at Apxlus in the back of his mind. *This has been too easy*, he thought. He stopped Asael as he was about to push the door open.

"Stop," Apxlus commanded. Asael froze his hand in mid-reach, and waited for his commander to continue.

"What do you hear, Asael," Apxlus asked. The warrior listened intently for the sounds that his commander heard. There were none.

"The battle has stopped. There are no more blaster shots, either outside or inside," Asael stated. He pulled his hand back from the door, and activated his sheath blaster. He pushed the door open just enough to see past the doorjamb. The rain was still coming down, but there was no sight of Moak, Anacen, or any of the garrison around the landing platform. None of the security lights were functioning, leaving the surrounding area in darkness.

"My Lord, when we exit to outside, we will be targeted by any forces that are left. Asael and I will shield you with our bodies. Should we fall, continue running directly into the woods. One of the warriors will meet up with you and escort you to safety. Do not come back towards the building." Apxlus thought he saw a nod in the darkness, but couldn't be sure. He made no other sound.

"Asael, when you push the door open, cover us towards the landing platform. We will run to the right and back along the pathway we came in. Follow after us, and provide us protection on our left flank and rear. I will cover the front and right flanks." Asael clicked in his throat to acknowledge, and then threw the door open.

The sound of the rain increased in volume once the door was open. Asael quickly exited the hallway, with Apxlus and the Son of God directly behind him. The rain drenched the trio almost immediately, waterlogging their clothing. Asael continuously surveyed the area, peering through the blackness trying to see any movement. Apxlus was on the other side of their Christ, going through the same exercise. Not seeing any movement, they continued in a jog towards the tree line. Leaving the cover of the building, they thrust themselves into the open area between the detention center and the tree line, waiting for the inevitable barrage of blaster fire to rain down on them. When it did not, Apxlus glanced over at Asael, sending him a look of concern. *We're walking into a trap*, he thought. Asael seemed to be concerned with the same thought, catching Apxlus' glance and sending his own look of concern back.

As they passed the halfway point to the tree line, they heard what sounded like one of their warrior brethren clicking loudly from beyond the thicket edge to get their attention. Apxlus swung around to his right to see what they were being warned about. In the distance a pantheon of lights in the sky could be seen quickly approaching. Quickly counting, he guessed the oncoming ships numbered above twenty. He wasn't sure what type they were from the lights, but he guessed they were attack craft. *Probably the teeth of the trap*, he thought.

As they slowed to enter the thickets of trees, Moak and Anacen showed themselves, sheath weapons activated.

"Apxlus, something happened to the forward warrior groups. We observed some intense fighting as they entered the building, but haven't seen or heard anything since shortly after they breached the front of the detention center."

"We cannot be concerned with them now. Our duty is to protect Him," Apxlus responded, motioning towards the man standing slightly behind him. Moak and Anacen realized they had not even acknowledged His presence up to this point. Almost in unison, both knelt before the man, offering their devotion and protection with their lives. The man raised His hand and commanded both to rise, but said nothing else.

"Asael and I will escort our Lord to the ship. Wait here for Secael and Athes. Secael may need your assistance; Athes was wounded." Both of the warriors nodded in understanding, and parted to let the trio pass. Apxlus and Asael slid past the two, pulling the Son of God along with them.

With the rain still coming down heavily, it was

difficult to see through the trees. Apxlus took the point, with Asael bringing up the rear. They heard what sounded like a low rumble of thunder off to their right. Looking that way through the trees didn't reveal the source, but both warriors guessed that it was more reinforcements joining the group of oncoming lights.

Choosing to sacrifice safety for speed, the trio ran at three-quarter pace through the underbrush, slipping and sliding on the mud and wet leaves. As they neared the clearing that the ship had landed in, Apxlus stopped and knelt on one knee. Dropping his staff to his side, he held up his left hand, and closed his eyes to concentrate on a vision of fire. He imagined the warmth of the flames licking at his fingertips, and the bright light that the ball of fire would give off. Within seconds, he could feel the palm of his hand growing warmer, until it combusted into an orb of fire. Holding up his flaming hand, he used it to signal to the cloaked ship.

The ship materialized from the air, slowly fading into view as if a fog was clearing. Apxlus snuffed out the flame on his hand as Asael grabbed Christ and began moving towards the side hatch that was sliding open. The ship's antigrav engines powered to life, and the running lights on the ship began to brighten the raindrops falling around the hull. Landing lights flooded the wet ground and surrounding area with light, making it difficult for anyone to hide from view.

Naoh met them at the door, helping the trio into the ship. Apxlus turned to look over his shoulder, searching for the lights in the sky that had been converging on the complex. With the clearing suddenly illuminated from the ship's lights, it was likely that they were noticed by the enemy forces.

"Where are the others?" Naoh asked, walking

towards the cockpit. Asael had taken Christ down the corridor towards the reflecting chamber that Apxlus had set up.

"Athes was wounded. Secael has gone back to get him. Moak and Anacen are waiting to assist in the extraction. We need to run the sensors and find out where the other two groups are." Naoh hurried into the cockpit, sliding into one of the pilot seats. Apxlus followed him, seating himself in the other. Hurriedly pressing buttons and entering information, Naoh and Apxlus didn't notice Asael enter the cockpit.

"Commander, Moak and Anacen are on their way to the ship – Secael and Athes are not with them. Moak reports intense fighting in the vicinity of Secael's last known position. The area where they had stationed themselves for support of Secael's retrieval of Athes was in danger of being overrun. Awaiting orders, Commander." Apxlus nodded, but did not look away from what he was doing.

"Asael, man the weapons package console," he ordered, interpreting the wealth of information that the sensors were feeding him. A large contingent of aircraft was in the vicinity of the detention center. Some were already on the ground, emptying out life forms by the dozens. Others appeared to be moving in ever broadening circular patterns, apparently searching for the infiltrators.

"Apxlus, the sensors have located most of our warriors. The majority of them are in the complex itself, towards the front. There are two near the rear of the building. There are several that the sensors cannot detect." Apxlus grimaced at the report. Most likely the two groups were trapped together in the complex, hemmed in from the outside forces, with their only way to get out having been caved in by Apxlus' orders. The others were dead, or captured and out of sensor range. He assumed that the isolated two in the rear of the building was Secael and Athes.

Several of the ships in the air started to slowly move into position around the *Nowrimo's Revenge*. He silently asked for God's forgiveness for what he was about to do.

"Naoh, we must get out of the system immediately," he commanded. Naoh swiveled in his seat to face his commander.

"And leave all of our brethren behind?" Naoh asked incredulously. He held Apxlus' gaze. "No, we cannot do that to those warriors."

"Naoh, now is not the time to be disobedient. We must leave this planet at once, or we will not leave at all."

"We can fight *with* them, assist them in their escape in to the wo..." Apxlus waved his hand and cut him off.

"To have them hunted down like animals, one at a time? This is all a trap. The enemy only let us return to the ship so that it would have to come back into dimensional space, allowing them to find it." He paused, resigned to the choice he was making. "We have no choice. In order to protect our Lord, we must leave the others behind." Silence ensued, with Naoh glaring at his commander. Apxlus waited for a few seconds, then continued. "You know there is no other choice."

Naoh clicked several times in his throat, signaling his anger. He held Apxlus' gaze for a second longer, then swiveled back to his control panel. Forcefully punching at the controls, he reviewed the remainder of the ship's systems while they came back online.

"Moak and Anacen are aboard!" Asael called out. A muffled clunk sounded below as the hatch closed, and was secured from the inside. Naoh guided the ship off the ground, rotating on its antigrav engines. The enemy ships were surrounding them, but curiously were not firing on the ship.

Apxlus moved from his seat, and yelled out of the cockpit for Anacen. He sat back down in the command chair, leaving the other pilot chair for Anacen.

"Apxlus, they are not attempting to stop us," Naoh stated.

"They won't risk destroying the ship. Not with Him on board." Apxlus switched on the all-ship communication channel.

"Asael, use the beam weapon only. You may fire at will."

Within seconds, the particle beam fired on the nearest hovering Fe-Ruqian ship, cleaving it into two fiery pieces. The *Nowrimo's Revenge* lurched forward on its antigrav engines, maneuvering towards the gap in the perimeter that had been created by the removal of the ship.

"Commander, the enemy has commenced another attack on the detention center. It appears to be mostly ground troops, but there is some weapons fire from a few of the support craft." Naoh pointed off to their left, just over the trees. The glow of the beam weapons and explosions lit up the rainy night sky.

"Asael, target the support craft attacking the complex," Apxlus ordered. *Let's give our warriors a fighting chance*, he thought. The particle beam shot out at the Fe-Ruq vessels engaged in the attack, quickly destroying the majority of the craft before the others retreated away from the complex. The wreckage of one of the aircraft crashed onto a large grouping of Fe-Ruq soldiers, trapping them all beneath the burning hulk.

"Engage the IDMD as soon as possible, and take the ship to orbit," Apxlus ordered. The ship's thrusters engaged, and the craft roared past the remainder of the ships hovering around them.

"Incoming aircraft, on an intercept vector," Anacen reported. The bright flashes of warning shots flew close to the viewshield, momentarily blinding the pilots. The image of the shots remained in Apxlus' retinas as he continued to watch through the forward viewshield. The sky was still black from the night and the clouds, and the rain continued to hit the viewshield, blurring their vision of the night sky.

"Evasive maneuvers," the commander ordered. Naoh corkscrewed the ship deep into the storm clouds, continuously checking the proximity of the intercept ships. "Asael, warn off those intercept craft." Asael responded by quickly firing a dozen times with the particle beam weapon, taking out several of the intercept craft, and causing the remaining ones to back away from their ship.

"Thirty seconds to orbit," Naoh called out. "Anacen, you have the controls. Initiating the IDMD. Stand by." Naoh switched to the IDMD control panel, bringing the delicate controls to life in preparation for operating the unit. The sensor panel beeped various warnings, but the most incessant was the proximity warning sensor, reporting the increasing number of suborbital craft and interstellar ships that were closing in on them or their projected escape vector.

The next half-minute was intense, as the number of enemy ships increased by the second, many firing warning shots ahead of or behind the *Revenge*. One errant warning shot glanced off a rear shield, scorching a line in the hull. Just as the ship was about to enter the vacuum of space, the IDMD engaged and the ship faded into interdimensional space, leaving the Fe-Ruqian ships behind.

All aboard the *Revenge* sat still for a moment and breathed a sigh of relief. The enemy ships could still be seen visually, but did not appear on the sensors; nor did they on theirs.

"Naoh, Anacen, well done. Plot a course to one of the moons of Jethl. We will bide our time there before attempting to leave the system. I anticipate that it will be very difficult to get out of the sector. We may need to wait for an opening in the outer defenses." With that, Apxlus stood and left the cockpit, leaving the two warriors to pilot the ship away from Je-Fin.

CHAPTER XII

"General Odine, I have a situation update for you," the young aide reported. General Odine waved her in as he listened to a briefing from one of the field commanders at the detention center. He glanced at her quickly, motioning for her to report her information, then turned back to listen to the field commander.

"The colonel in command of the Devilspear wing reported that the target ship was allowed to escape unharmed into orbit. One of our defense platforms tracked the ship until it either jumped on a thread or utilized an IDMD."

General Odine didn't turn to face her, instead choosing to respond to a statement by the field commander. "I want some of them alive, Major. Limited losses are acceptable. Also, I just received a report that their escape ship has departed the planet atmosphere and left for parts unknown. Make sure that all of the prisoners know they've been abandoned here. Report back in two hours. That is all." General Odine switched off his communication device and turned towards his aide.

"Did they jump a thread or use an IDMD," the General asked her. The aide glanced down at the data tablet, then back up.

"It doesn't say which, sir. Just that one of the two was used." She nervously stood in front of the General, waiting for him to respond. He was infamous for ending the lives of those that brought unfavorable reports. She was certain that her report was not going to be viewed positively.

General Odine sat in his chair for a minute, pondering the information. Jumping on a thread wouldn't gain them anything. One of the defensive platforms could surely track the exit vector, leaving them plenty of time to prepare an interception force at the end of the thread. With the importance the former prisoner held for his enemies, he was fairly certain that they would have used an IDMD to try to evade detection and capture. They wouldn't risk fighting their way out, not with their precious cargo. He smiled outwardly, realizing that his enemies had limited choices for success.

"Thank you for the information," he said to the aide. She stood there, expecting some act of violence to befall her. "You're dismissed," he said, waving her off once he saw she wasn't leaving. She backed up a step and then turned and walked out of the office, sneaking a look back at the General.

General Odine pressed a combination of keys on his data table, and a hologram of a naval officer appeared above his desk.

"Rear Admiral Krawol, the Shalothan force has entered interdimensional space with their target. I'm sending over the latest information from our orbital platforms." General Odine flicked a piece of lint from his coat sleeve. "Everything appears to be falling into place for our plan. I want the crew of that ship alive."

"And their cargo?"

"Alive or dead. Either way it doesn't matter. He

won't be going to Shalotha under any circumstance." He straightened his coat and tugged on both sleeves to even them out.

"Understood General. We have our fleet in place now."

"If they somehow escape your forces, it would not be in your best interest to return with the fleet, is that understood?" General Odine lifted his head so he could look directly at the hologram of Rear Admiral Krawol.

"Yes, General," Krawol said, bowing his head in obedience.

"Send updates every two hours on any reported activity. They may drop back into dimensional space well before Ru-Nula. I would advise that you watch not only the system borders, but the planets just inside the outer-ring, such as Feu-Jegt and Jethl. That is all." General Odine turned off the hologram projector and stood up, stretching his legs. In a few hours he would participate in the holoconference with the heads of the surrounding sectors to condemn the unwarranted attacks on Je-Fin by the ruthless and warmongering Shalothans. The creative surveillance images that his intelligence team had put together would support his admonishment of the Shalothan government. He thought about how he would pressure the other sectors to support him in his condemnation of the attack. And then he would slowly work that condemnation into the basis for breaking the truce. He smiled at the thought.

The *Alaurian Spirit* had made good time to the Fe-Ruq sector after changing course based on the new information that Captain Pollard had given the senior officers. Unfortunately, they had arrived after the Shalothan ship had entered the primary system, but just in time to be greeted by a large Fe-Ruqian fleet that had moved into position to patrol the sector border. One of the fleet vessels had contacted the *Alaurian Spirit* for identification, and Captain Pollard saw no danger in providing it to the captain of the vessel, the *Censer.* The captain of the *Censer* was persistent in his quest to seek the truth about why the *Alaurian Spirit* had been heading towards the Fe-Ruq border.

"Captain Pollard, how can you be so arrogant as to assume that your statement would just be accepted as truth?" Captain Cellif Tarvold asked quietly. He suspected the USF vessel was tracking the Shalothan vessel, as were his fleet vessels, but he didn't want to be lied to about it.

"With all due respect Captain Tarvold, I stand by my statement. We are merely running the ship through some tests. You have access to the orbital ship dock records at Mars. Check for yourself. This ship was in hibernation in a shipyard less than a week ago," Captain Pollard argued, with a hint of indignation in her voice. She wasn't worried about an attack from the *Censer* or any other Fe-Ruq vessel, but she certainly didn't want to be detained any longer than absolutely necessary. She assumed the Shalothan vessel had jumped on a thread to get to Je-Fin, but she couldn't be sure unless she could have the sensor sweep the area for them. The problem was that if they turned on the sensor sweep, the entire Fe-Ruq fleet would know that they were looking for something, which would contradict her explanation of simply running tests on the ship. Even if the story had been true, it would not have been in good form to run a sensor sweep so close to a sovereign sector's border. It certainly would not have gained her any respect among the other captains of the fleet.

"Captain Pollard, you and your ship are within ten thousand kilometers of our sector's border. There is an entire universe out there, yet you choose to run your 'tests' just outside our borders. Captain, your decision to operate your command so close to our border could be interpreted as a provocative move in an attempt to engage us in war. Being a rational man, I have no doubts that an attempt to attack our sector with a single ship is not the truth that you are so desperately trying to hide. However, if you continue to lie to me about the reasons for your being here, I will have your ship impounded, you and your crew detained on one of our ships, and have you deported back to your system. With that being said, are you willing to tell me why you are here?"

Commander Marshall Tennison looked over at Captain Pollard. They were certainly in a poor position at the moment. Telling Captain Tarvold the truth might not prevent them from being physically detained by the fleet anyway. He preferred for them to turn and leave, hoping that the fleet wouldn't pursue them. They way he saw it, they were there for the same reason, and probably wouldn't waste the resources to chase after a USF vessel that was outside its borders, regardless of how close it actually was.

Secael sprinted across the open field, scanning left and right as he ran. The blackness, which permeated the field only minutes before now, gave way to a harsh light that bathed the field in white, originating from several aerial vessels that had converged on the area. Slapping his hand on his blaster sheath, he twisted and fired a few random shots at the lights, hoping that one of the unaimed shots would find its mark. The lights still shined down as he reached the leading edge of the building.

Slowing down as he approached the door that he and Apxlus seemingly had just left, he could hear weapons fire suddenly ring out amid the sounds of the storm. The high-pitched whine of the laser battery pierced through the rain. He wasn't sure how many had arrived or how many were actually firing, but he could distinguish that the blasts weren't hitting anything solid.

Keeping his blaster sheath activated, Secael raised his left hand and concentrated on creating fire in his palm. Now was not the time for stealth, he decided. With their ship ready to take off, he had precious few minutes to retrieve his comrade and return before they vectored off planet towards the outer-system boundaries. Stepping into the darkened vestibule, he glanced behind him once more to ensure that the garrison soldiers were not following him in. His left hand burning with flame, he waved his arm slightly to cast the light around the walls and down the hall. Seeing no one else was in the immediate vicinity, Secael made his way towards the hole blown in the far door. As he approached the secondary entrance, acrid smoke filled his nostrils, causing him to duck his head slightly to avoid the unseen wisps of smoke. He listened intently for a few seconds for any sign of activity on the other side of the door, in what had been a guard station area. Hearing only the distant sounds of a battle playing out, he could discern nothing in the immediate area. He cautiously stepped through the hole, keeping his blaster pointed ahead of him.

He stepped towards the remains of the guard station

desk, scanning the area repeatedly to watch for a trap. As he stepped to the side, he could see the legs of a Shalothan warrior protruding into the open. Athes' body had been moved from the position that he had left him in. Whether it was Athes himself trying to move, or one of the soldiers, he could not know.

"Athes, can you hear me," Secael whispered as he slowly approached the body. There was a slight stirring from the body, and then nothing. Secael positioned himself next to the upper torso of Athes, and knelt down to inspect the wound. The blast that had found its mark on Athes' arm was stronger than a typical handheld blaster of the Fe-Ruqian military. He guessed the garrison had a few blaster rifles on the premises, which would explain the higher power of the shot. A Shalothan's biological armor could withstand a typical blast-shot, especially one that was fired blindly instead of aimed at the soft tissues left unprotected by the body armor.

"Athes, we must go now," Secael said, switching his focus from Athes to the room around him, and back to Athes. The injured Shalothan's eyes flitted open, and he looked at Secael for a moment before speaking.

"How bad is the injury," he asked Secael. Secael glanced down at the warrior's upper arm, and held his flaming hand above the arm so he could examine the wound. The keratin armor had been hit dead on, burning a clean hole through the surface and into the tissue and muscle below. The hole was large enough for Secael to have put his first two digits in, and, although cauterized from the blaster shot around the penetration point, the tissue underneath still bled some, pooling underneath the arm and shoulder of Athes. The damage was not life threatening at this point, however the risk of infection was high if not treated quickly. The advantage the Shalothan species had over most other species in regards to tissue damage is that their biological processes had developed over time to a point where they would regenerate the damaged tissue in a short amount of time. The keratin armor took considerably longer to regenerate, but injuries that could render a human's arm useless for long periods of time may only disable a Shalothan for a few days at most. This particular injury, while bad, was not nearly as disabling as Secael originally had thought.

"You're still losing blood in the wound. I can't tell if regeneration has started yet, not by the light of the fire. We need to get out of here, but I need to stop your bleeding. You know what must be done, yes?"

Athes grimaced slightly at the thought, and nodded an affirmative. "Do it quickly."

Secael held the warrior's gaze for a moment longer, then thrust his burning left hand into the open wound on Athes' arm. The flesh sizzled and burned, and the smell quickly filled the air around the warriors. Athes clenched his right hand into a fist, and let out a small groan, but those remained the only outward expressions of his pain. Secael pressed his fingers on all sides of the wound, burning the raw tissue until it stopped bleeding. Within a few minutes, he could see no more blood coming from the wound.

"Athes, we must go. They cannot wait for us much longer." Secael attempted to raise the wounded warrior, but Athes waved him off.

"Is the Son of God safe?"

"He is on the ship with Apxlus and the others. They are waiting for us."

"What about our brethren that coordinated the

frontal assault? Are they also back on the ship?"

"I do not know that answer. It did not appear that they had made their way back to the extraction zone when we arrived. I heard fighting in the distance as I came back, and dozens more military craft are in the area. It appears the battle is unfinished."

"We must join them then," Athes said, struggling to prop himself up with one arm. Secael snuffed out the flame on his hand, and slid his arms under Athes' shoulders and lifted him up. Athes steadied himself with a hand on Secael's shoulder.

"Did you happen to see my staff," he asked Secael. The other warrior was about to answer when they heard an explosion rip through the hallway that led outside. Both ducked down reflexively to avoid flying debris. A man's voice could be heard issuing orders, presumably one of the garrison commanders. Peering around the remnants of the station, both warriors could see the silhouettes of two soldiers as they tentatively made their way down the burning hallway, weapons drawn and ready.

"I will take these two. Go to your left. That is the cellblock corridor. I will meet you at the far end. We can make an exit down there." Secael pushed Athes' right shoulder towards the direction he was talking about. Athes clicked in acknowledgment and crouch-walked out of Secael's view. A second later a small flame could be seen, appearing to float in the blackness of the darkened building.

Secael waited for the two soldiers to get a bit closer towards the remnants of the door frame that had held the secondary door. Flames licked the sides of the frame, and the remaining piece of the door hung precariously by a strand of twisted metal from one of the sidewalls. Studying the soldiers as they approached, Secael noticed that these soldiers weren't wearing the same type of uniform that the garrison soldiers had been wearing. They also sported higher powered weapons than a typical infantry unit. Guessing they were special operations soldiers, he assumed they each had optical implants that allowed them to see in the dark. He had precious few seconds before they would be past the fire, into a position that would provide them with a clear view of the room, and with it – him.

He targeted the soldier on the left, slightly ahead of the other soldier. Taking aim at his head, he fired two quick shots in succession, leaving a headless body crumpling to the ground. The second soldier dove to the ground, spraying blaster fire into the room. Secael crouched low to the ground and took out the second soldier with another precise shot. The soldiers' commanding officer yelled into the corridor behind them, ordering them to call out their status. Secael took the opportunity to make his way towards the cellblock corridor, feeling along the wall with his hand rather than creating a flame again.

As he reached the entranceway, he heard more soldiers shuffling into the burning corridor behind him, intent on making it further than their two fallen comrades. Remembering the layout of the cellblock area, Secael broke into a trot to quickly make it to the other end. Athes clicked in his throat as he approached, and he clicked back to signal Athes it was he. Just as he arrived at the end of the corridor, the ground shuddered, and a deafening sound erupted outside the building walls. From the way they were positioned, Secael guessed that it was towards the front of the building.

"Perhaps our brethren are not finished fighting yet,"

Athes suggested, a smile that could be heard in his voice. Secael focused on creating fire on his left hand again, and used his right to map out a square with the last bit of explosive gel. The bead of gel ran out before he actually completed the square, but he knew that the hole would be more than adequate for their use.

Both warriors backed away and crouched in the doorway of a nearby cell that was open. Taking careful aim in the dim light, Secael fired at the bead of explosive gel, causing an explosion that sent the wall hurtling outward away from the rest of the structure. As the smoke cleared, both saw that the area beyond the hole was filled with light, and water poured from the ceiling. Cautiously moving towards the hole, Secael saw that the room was actually an open area on the outside of the building, and the water pouring from the ceiling was actually the rain coming down. Peering out of the hole, he could see the sources of the light circling in the sky above, searching for the attackers. Beyond the field of light, the terrain gave way to more trees and bushes.

Calling out to Athes to follow, Secael ducked through the hole and ran towards the trees. As both became visible in the search lights, weapons fire lanced out from several of the ships circling above, strafing the ground that they ran across. Both offered return fire into the sky, with neither taking the time to aim at their targets. Secael noticed that this open expanse was a bit wider than the one on the other side of the building. He risked a glance behind and saw Athes lagging behind, his wounded arm hanging at his side as he ran. Secael slowed to provide cover fire for Athes as they neared the edge of the trees. Just as they reached the edge of the thicket, more explosions rocked the detention center, sending a giant plume of billowing fire and smoke into the stormy night.

The two warriors surveyed their surroundings. The thicket provided cover for now, but ground troops would inevitably be securing the perimeter of the building as they arrived. In the night sky, it appeared that an aerial battle was ongoing, with flashes of red lighting up the low-lying clouds. The burning wreckage of some large vessel could be seen towards the front of the building. The front corner of the damaged structure and the natural terrain blocked much of the view, but pieces of the wreckage could be seen littering the battlefield. The building itself was now engulfed in flames, and several portions of the outer wall towards the front had collapsed in on themselves, revealing the burning interior of the building. As Secael absorbed the view, a thought exploded into his head; a detail that he hadn't noticed before. *Where were all the others prisoners? There were no other prisoners in what supposedly was a maximum security complex!* The sobering reality of the situation struck him like a blow from a staff. *This was a trap.*

CHAPTER XIII

Captain Pollard's conversation ended in a stalemate when both captains received urgent incoming messages at seemingly the same time. Realizing the only person who would be contacting her on her personal communication channel was Admiral Caturorglimi, she hastily closed the open transmission with Captain Tarvold and retreated to her state room to take the incoming call.

Arriving in less than a minute, she let herself fall into the chair at her data table to compose herself before taking the message. Straightening her uniform top, she maneuvered in her seat to put herself before the communication console, and switched on the unit to open the communication channel.

"Captain Pollard here. Secure transmission."

"Captain, this is Caturorglimi. We have an unforeseen situation developing. Government leaders in several sectors just took part in a holoconference with General Odine of the Fe-Ruq sector. According to statements made by the General and his staff, a maximum security detention center on Je-Fin was recently attacked by Shalothan warriors, and the attackers kidnapped an individual of interest. I've forwarded a copy of the communication and their statements. You are to review it immediately. I will stay on the open channel to answer any questions.

Captain Pollard acknowledged the order, and quickly pulled up the information on her data table information screen. The data video began playing, displaying an image of General Odine surrounded by advisors addressing the leaders on the holoconference. The leaders dispensed with formalities quickly, and General Odine had one of his advisors begin showing a recording. The General spoke while the image played, providing a narration for the images.

"The attack began when the unidentified craft ignored repeated attempts at being hailed by our defensive platforms, and then proceeded to violate the planetary airspace without authorization." The image showed a frigate blasting into the atmosphere, destroying several Je-Fin atmospheric patrol craft while spiraling and weaving its way through a maze of defense craft.

"Notice the way the craft continues to maneuver in order to eliminate as many interceptors as possible. The total loss during this initial entry phase was at least seven defensive patrol craft, including the loss of life for each of the pilots and crew." The image stopped, and the General paused for a moment before continuing.

"These next images are from multiple stationary surveillance recorders situated at various points on the complex. Notice the savagery with which the Shalothan intruders massacre the unsuspecting garrison soldiers." Bringing the recording to life again, the images displayed what appeared to be a state of the art, multi-level detention center heavily armed with patrols and outer defenses. The image cut to what appeared to be an entranceway into the facility, clearly showing at least six Shalothan warriors fighting with troops on the ground. In the span of a minute, the recording showed the lethal precision with which the Shalothan warriors cut through the detention center garrison. Bodies of the Je-Fin soldiers quickly littered the newly minted battlefield.

"Unfortunately for the Shalothan attackers, one of our perimeter recorders captured a group of the warriors escaping back into the woods with an individual from our facility. Based on this upcoming segment, one can only assume that our former prisoner is important enough that the Shalothans blatantly entered our system to extract their agent." The image jumped again, this time to show what appeared to be more Shalothan warriors running across an open stretch of field into the woods, taking the Je-Fin fugitive with them into the woods. The advisor stopped the image again, and paused for the General to speak.

"The battle at the detention facility proved to be costly, as early estimates indicate we may end up with over one hundred casualties. We have not confirmed exactly how many Shalothans attacked the facility, but our early analysis has indicated over thirty warriors. Outrage is not a strong enough word to describe our response to this barbaric attack. I can only hope these next images can accurately instill the sense of anger that the Fe-Ruq government suffers from on this sad day." The General nodded slowly towards the advisor controlling the images. The image resumed motion, and the images switched every few seconds. It began with an image showing dead troops in the woods, followed by images of the injured lying on the ground near a wall. Later images showed the burning wreckage of a military craft on the ground, and dozens of corpses on what appeared to be a battlefield. It finished with footage from inside a building showing a fierce battle raging between detention center garrison soldiers and Shalothan warriors. The recording stopped once more, pausing with an image of a dead Je-Fin soldier filling the viewscreen, blood darkening the chest area of his uniform.

"These last images are of the violent escape of the Shalothan attack force as they exited the atmosphere." The recording restarted, showing a frigate blasting its way through the atmosphere, destroying several more Je-Fin craft in the process. The recording stopped and faded away, and the General waited a few moments before speaking.

"The planet of Je-Fin, as well as the system and sector of Fe-Ruq, denounce these actions of war by the Shalothan people. The prisoner they took is an individual that is of utmost importance to us, and we demand that he be returned. In addition, we request that each of you formally condemn these attacks, and support our request for economic sanctions on the systems and planets within the Shalothan sector. Please take our requests to your advisory councils. I would like us to reconvene within one standard day."

The image of the holoconference faded as the recording ended. Admiral Caturorglimi's voice piped in over the channel.

"Thoughts Captain?" Captain Pollard sat back in her chair, biting the inside of her cheek. She wondered if what she had just witnessed was actually true.

"Have our intelligence agents reviewed the footage for the authenticity of the recording? Why wasn't the Shalothan Primary invited to the meeting to explain or deny the attack?

"Unfortunately, the Fe-Ruq military is not releasing

the recording. The official statement is that the footage reveals highly sensitive security information, were someone to have the footage to examine. Obviously, my first thought was that it was a total fabrication. However, we had suspected that the transport frigate that left Shalotha a few days ago would be destined for Je-Fin. The parties involved assumed it would be a stealth mission, and that the Fe-Ruqians would deny that they lost a political prisoner, to save face more than anything else. For the Fe-Ruqians, specifically General Odine himself, to not only be the initiator of the meeting, but to divulge all the details that they did, makes me suspect that at least some of the details involved are true. Why go to all the trouble to make something like this up?" An image of the Admiral had replaced the paused image of the recording. Angelina waited for a moment to see if her commanding officer had any further information to add to his explanation. Hearing none forthcoming, she repeated part of her initial question.

"What about the Shalothan Primary? Why not ask the governmental leader of the system suspected of carrying out the attack?" Angelina hoped that he would provide at least a guess this time.

"Two theories on this one. The first is obvious; the Fe-Ruqians didn't want to give the Shalothans a chance to explain or deny that they had sent someone to basically kidnap the supposed Son of God from Je-Fin. Allowing it to turn into a political debate and giving the Shalothan Primary a chance to deny that the attack was government sponsored would only hurt any demands for formal retribution from the Fe-Ruq leadership. Other sectors could very easily view a denial by Primary Radael as confirmation that it was more of an independent terrorist attack by religious zealots, thereby undermining whatever support Odine was attempting to rally."

"And the second, sir?"

"The Fe-Ruqian version of the events don't match the truth, and they want to stoke the fires of outrage from the other systems quickly enough to allow them a reprisal attack without penalty from other systems. The longer the allegations are out there, the more likely that others sectors will back down from supporting the Fe-Ruqians, regardless of what actually happened. Allowing the Fe-Ruq military to initiate return strikes against Shalothan interests will only start another galactic war, and the other sectors dread being pulled into another conflict. The Fe-Ruq sector is about the only one left that could survive another prolonged conflict. General Odine may view this as a starting point to launch a counter-strike campaign against Shalotha, with thoughts of finishing their last major skirmish. The truce didn't sit well with any of the parties involved; it was necessary for the galaxy's sake. To a man, every Fe-Ruq military commander hopes for the day that they can exact their full revenge on Shalotha, unhindered by the parameters of the truce." The admiral finished, leaning to one side of the image to take a drink of water. Resuming his original posture, he wiped the corner of his mouth with an out-turned thumb, and visibly took a breath.

"Captain Pollard, regardless of what the truth is, the galaxy is now precariously close to being thrown back into a massive conflict. To avert this, several of our own ambassadors contacted General Odine's staff immediately following the holoconference that you just viewed. We as a sector cannot suffer through another protracted conflict. As military resources go, you're quite aware that every facet of our defense forces struggle with adequate supplies. You yourself are on a refurbished frigate rather than a vessel more suitable to your mission. The ambassadors and the advisory staff from Fe-Ruq have come to a tentative solution; the Fe-Ruqians want their prisoner back. In exchange for his return, they will not escalate the incident any further than it has already gone. As such, Captain Pollard, your mission objectives have changed once again. Primary Radael should be receiving the solution parameters within an hour. The communiqué detailed what he and his regime need to accomplish in order to prevent further hostilities. Basically, the Shalothan vessel will be intercepted, and expected to hand over the prisoner to a third party. The Fe-Ruqians have agreed to release the attacking vessel and its remaining crew once the prisoner transfer has occurred. Captain, you and your crew will be the third party representative at the transfer station."

Captain Pollard broke in, "Admiral, I respectfully object to this mission."

"This is not a request, Captain."

"Admiral, if I make speak freely. We are not equipped for prisoner transfers. Most of our holding capacity is already being used to store our officers' clones. This political prisoner cannot safely be held captive on this vessel."

"Let me remind you that we're speaking about a man claiming to be the Son of God. Not the worst planetary killer in galactic history. Not a mad Shalothan warrior. Nothing violent. *He claims to be a man of peace.* He's a political prisoner at this point, no more, no less."

There was a long pause between the two, as Admiral Caturorglimi and Captain Pollard stared at each other through the holo-image. Captain Pollard broke her stare first, looking down at her data-table to compose herself. Within seconds she faced her superior officer again.

"Admiral, where exactly is the transfer waypoint?"

"The Fe-Ruqians seem to think that the ship was heading towards the outer system rings. Primary Radael has been instructed to inform the ship's crew that they are to meet with your ship and a Fe-Ruq military escort in low orbit around Jethl. You will be escorted in system by a," Admiral Caturorglimi paused to glance down at the data-pad in his hand, "Captain Tarvold. My understanding is that he is part of a detachment guarding the Fe-Ruq system borders. Once you've rendezvoused with this Captain Tarvold's group, you will travel to Jethl to await the arrival of the fugitive vessel. The transfer will be conducted in orbit. You will then be escorted to an undisclosed in-system planet while the fugitive vessel is escorted to the system border. Once you have arrived to the undisclosed location, you will complete the transfer process and return the political prisoner to a Fe-Ruq designate to be determined. Any questions?"

"Are we to remain in system after the transfer?"

"At this point, I would assume that you will be escorted out by Captain Tarvold. If that happens, you will return to your mission origination point and receive further orders there. If you are not asked to leave the system immediately, you are to attempt to determine where the Son of God is being transported. Once you have specifics, exit both the system and sector and return to your origination point. Do not transmit any information while in-system. Anything else?"

"Admiral, if this really is the Son of God, this seems as if we're abandoning him to the Fe-Ruqians, a system that, need I remind you, doesn't believe in God. I can only imagine what they will do to him."

"Captain Pollard, you are acting on behalf of the USF, not your church," the Admiral's tone of voice sharpened as he rebuked the captain. "The decisions made were made for the safety of not only our own sector, but of several others, including the ones that we brokered the truce agreement for. We have a responsibility to both the Shalothans and Fe-Ruqians to ensure that this does not escalate any further. Maybe He'll start His new Kingdom on Je-Fin." The last statement was made with sarcasm, and the captain actually thought she detected a sneer on the admiral's face.

"Yes sir, Admiral," Captain Pollard replied.

"Unless you have any other questions, you are dismissed. Admiral Caturorglimi, out."

"Captain Pollard, out," Angelina stated, but the communication had already faded to black before she finished her end of the sign-off. She leaned back in her chair and pondered the effect that this would have on the galaxy should the general populace learn of the supposed return of the Son of God. If the other systems of faith learned of this situation, there would be no avoiding another conflict. Hordes of the faithful would probably descend on the location where the Son of God was being held, demanding his release. Depending on the military forces present, it could be a protest in vain, or a massacre waiting to happen. In either situation, the Fe-Ruq system proper would be inundated with believers, mostly to one planet, sapping resources and creating a security nightmare for the planetary defense forces. And, if someone were to plan ahead far enough, they stood a chance of having a healthy portion of believers *and* the Son of God all in one place at the same time, creating a perfect opportunity for an attack. For an anti-religious government such as the Fe-Ruqians, it could be too tempting of an opportunity to pass up. Captain Pollard envisioned General Odine sacrificing one of his planets just to rid the galaxy of people of faith. It was not something that General Odine was incapable of. The question would be whether he would actually choose to commit genocide on such a highly visible level. Such an act would spell the end of the galaxy as they knew it, for it would become a religious crusade on a scale the likes of which history had never seen.

Captain Pollard clicked on her communication board and called for her senior officers to report to the bridge. She would need everyone to be briefed and ready to go. She just hoped that none of her crew decided to take matters into their own hands to protect the Son of God.

CHAPTER XIV

Radael Asalor sat in his transport flanked by two warriors, while the remaining warriors in the Primary's personal honor guard escorted the craft to its destination in their own atmospheric patrol craft. The morning had began easily enough, with Radael meeting with an agricultural advisor on the reconstruction progress of the governmental agricultural farms in the southern hemisphere. The past decade had put a strain on their production. First through the massive output necessary to sustain their hungry war machine, and then by the utter devastation incurred through the planetary bombardment that the Fe-Ruqian war craft had rained down on them for wake periods on end.

Staring through the transport viewshield, Radael pondered what the immediate future held for not only Shalotha, but the entire system under his responsibility. The interruption by one of his military advisors and the subsequent request of his presence at an emergency advisory board meeting suggested that something had gone terribly wrong in the covert operation on Je-Fin. He had not received any information from Reaz Apxlus since he had sent word to his trusted friend that his mission was to begin, nor had he expected to. But now, on a day when he should be working on rebuilding his planet, he faced an uncertain future; one that could threaten to destroy everything he had worked for.

The transport glided into the narrow portal at the base of the sleek monolithic obelisk structure. The massive piece of construction had been created by the ancient masters centuries ago as a gift to their gods, the false gods the Shalothans had worshipped before their race had found Christianity. Now the structure served well as the headquarters for the Advisory Board and their respective support staffs. The construct rose two hundred meters into the air, tapering to a point that was built of the same material contained in a viewshield. The transparent material allowed light to filter in during the wake period, and light to shine from within during the sleep period. Built of the black kranistone from Shalotha's deep-sea mines, it loomed over the sprawling gardens colored with the red blooms of tens of thousands of typher plants, creating a striking contrast to all in visual range of the building. From a distance, the black structure resembled the tip of a dagger rising out of a pool of blood.

Settling down onto the stone surface within the hangar bay, Radael and his warrior escorts descended from the transport ramp before the antigravity units in the transport had powered down. The sound of boots marching in unison across the stone floor echoed in the chamber as he and his honor guard strode in haste towards one of the far service lifts. His agricultural advisor had preceded him here once Radael had received the urgent message. All of his Advisors were expected there, either in person or by means of secure holotransmission.

Reaching the second-to-highest level of the structure, his honor guard led the way to the wide stairway that ascended into the pyramid shaped room that was the meeting chamber. Striding up the stairs and into the room, Radael and his companions were bathed in the sunlight pouring in through the transparent walls, which sloped upwards into a point at the apex of the room. Seated around a long table in the center of the room was the majority of the advisory board. A few seats were empty among the twelve advisors, and aides rushed to setup a machine in each empty location to allow the absent advisor to participate via holotransmission. The lone seat at the head of the table was the exception, as that particular seat was reserved for the Primary.

Radael turned to each of his advisors, and extended greetings. Several of the advisors seemed subdued and quiet, causing concern for the Primary. The aides finished their duties, and were ushered out of the room. Only the advisors, the Primary, and his two honor guards remained.

"Primary," one of the advisors began, "I received an encoded message nearly two hours ago from an out-system contact, indicating that a Shalothan strike force was the subject of a massive military exercise within the Fe-Ruq system." The advisor, Risap Sateron, was the most senior of the advisors on the board, and as such had ascended to the rank of the Chief Vizier for Radael's staff. Risap's keratin armor was faded to a whitish-gray color, and the ridges along his cranium were worn down from time. The skin on his face sagged, giving the appearance of sadness.

"Perhaps you can explain why our forces are in the Fe-Ruq sector, let alone the primary system?" A different advisor, a large warrior with battered armor and a black tunic, interjected with this question.

Radael's head swiveled on its neck to face the

opposite side of the table, and in turn the advisor posing the question. Laniz Tesuh, whose official title was General of the Armies, sat three seats away from Radael, eyes burning into his Primary.

"General Tesuh," Radael began, addressing his advisor with his formal title. "Perhaps *you* can explain the blatant show of disrespect towards your Primary?" Radael glared back just as fiercely at General Tesuh, refusing to allow such absence of respect in his presence.

General Tesuh clicked in his throat lightly, then bowed his head slightly in deference to Radael.

"Forgive me, *Primary*. I merely seek to understand why some of my warriors would be on a mission that I have no knowledge of." General Tesuh uttered the title of Radael with contempt. The General leaned forward in his seat, still searching the face of Radael for a sign of weakness. Radael held his gaze for a few heartbeats, then turned to face the rest of his advisors.

"Before we get into accusations and explanations, I would like to know the content of this message that you received," Radael stated. He nodded towards Chief Vizier Sateron to provide the information. Sateron began, detailing the events that had led to a message being sent on a personal communication channel to his chamber. Revealing the message source was from a contact within the USF, he indicated that he believed the content, and shared the details with the group. The USF source reported that a holoconference had taken place, with General Odine of the Fe-Ruq system condemning Shalotha for the attacks. Images of Shalothan warriors were broadcast for all of those participating in the holoconference, along with damning scenes of violence and death, and lastly, of the alleged kidnapping of a political prisoner. At the conclusion of the report, Sateron fell quiet and waited for Radael to speak.

"The details of this report are very disturbing. General Tesuh, how could so many of our warriors experience such a catastrophic lapse of discipline all at once? More over, I suspect that perhaps they were provided with resources to get off-world safely without detection. Surely, our planetary defenses are not so weak as for you to suggest that we could miss a contingent of warriors departing without proper clearance. Have you any theories on how this could have occurred so easily?" Radael spoke evenly, but the tone of his voice carried a tinge of anger in it. General Tesuh sat stone faced in his chair, acutely aware that every being in the room was watching his body language, waiting for a facial twitch or slight bowing of the head that indicated a weakness in the General's façade. None was forthcoming, and an uncomfortable silence permeated the air in the chamber.

"Primary, I propose a solution." The voice came from further down the table, from the Vizier of Hlos, the innermost populated planet in the Shalothan system. A member of the trade caste, the political prowess of Moam Odatec had served him well in his rise to power. By rank, his Vizier-ship was the lowest in importance among the four planetary Viziers, as his planet was the smallest by population in the system.

Radael nodded for him to continue, and all heads turned towards the Hlos Vizier.

"Based on the report, the solution seems apparent. This rogue group of warriors has the political prisoner with them. If they successfully return to the Shalothan system, it will appear that it was a sanctioned attack on the sovereignty of Fe-Ruq. It is doubtless that a military attack by the Fe-Ruqians would be unavoidable. Our systems cannot suffer any further destruction if we are to restore ourselves to our former glory. Protecting a few warriors in return for the loss of life of tens of millions of our brethren is not acceptable. We must denounce this attack, and assist the Fe-Ruq government in the return of their prisoner. If our own forces were to capture the group, we could return the prisoner to the Fe-Ruqians as a token of good faith. The undisciplined warriors can be dealt with in private," Odatec glanced down at General Tesuh, "and the leadership in our military addressed at a later time." Odatec quieted down, and several of the advisors looked around at one another, awaiting the Primary's position on the solution.

"Vizier Odatec's solution seems to be the most logical I can think of. Is there anyone else that can propose a different approach to resolution, one that will not pull us into another conflict?" Radael looked at each of the advisors around the table, waiting to see if any of the leaders on the advisory board would suggest a different solution. Receiving none, Radael continued with a course of direction.

"General Tesuh, you will dispatch several ships to the sector border, on a vector towards Fe-Ruq. Should the rogue ship approach Shalothan space before we contact the Fe-Ruq government, they will intercept the rogue warriors and detain them. Otherwise, they will await communication from you. The Chief Vizier and I will negotiate a handoff location so that the prisoner can be transferred back to them. We will provide this to you for their use. I would anticipate that you will provide the proper leadership to your forces. Do you have any questions, General?" Radael held General Tesuh's gaze before smiling slightly and looking around the table.

"If there are no other concerns, then I suggest we focus on creating a contingency plan should General Tesuh's detachment fail to stop the returning warriors. Let us begin with the assumption that a return to Shalotha would precipitate an outright attack by the Fe-Ruqian military at best, but possibly a multisector contingent at worst." Primary Radael and eleven of his twelve advisors spent the next several hours strategizing what to do should there be an attack on their sector. The lone advisor not participating, General Tesuh, sat quietly in his seat, listening to everything.

The emergency meeting had ended, and Radael signaled to Chief Vizier Sateron and Vizier Odatec that he wanted them to stay behind as the other advisors departed or signed off from their holodevices. The sky had turned a deep red, casting long shadows throughout the chamber. The illumination globes embedded in the floor of the chamber were beginning to glow faintly with a white light to oppose the intruding darkness.

Once everyone but the three politicians had left, Radael motioned them to sit down.

"Risap, what was your impression of our comrade, General Tesuh?" Radael looked at both advisors, but returned his gaze to Risap to await an answer.

"Primary, he knows that he's in a situation that cannot work out well for him with any outcome. He senses that you're aware of his intentions, I believe."

"Vizier Odatec, what was your impression?" Radael sat still, observing the younger advisor.

"Primary, I expect that General Tesuh quieted

himself because he does not have the amount of allies on the advisory board that he covets, especially if he were to act on the rumors that he is planning a coup."

Radael nodded, thinking through the possibilities.

"I expect that General Tesuh will bide his time before seeking his revenge. If it's truly a higher position of power that he covets, then he will need to count the majority of the advisory board as his allies. By definition, that would mean most of the advisors would need to be my enemy. Hence, the reason why we did not go to the board with Apxlus' mission. While all understand the possibility that the Son of God is on Je-Fin, none dare make accusations that this rogue group of warriors traveled to Je-Fin on someone's order, regardless if they are bringing back our Savior." Radael watched young Odatec's reaction to his statement, gauging how much understanding the young Vizier had of the situation. Seeing some confusion, Radael began to explain his rationale.

"Vizier Odatec, let me enlighten you about the conflict between General Tesuh and I. The esteemed General loathed the fact that I accepted the terms of the truce without consulting him. He feels that I am a weak leader, and that for Shalotha to return to our former glory we need a powerful militaristic leader, much like the Primaries of old. His contempt for me is widely known, however it may not be well understood by many of the advisors. Most of you on the advisory board are not true warriors; most of you were raised in other castes, and perhaps had a taste of battle during the last inter-sector conflict. General Tesuh, on the other hand, is bred from a long lineage of great warriors, and is extremely proud of his ancestry. He was on the losing side of our most recent Civil War, and was selected as an advisor for this board not because of his strengths as a politician, but because it was negotiated during the surrender. Unfortunately, he was the warrior that signed the surrender documents, and submitted them to the highest ranking official on the victorious side, which happened to be me. During the inter-sector conflict, it was under his command than many of our greatest losses came. Whether an attempt to make our decisions look poor, or just a lack of leadership on his behalf, no one can be sure. But he does hold the highest rank within our military command structure, and as such has powerful resources at his disposal. I would not put it out of the range of possibilities that he is planning to reignite a civil war, if only to restructure the government, with himself in a top position of power. Should a civil war result in my untimely demise, he would be no worse off for the loss." Radael paused for either of the advisors to ask a question. Moam Odatec recognized his opportunity first.

"Primary, Chief Vizier Sateron. If General Tesuh is such a threat, then why are we entrusting him to head off a possible conflict that would draw us back into war? If he's successful, then wouldn't he be redeemed as a warrior and leader?" Radael and Risap chuckled softly. Both looked at each other, and Radael nodded for him to explain the reasoning to Moam.

"General Tesuh is a threat that we all agree needs to be removed. The current situation provides several opportunities for us to negate his power. Most importantly, realize that the advisory board is fractured in three regarding our decision to handle the information pertaining to the supposed appearance of the Son of God on Je-Fin. The revelation that a covert group of warriors was sent to Je-Fin will cast a shadow of distrust on General Tesuh. Many will suspect him of attempting to circumvent the advisory board, and that distrust alone will alienate two of the three factions on the board. He does not know that we've already agreed to meet with the *Nowrimo's Revenge* under the auspices of facilitating a prisoner transfer. We have already dispatched several other vessels to the actual transfer coordinates, and will be supporting the safe return of our Lord to Shalotha. The USF contingent is not aware that we will back out of our agreement, and are sending one or two vessels at most. The Fe-Ruqians will probably have several of their fleet vessels ready, just in case. We anticipate a battle, but we have confidence that Commander Apxlus will be successful. For General Tesuh, he is in a no-win situation. Should he stop Commander Apxlus and our Savior, he will effectively prove himself as a warrior that acts contradictory to the needs of the Republic of Shalotha and her people. That alone will earn the contempt of the two thirds of advisors that felt we should aggressively retrieve our Lord from Je-Fin. Should he fail to stop them, his inability to stop even a single vessel from re-entering sector territory would be a further indictment of his inability at leadership. The remaining advisors would look upon that failure as a warning not to side with him on any internal conflicts within the advisory board. The other advisors would ascent to his removal from position, provided one of the Viziers demands it of him officially." Chief Vizier tilted his head slightly after the last statement, narrowing his eyes at Odatec. Moam understood the implications in his words.

"Primary, Chief Vizier Sateron. Should General Tesuh fail in his duties, I will demand that he remove himself from the advisory board on the grounds that he is not fit for duty in his position. Perhaps Commander Apxlus would be available to fill his role on the board? I'm confident that his successful return with the Son of God would generate a vast amount of support for his ascension to the position."

Radael and Risap glanced at each other and smiled knowingly. Looking back at the Hlos Vizier, Radael smiled widely.

"Vizier Odatec, I think that is a very wise choice."

Athes and Secael stopped to rest for a moment. The rain was still pouring through the tree canopy overhead. The warriors had circled back around along the edge of the trees, around the flight deck and dock wells, through the thicket, and to the edge of the field that the *Nowrimo's Revenge* had landed in. The grounds surrounding the complex were quickly filling with fresh Fe-Ruq military soldiers and Je-Fin planetary defenders, bent on capturing any remaining Shalothan warriors alive, however, this open area where the *Revenge* had been was still unsecured. Both warriors knew that the field wouldn't remain that way for long.

Secael risked lighting his hand to signal the ship, in hopes that they were still cloaked with the IDMD. After waiting and waving the flame for thirty seconds, Secael snuffed out the flame and retreated with Athes deeper into the trees. It was evident the ship was no longer on the ground, although there was no way they could tell if it had just relocated to another side of the complex, left the atmosphere, or had been destroyed while in flight.

"Suggestions on improving our situation?" Secael asked. He was down on one knee, peering through the darkness in between flashes of lightning, searching for any possible enemies in the area. Athes held a hand over his wound, protecting it against the rain and anything that could brush up against it, such as branches or leaves.

"Vacate the area immediately. We have no ship, no support, no ability to communicate off-world, and cannot pass ourselves off as the natives." Athes clicked several times after the last portion of his statement, indicating he made it in jest. Secael grunted his reply, and nodded in agreement.

"We could go back and fight with our brethren, provided they are still alive and on the ground near the complex." Secael offered the option despite knowing that it was not a sound strategy for them. Athes shook his head.

"If we go back, it's only to find a way off-world. They would not expect us to attack them now, not after such heavy losses on our side. We have the element of surprise again."

"We do not know if we had heavy losses. We have no knowledge of anything at this point," Secael reminded him. He glanced up through the trees at the bright flash of lightning that lit up the sky. In his peripheral vision, he caught sight of a silhouette of a humanoid figure off to his left.

Not making any sudden motions, Secael clicked softly to get Athes' attention. "We have visitors. To my left, roughly thirty meters or so. I saw one during the last lightning flash."

Athes looked to his right without moving his head. He strained to see through the darkness, but saw only rain and shadows among the trees. He twisted his right arm and slapped it against his thigh, activating his blaster sheath. Secael reached over and tapped his as well, causing the weapon to slide down into his hand.

Lightning flashed again, revealing that the one silhouette had multiplied to several, each spaced a few meters apart in a rough semicircle less than thirty meters from their location.

"They know we're here," Athes whispered. Secael only nodded, realizing that the group starting to surround them most likely had located them using a heat sensor. "Run, or fight?" He looked at Secael through the driving rain, trying to catch a glimpse of his face for his response.

"Fight," Secael whispered back, "but we wait until they're close." He hefted up his staff, indicating that he wanted to use that rather than his blaster. It made sense to Athes. Fighting in the dark, the blaster shots would only draw their enemies' eyes to the point of fire, whereas fighting with the staff gave them the advantage.

Both warriors stepped into a crouching position, facing the semi-circle of men coming towards them. Secael was angled slightly to the left to face his attackers once they advanced. Athes gripped his staff in his right hand, and balanced the end of it in his left. His wounded arm still pained him severely, and he feared it would be virtually useless in battle. Almost at the same time, the warriors caught scent of the advancing soldiers through the rain. Secael lifted his head slightly to get a better smell with his nostrils.

"The grace of God be with you Athes," Secael whispered to Athes. The wounded warrior did not respond, but merely braced for the battle that was about to begin.

One of the soldiers closest to Secael came within striking distance first, only a few meters away. Secael rotated his staff just slightly, then jumped forward and swung his staff upwards at the soldier's weapon. The soldier was prepared for an attack, but wasn't quick enough to evade the staff, firing a salvo harmlessly into the air as the force of the rising staff knocked the weapon out of his hands. Secael brought the staff back down on an angle, slashing across the soldier's throat with the barbs on his staff. The soldier staggered to the ground, holding his hands near his throat, stemming a gush of blood. A few of the nearby soldiers were yelling in Secael's direction, but he could not understand what they were saying. He also heard the grunting of Athes only a few meters away, engaged in his own battle with the soldiers.

Another soldier fired at Secael as the first soldier fell. The blaster shot sizzled past his head, scorching a tree behind him and superheating the wet bark into steam. Secael swung his blaster arm up and fired two quick shots, but the soldier had anticipated his move, ducking out of the line of fire. Another soldier moved towards him from the left, weapon raised. The second soldier was still crouching, close enough that Secael could see that he had drawn a bead on him.

Secael flung his staff towards the crouching soldier, twirling it through the rain into the side of the man's skull. The staff banged off the protective headgear the soldier wore, knocking him to the ground, but the split second distraction allowed Secael to bring his right arm across his body and fire at the soldier to the left. The blaster shot flashed through the rain, its path quickly ending in the soldier's chest. Secael took two long strides towards the soldier he had knocked to the ground with his staff and stepped on the weapon in his grasp, holding it to the ground. He fired a single shot into the face of the soldier, causing the body to permanently slump against the ground. He moved to the first soldier he had attacked, and saw that he was still alive, clutching his throat. He put the soldier out of his misery with a single discharge from his blaster.

Athes felt the air rush away from him when Secael set himself into motion against their attackers. He reacted immediately, launching himself into an attack against the remaining soldiers. He sidestepped to his right, stutter firing across the line of men, hoping to catch one or two of them before they were in too close. One of the first shots felled one of the soldiers, but the others reacted quickly and dropped to the ground. Crouching down, he ran to his right in an arc that would bring him around the side of the group. He slapped his blaster sheath closed and grabbed his staff in his right hand, firmly planting the tip of it into the ground. Throwing all of his weight forward as he jumped up, he used the staff as a cantilever, vaulting through the air into one of the soldiers. He landed on top of him, quickly swiping the knifelike ridges on the back of his hand across the soldier's throat, slicing it wide open. Rolling to his right, he pulled the soldier's body on top of him, using it as a shield against the other two soldiers. Several blaster shots tracked through the rain, sizzling into the ground and then into the back of the dead soldier in front of him. He tapped the top of the blaster sheath against the headgear of the dead soldier, reactivating it for use. From a prone position he fired at the two soldiers, hitting one in the shoulder, but missing the other one completely. The latter ducked to his right, then crouched down behind the trunk of a large tree. Athes scrambled to his knees and crawled behind the nearest tree. He could no longer see the other soldier, but heard two quick blasts of weapons fire from the general direction of Secael.

Athes dropped down onto his stomach, and pulled himself hand over hand through the underbrush away from the tree to his left. He heard another blaster shot in the vicinity of Secael, but could not see what was happening. He peered through the rain dripping down his face and spattering against the leaves of the scrub brush surrounding him. As he moved, the other soldier came into sight, speaking into some device. His back was to Athes as he seemed to peer around the trunk of the tree searching for him. The sound of another blaster shot sliced through the air, and Athes made his move. In one deft motion he leaped up, and pointing the keratin ridges on his right hand inward, he wrapped his arm around the soldier's neck, pulling the ridges across his throat. The body quickly slumped in his grasp, and he let the corpse slide to the ground.

Glancing around the tree, he saw Secael firing his weapon into a soldier on the ground. A quick survey of the immediate area revealed that no other soldiers were standing or moving.

"Secael, this one was reporting in. It's a matter of time before ten times the number of soldiers converge on us. We must leave, now!" Secael looked in his direction and nodded, then gathered his staff to him. Athes quickly did the same. "We must get off-world immediately. We will not survive here through another wake period. Secael, we must take one of their ships."

The warrior nodded, and turned towards the general direction of the area they had just escaped from. The rumbles of thunder had lowered in volume, and the rain began to slow to a drizzle. Both warriors realized they were quickly losing any advantage they had. Secael broke into a slow trot, pushing his way through the underbrush, using his staff to knock low branches and bushes aside. Athes followed closely, peering through the darkness on either side in an attempt to spot more of the enemy soldiers. The flashes of lightning still lit up the sky, but it was distant, failing to reveal any of their surroundings.

They backtracked through the woods without incident, arriving at the edge of the thicket nearest the dock wells and flight deck. Several groups of soldiers patrolled the edges of the woods, and the building itself seemed to be surrounded by crews doing something near several locations along the base of the complex walls. They watched the scene for over an hour from their stomachs, lying in the thick underbrush. Athes tapped Secael on his arm and directed his attention towards the front of the complex. From their angle, they could see part of the burning wreckage of a crashed atmospheric fighter. But it was the swarm of medical droids bringing bodies out of a small transport that caught their attention. The droids were taking the bodies to various, random locations on the battlefield, and propping them into different positions. Some even used a blaster on the bodies, firing into them, while a vid-droid hovered nearby, seemingly recording pictures of the body and of the wreckage.

The crews near the base of the complex began backing away from the building, and waving towards the nearby transports that were on the ground. Both warriors watched in earnest as the defensive air perimeter began to dissolve, and all the ground patrols began returning to a rally point several hundred meters away from the front of the complex. Within minutes all the atmospheric fighters had left the immediate airspace, and none of the soldiers remained in the area.

"Get up," Secael ordered. Athes glanced over at his comrade, unsure that he had heard correctly. Waiting only a second or two for Athes to respond, Secael reached down and dragged the warrior to his feet, pulling him deeper into the woods. "We must get away from here now. Run!"

Athes obeyed the order, following Secael through the underbrush and trees as quickly as they could manage without tripping and falling. They had made it about fifty meters into the woods directly behind the dock wells when a flash of light lit up the sky behind them, briefly turning the darkness into daylight. A second later, a shock wave hit both warriors from behind, knocking them unconscious.

The light slowly faded into his consciousness. There was no feeling in his body, only awareness that he lie face down on the ground. At first, there was only dim light, but the light grew in brightness until his eyelids flickered open. The leaves on the ground slowly came into focus, and Athes breathed in deeply.

Moments passed as his mind tried to move his body. Minutes or hours, he wasn't sure, but finally his thoughts of movement resulted in a twinge in his hands. Slowly forcing his body into motion, he dragged his arms up towards his shoulders, pulling them lifelessly towards his torso. Feeling began to return in waves. So did pain.

Athes pulled his knees up under him, and pushed himself up off of the ground. Mud and leaves stuck to his body in various places, leaving bare spots on the ground. His sense of smell began to return, and he caught the faint whiff of a smoke. The faint whiff quickly gathered into an overpowering smell that washed over him as his sense of smell came fully back to him.

Sagging against the pain that racked his body, Athes held himself up on his hands and knees until he found the strength to stand. Getting vertical, he twisted around to survey his surroundings.

The pitch-black of night had given way to an overcast sky; morning or afternoon, he wasn't sure which. Black smoke billowed into the sky from the flattened rubble that had previously been the prison complex. Tens, if not hundreds of trees nearest the building had been burned in the explosion or simply blown over from the shock wave. His memory began to return, and he recalled that he had been running away from the building. *They* had been running away from the building.

Athes staggered through the flattened underbrush, searching for Secael. His comrade was only a few meters away, lying crumpled in the broken branches and mud near the base of a broken tree. Kneeling down beside him, he checked for signs of life. Secael was breathing.

CHAPTER XV

Captain Pollard sat alone for a moment, collecting her thoughts. The hailing light on her communication board blinked on and off in hypnotizing fashion. Undoubtedly it was the captain of the *Censer*, Cellif Tarvold. She didn't want to have the conversation with the Fe-Ruqian captain just yet, having just finished with the Admiral. Heading into enemy territory, led by a enemy's military escort to facilitate a prisoner transfer was not high on the list of items she had wanted to accomplish as an officer. Yet, there the blinking light was, awaiting her response to begin the journey into Fe-Ruqian space.

Captain Pollard activated the communication system and opened a channel for the individual that was hailing her.

"Captain Pollard here. Secure transmission."

"Captain Tarvold here. I'm hoping that your 'urgent call' was of the same nature mine was?" Captain Tarvold's image stared blankly back at Captain Pollard.

"If you mean the message that we're to be escorted by your ship to the transfer point, then I would have to say yes, it was of the same nature."

"Captain, the *Censer* and the *Lillian* will be accompanying you to Jethl. You will power down all weapons systems at once. We will be running continuous sensor sweeps against your ship to ensure continued compliance. Please don't mistake our escort as being friendly. Should you happen to activate your weapons systems at any time within Fe-Ruq space, I shall have the pleasure of personally ordering your ship to be blown to particle dust. Are we clear on your requirements, Captain?"

Captain Pollard leaned back in her chair, anger rising in her throat. She had no choice but to acquiesce to the demands, and the arrogant captain of the *Censer* fully understood that he had the upper hand.

"Captain Tarvold, please allow me twenty minutes to communicate the new orders to the crew and have the weapons systems sufficiently powered down. I will contact you as soon as we're ready. Pollard out." Captain Pollard jabbed her finger to cut off the transmission, leaving her in silence once again. She leaned over and sent word for her senior officers to join her immediately.

Athes gently shook the limp form of Secael, trying to rouse his comrade from unconsciousness. He continued to look around, suspicious of the surrounding trees. He could not smell anything except the reeking stench of smoke from the destroyed prison complex. The longer they stayed in one place, the easier it would be for Fe-Ruqian soldiers to return and find them. In the condition he was in, Athes did not feel confident that he would be able to ward off an attack and safely move Secael out of the area. Leaving him was not an option either.

The Shalothan warrior decided to drag Secael further into the surrounding woods, intending to put substantial distance between the battle zone and themselves. At the very least, they needed to find a way off-world, and it didn't appear that there was anything usable in the area.

Taking care to still be careful with the injured Secael, Athes quickly moved his brethren by dragging him behind him. He didn't have the strength to lift and carry Secael, and feared that such an effort would cause himself too much pain to continue. Besides his original injury, his entire body ached from being thrown from the blast, and he was certain there were other injuries that he hadn't diagnosed yet.

The excursion went slowly, to the point that Athes felt they would be discovered at any moment. Over the course of the few hours that he had been moving, at least two pair of sub-orbital fighters had flown high overhead, presumably on patrol. Guessing that the units were based out of another base somewhat nearby, he tried to recall his pre-drop briefing for any information that may have indicated exactly how far away the base was.

Stopping to rest, Athes laid Secael down and moved some brush so that it shielded Secael from view from above. Athes clambered underneath some other brush and lay prone, trying to regenerate himself. Glancing at the still unconscious Secael, he assumed that whatever injury Secael had sustained in the blast had caused his body to go into a regenerative coma. During the last few hours he had periodically stopped and checked on Secael, trying to awaken him. Each time his body exuded immense heat, a sure sign that the regenerative processes were in progress within his body. It was a positive sign, but still didn't help their predicament. It could be days before Secael came around, depending on the severity of the injury.

Day turned into early evening, and Athes stopped once again. Doing a quick calculation in his mind, he figured that they couldn't be more than four or five kilometers from where they had started. Unlike a typical mission, the darkness would not be working to their benefit. Not knowing the lay of the land, nor exactly where the were, Athes decided to try and make camp. The typical Fe-Ruqian patrol craft carried thermo-sensors that would make it very easy to detect the two during the cool night. *Especially with Secael's processes still emitting such heat*, Athes thought.

Realizing there wasn't much else to do to shield them from observers high above, Athes decided to create a safe zone for them to spend the night. Locating some thick branches in the area, Athes began using them as crude digging tools to carve out a shallow hole in the ground. Frequently listening for any change in the wildlife that would give away approaching predators or enemies, Athes dragged Secael into the concave area and positioned him so that his body lay straight along the deepest part, with his head resting against the lip of the hole. Making certain that he would still be able to breath, Athes pushed the dirt around the sides of the hole back on top of Secael, covering up his entire body save for the portion of his head containing his mouth and nose, effectively hiding the thermo-signature from any sensors. The gambit wasn't guaranteed to keep ground-based and hand-held sensors from seeing the exposed portion and discovering him, but aerial sensors wouldn't be able to separate the small blip from a ground rodent signature.

Athes repeated the process for himself, careful to leave the surrounding underbrush as undisturbed as possible. He wasn't able to fully immerse himself into the ground to the level that he had covered Secael, but he felt comfortable that his head and portion of upper torso would not be so easily discovered from above.

Calming himself, he steeled himself for a long night of solitary watch.

The *Alaurian Spirit* sped through the soundless vacuum of space, flanked by the glistening vessels of the Fe-Ruq empire. Distant stars hung in the blackness of space, providing little light for the trio as it traveled through the emptiness. Commander Tennison looked over the sensors again, and found them reporting the same thing that they had two minutes ago – no other vessels in the area.

The trip had been delayed right from the beginning with the Fe-Ruq fleet taking almost a full standard day to maneuver and set up on the system border before allowing the escorts to depart with the *Alaurian Spirit*. The wait had put all of the USF officers on edge, particularly Marshall Tennison. He constantly watched the Fe-Ruq vessels for any sign of trickery or deception that would announce an attack. Even now, almost twelve hours away from the edge of the system, he still felt unnerved at being flanked by two Fe-Ruqian military vessels with no other USF vessels within two days of their location. If the *Censer* and *Lillian* decided to attack the *Spirit*, the battle would be brief, and the outcome would most likely not be in the *Spirit's* favor.

Tennison didn't like the situation.

"Athes." A long pause. "Athes, are you near?"

The voice jolted Athes to alertness. *How long have I been asleep*, he wondered.

"Athes, can you hear me?" the voice whispered.

Darkness still encompassed the surrounding area, but the faint hint of daybreak could be seen through the tree canopy above.

"Secael, lay still. I'm over here. We're safe, for now."

"I can't move anything, Athes."

"You're covered in dirt, to shroud you from any sensors. Your heat emissions could have given us away had you been left out in the open. Don't try to get out yet. There could still be patrols nearby. We're not that far from where we started. We'll wait until the day begins to warm before we move again."

"What happened?"

"They bombed their own prison. I assume they didn't want anyone to know what had happened there. How much do you remember?"

"Only shadows of what happened after we fought the soldiers in the woods."

"We saw them clearing out of the area, and then we tried to run from the blast area. We figured it out too late, and were caught in the shockwave. You've been unconscious for over a full wake cycle. How do you feel now?"

"I can't sense any major damage, but I can't move either. I won't be able to fully diagnose until I'm free."

"Soon brother, soon."

The senior officers of the *Alaurian Spirit* sat in silence listening to Captain Pollard's explanation of their new orders. Commander Tennison shook his head slightly at the revelation regarding the weapons systems, but other than that there were no outward signs of displeasure with the directive. Captain Pollard finished, and waited in silence for any of the officers to speak.

"Captain, if I may," Tennison said, breaking the silence. "We're going to be deep in Fe-Ruq territory with our weapons systems powered down. Does that also mean sensors? What about shields?"

"Good question Commander. Captain Tarvold only specified that we were to power down weapons. We'll leave sensors in passive scanning mode until further notice. I'm not powering down the shields, regardless of what our escorts want. No one is sure what the intentions of the rogue ship are, so it's quite possible that we're fired upon when at the transfer point, or before. I wouldn't discount the possibility of a second Shalothan vessel in system, especially if they believed they were going after the Son of God. The question will be how dedicated they are to Him, and what they'll be willing to do to get Him out of the system."

"Captain, we know the Shalothans can be fanatical about religious objectives," Lieutenant Soloman stated, "so it's probably safe to assume that they will stop at nothing to complete their mission. It's highly unlikely that they will just hand over a being they believe to be the Son of God."

Captain Pollard nodded her head in agreement.

"Which means, what? They'll not go to the transfer point? They'll have an ambush waiting? The way I see situation developing is that they'll try and avoid detection and exit the system without going to the transfer point. I wouldn't be surprised if Captain Tarvold and his crew are going over the same scenarios right now. It appears, based on ship movement, that a majority of the Fe-Ruqian ships are staying near the system borders, most likely in an attempt to stop the Shalothan vessel or vessels from fleeing. Commander Tennison, I want you to personally monitor sensors for any sign of incoming vessels. There is no help for us here if we're attacked, so let's make sure we at least know it's coming so we can maneuver behind our escorts. Any questions?"

None of the senior officers gathered indicated they had questions, so Captain Pollard dismissed them. *The only problem is, what if it's our escorts that do the attacking?* she thought to herself. She didn't have a good feeling about their new orders.

Daybreak came and went, and the skies above quickly turned dark gray, foretelling another stormy day. Athes dug himself out of his cover and assisted Secael out of his, careful not to move too quickly should Secael still be injured.

Both reevaluated themselves, determining how serious their injuries were. They concurred that Athes' injury was still the most serious, but appeared to be healing already. Neither could detect any external injuries for Secael, and agreed that some type of internal injury had occurred, causing Secael's intense regenerative state. Both still ached from the shockwave, but neither were concerned with any lingering effects.

After scrounging for food among the underbrush, they set off along the same vector that Athes had used the previous day. The dark skies soon began to empty, drenching the entire area, but also providing some protection against aerial patrols. The rain continued throughout the day, making the footing worse with each passing hour.

The skies were darkening as evening approached when Athes suddenly stopped. He motioned towards Secael, and both dropped into a low crouch. Athes pointed towards his ear, and Secael tilted his head upwards to listen for any strange sounds. For a moment, he wondered if the rain had finally affected Athes' hearing. He could hear nothing except the rain hitting the upper leaves of the canopy and the dripping sounds as the rain drops fell to the ground and soaked the underbrush. He was about to move forward when streaks of light sizzled across his field of vision from left to right, momentarily blinding him in the fading light.

Both Shalothans dove to the ground, slapping their blaster sheaths as the fell. Athes maneuvered himself into a kneeling position, while Secael continued to lay prone, propped up on one elbow while that hand supported his firing arm.

Flashes of light continued to lance through the trees at a level about a meter off the ground. Tree bark and water evaporated into steam where the streaks of light connected with trees, indicating that they were coming from a weapon.

"They're going to flank us if we stay here!" Secael said, voice raised so that Athes could hear him above the sizzles and pops that were occurring closer to their position.

"We don't know how many there are. We could be heading into a trap. We don't know how long they've been tracking us." Athes lifted himself up slightly and fired a few quick bursts from his weapon, randomly firing into the trees.

"Athes, we cannot just sit here and wait for them to overtake us." Secael tilted back and forth, attempting to see his adversaries through the rain and darkening forest.

Athes was about to answer back when a sonic boom knocked both of them to the ground, rattling their bones. The weapons fire ceased for a brief moment, then resumed with more intensity.

Secael leaned over and grabbed Athes' wrist. Athes swiveled to look down at the warrior.

"We must go now. You know this," Secael said as he nodded upwards, indicating he was concerned about the air support that recently arrived. Athes nodded, then crouch-walked towards the same direction they had been traveling in. Secael pulled himself up and followed, careful not to bounce too high lest he fall into the firing line.

They had made it approximately twenty meters when weapons fire began pouring in from a different direction, this time from behind them. The blasts weren't accurate enough to hurt them, but certainly limited what direction they could go in. The new bursts of fire were targeted more to their right, and closer to the ground, hemming them in from that side. The original direction of attack still provided a blistering covering fire, keeping both of them from running, and effectively herding the two of the forward along the same vector they had been traveling on.

"We need to take out one of the shooters!" Athes yelled towards Secael, returning fire towards the direction of the original attack. Secael spun and fired behind them, towards the rearguard attack. His bursts of fire were quickly returned, with the attackers coming perilously close to zeroing in on the pair.

Athes was about to move to his left towards the attack when two trees a few meters in front of him splintered in half, falling in towards each other. The *whumpf whumpf whumpf* of a heavy blaster filled the air almost at the same time, sawing through the surrounding trees and carving a large swath out of the forest. Athes and Secael both dove for the ground, careful to watch for falling pieces of the trees.

Whumpf Whumpf Whumpf. Two other trees behind them exploded into burnt splinters.

Whumpf Whumpf Whumpf. A tree to their right was hit by the first blast, with the falling trunk hit a second time, splitting that into two smaller pieces.

All of the trees within a radius of five meters quickly succumbed to the heavy fire, leaving smoldering stubs and blackened wood surrounding them. The heavy fire stopped, and voices could be heard shouting orders, some very near. Secael looked over at Athes, and slapped his wrist sheath to deactivate his weapon. They both knew that they didn't have the firepower to compete against their attackers. High above, the sound of sub-orbital craft approaching filled the air, making it difficult to understand the voices. Athes looked around, and finally seeing how many attackers there were, deactivated his wrist sheath as well. Dozens of soldiers faded into view as they approached from the depths of the forest. All had their weapons trained on their position, and appeared from every angle.

"Shalothans," one of the soldiers called out in the Shalothans' native tongue, "remain on the ground. You are now under Fe-Ruq detention orders. Any attempt at fleeing will result in fatalities."

Athes clicked in his throat at the sound of the Fe-Ruq soldier speaking his native tongue. Secael was surprised as well, but did not react the same as Athes. He merely slipped his wrist sheath off and dropped it to the ground, leaving his hands void of any weapon. Glancing over at his comrade, he saw that Athes was defiant in relieving himself of his weapon, choosing to stand and stare down his foes.

"Athes, disarm," Secael whispered. "They won't take any chances with us. We need to stay alive a little longer."

Athes looked over at Secael questioningly.

"We need to ensure the safety of our Lord. We're of no help if we meet our end here." Athes nodding in understanding, but didn't move. He stood rigid, gaze focused forward.

Five Fe-Ruqian soldiers advanced on the two of them, one standing directly in front of them, and the other four surrounding them as if standing at the corners of a box surrounding the Shalothans. The one directly in front of them waited until the soldiers were situated, then spoke.

"Pick up your weapon," the soldier said in Shalothan. Neither Secael nor Athes moved, but each stole a glance at the other out of the corner of their eyes. Seeing that neither was moving, the soldier repeated the order. Secael hesitated at first, then slowly bent down to pick up his wrist sheath. He expected a blow to the back, a shot to the head – anything really – as soon as he touched his wrist sheath, but nothing happened. He quickly picked it up and stood upright, keeping his weapon in plain view. The soldier who had ordered him to pick it up nodded at him.

"Put it on."

Secael put his wrist sheath back on slowly, watching the soldier. When Secael was finished, the soldier waved to another soldier further back, and spoke something in a tongue that his cochlear implant translator didn't understand. The soldier walked off into the darkness, returning seconds later with two long sticks, one in each hand. Secael immediately knew they were Athes' and his staffs. The one soldier walked up to Secael and held both out, presenting either for him to take. Secael selected his, and watched as Athes moved to take his back. Both looked back to the soldier who seemed to be in command, and waited for him to speak.

"The both of you were part of the infiltration team, weren't you?" Neither Secael nor Athes made any audible sounds or showed any sign of understanding. "If you're not, then I'm guessing that you're aware of that team, and who they rescued from the staged prison. Either way, I need you to help us." Both Shalothans stole questioning glances at one another, but still remained silent.

"The man you rescued – you truly believe this is some kind of God?"

"No, He is the Son of God," Athes corrected. The soldier turned to Athes and took a step closer.

"Then why was he here? On a planet that doesn't believe in him, in a system that doesn't care for him?"

"What do you want from us? You mentioned you need our help," Secael interjected.

"My name is Aedge. I was there when he appeared. I saw the bright light, and heard the voice. I want to find out if he's really who you think he is."

Athes looked at Aedge and clicked in his throat.

"Do you think that we will share anything with you?" Athes breathed in a low voice. He clicked again in anger, imagining the hand in his capture that this soldier had played.

"I hope that you will help. After all, your team was successful in getting him off-world. You have no way of getting out of this alive without our help," Aedge spread his hands towards the other soldiers, "I was hoping that you would want to reunite with your team.

We can get you off-world."

"Seeing our brethren again holds no interest for us," Secael said. "We serve our Lord now, not any government or body."

Aedge looked at the other soldiers, and dismissed them with a nod. He waited for the four soldiers to retreat further away before speaking again.

"The soldiers surrounding you have all heard of what happened. I was there, as were a few others in the group. Word has spread fast about your God's arrival an—" Secael cut him off.

"He is the Son of God."

Aedge nodded and continued. "Word has spread quickly about the Son of God's arrival. There are many of us who are torn; we know what we believe, or rather, what we were taught. But we also know what we saw. Whatever it is, our superiors tried to silence anyone who was there. They didn't want anyone to spread the word about what had happened. Most of the soldiers in attendance that day were taken off-world and reassigned. Some of us were assigned to the satellite post that the two of you were headed towards. We were notified of the assault prior to you arriving, as if someone knew you were coming. We had orders to wait until you had taken the prisoner, then proceed to the training facility to reinforce the garrison that was already there."

Athes leaned forward and interrupted him. "A training center? We were told it was a prison complex."

Aedge looked first at Athes, then at Secael. "It was a mockup of an older prison system. It was used primarily for training new recruits and practicing maneuvers. I saw the orders myself. General Odine ordered the prisoner moved there, along with the garrison. At first I thought we were going to hide the prisoner, but several messages were sent unencoded to deep-space outposts about the move. I assume your intelligence intercepted the messages, which is why your team was sent here. I'm not an intelligence agent, but it appears you were set up. Odine probably wanted Him out of here, just for the fact that His existence undermines every statute and teaching that the Fe-Ruqians have ever had." Aedge paused to look around, and slung his rifle over his shoulder.

"You still have not explained why or how you want us to help you," Athes said. He looked at Aedge and held his gaze, waiting for an explanation. The night had fully taken hold, making it difficult to see even a few meters in the darkness. The rain still came down, and with the trees in the immediate area destroyed, it fell unimpeded on the three of them.

"After your team left, a special task force from headquarters arrived at the sight, and began recording images and staging battle scenes. Once they had enough recordings, they destroyed the building. I can only imagine how those recordings will be used, but I'm going to guess that they'll put Shalotha in a bad light. It will appear to anyone who sees it that you came into our system, took our prisoner, and killed dozens, if not hundreds of soldiers in the process. Odine will find a way to use that to his advantage. Honestly, I don't care about Shalotha one way or another, but I want to find out about your Son of God. I don't think Odine staged such an easy escape for Him if he was planning on letting Him live to speak about it, especially to Fe-Ruqians. I would assume that Odine has a plan in place to ensure that both Shalotha and this prisoner are dealt severely with as soon as possible. Your team might not even make it back to your system before other systems find out about your attack. It would make sense for the other systems to try and stop your team, and kill off the prisoner in the ensuing battle, just to maintain peace in the galaxy. To Odine, He's just another political prisoner; one with potentially the most power to disrupt his little empire. I doubt His loss will be felt throughout Fe-Ruqian space. But for those that want to learn about Him," Aedge nodded towards the Shalothans, "or for those that know of Him, His loss would be tremendous. I will get you back to your system, but you must help me meet Him. I need to know who He really is. If the rumors are true, I need to bring the truth back here for everyone that saw or heard about what happened. I need answers, and you need off-world."

"And if we don't agree to your offer?" Secael asked the question, but both Shalothans were thinking the same thing.

"That is the question, isn't it," Aedge smirked. "I will assume that finding transit off-world will be much more difficult without our help. This planet is more military than anything else, so the sight of two Shalothans walking near a satellite base may trigger some concerns. You'll probably put yourself at a huge disadvantage in trying to get off-world, maybe even impossible. Some of us will be leaving this planet in the coming week, with or without you. It'll take us a bit longer to find this God of yours, but I have a feeling that every system in the galaxy is going to know who He is and where He is pretty soon. And how will that look to your God when we tell Him that you refused to help us meet Him and bring His word back to our system?" Aedge looked from Secael to Athes, and back. Neither said a word to Aedge. Athes looked over at Secael, searching out his face for any sign of how he should answer. After several heartbeats, Athes spoke.

"We must confer, in private. This is not a decision that we can make lightly." Aedge nodded, and slowly backed away until he was almost lost in the darkness. Athes turned to face Secael, who was watching Aedge remove himself from their immediate position.

"Your thoughts, brother?"

"I do not trust him Athes. I almost would rather take our chances. I find it difficult to accept that a platoon of Fe-Ruqian soldiers happens to be in the same area of the forest that we are in, willing to commit an act that amounts to treason in the Fe-Ruq culture. They can find Him without our help, if that were truly the motivation."

"What then? We tell him our decision is not to take his offer? They can still kill us right here, even with our weapons. And what of his last statement – how would we look to our own brethren if it were to be discovered that we turned down a soul who requests the Grace of God?"

"Would we be turning down a legitimate believer, or merely seeing through the deceit?"

"Even if it is deceit, we can use this opportunity to help our Lord. Perhaps this is a blessing in disguise, Secael. We should not waste it." Athes looked out into the darkness and through the rain towards the direction of Aedge Faerre.

"It is settled then. We will accept his offer. Let us pray for our Lord's guidance." With that, both Shalothans bowed their heads and prayed.

CHAPTER XVI

"Commander, Jethl is now within visual range."

Marshall Tennison gripped the back of the command chair tightly, dreading the approaching planet. The gas giant was only a speck on the viewscreen, but the sensors were able to pick up everything in the surrounding vacuum of space.

The planet itself.

The moon of Jethl.

And an unidentified vessel in orbit.

"Commander, the *Censer* has issued a coded message providing us a location for our position during the transfer. It appears they are beginning to accelerate and separate from us." Tennison looked over at Lieutenant Guy and acknowledged his report.

"Inform Captain Pollard that we are nearing the waypoint. I'm sure she'll want to be up here for this." The officer sent a brief message to Captain Pollard's communication board in her stateroom and, receiving an immediate reply, turned to face Tennison once again.

"She's on her way commander." Tennison nodded and looked back out the view port. The *Censer* and *Lillian* had moved forward of the *Alaurian Spirit*, and were quickly putting distance between themselves and the frigate.

"Sensors indicate a vessel coming off a thread."

"Identification?" Tennison looked over his shoulder

as Captain Pollard arrived on the bridge.

"Coming up now. Shalothan battle cruiser. Transponder is broadcasting *Guardian's Gate*. They are approaching the unidentified vessel."

Captain Pollard and Tennison looked at each other, unsure of what the new arrival was doing. They weren't prepared for a battle cruiser to be the representative for the transfer, but then, why should they have expected anything else.

"Switch from passive scanning and activate all sensors. Execute a long range scan and identify all local threats. Navigation, identify all thread points within a parsec of the transfer point. We need to know where any help is coming from. Set up monitors on each one identified."

"Captain, do you want me to order the weapons powered up?" Marshall asked.

"No. We don't want to provoke anything. We just need to be cautious for now." Marshall nodded, but gripped the chair slightly harder. He didn't agree with the decision to leave the weapons systems powered down.

"Captain, the *Nowrimo's Revenge* has transmitted an encoded message to the arriving vessel."

"Decode that message, Lieutenant," Captain Pollard ordered. He affirmed that he would, then announced another report.

"*Guardian's Gate* is hailing all vessels. Patching through."

"-he *Guardian's Gate*. We are here on behalf of the Shalothan Imperium for purposes of the transfer. Repeat. This is the *Guardian's Gate*. We are here on behalf of the Shalothan Imperium. We are requesting all vessels to power down their weapons systems before approaching." The message began to repeat.

"Are we within range for a detail scan?" Captain Pollard asked. The sensor officer indicated that they were, and she ordered a scan of the Shalothan vessel.

"Sensors indicate they have their weapons systems powered down, and are entering the vicinity of the transfer point with shield defenses down as well."

"Are the *Censer* and *Lillian* reacting?"

"Both vessels have shield arrays operational, but weapons systems are not activated yet. The *Censer* is hailing the unidentified vessel. We're marking it as the *Nowrimo's Revenge*, but that is not confirmed. Analysis is in progress."

"Captain, perhaps we should request our escorts to hang back with us. It won't make much sense if they spook the *Revenge* into taking off," Marshall suggested.

Captain Pollard thought about it for a moment, then shook off the thought. "We can trail the *Revenge* if they depart. I'm more concerned about the Fe-Ruq vessels making that Shalothan battle cruiser nervous. I don't think we have anything to worry about from the *Revenge*."

"Analysis complete. Unidentified vessel is confirmed as the *Nowrimo's Revenge*. Sensors indicate shield arrays are intact, however weapons are powered down. The vessel is currently stationary."

The crew on the bridge sat in silent for a few minutes as they watched the moon of Jethl grow in the viewscreen. The Fe-Ruq vessels had slowed their approach, and from the viewpoint of the *Alaurian Spirit*, the Shalothan battle cruiser *Guardian's Gate* was stationary, sitting below and behind the *Nowrimo's Revenge*.

Captain Pollard leaned over and touched the all-ship communication button on her command console.

"All hands to battle stations. All hands to battle stations. We are approaching the transfer point. Standby for transfer orders."

Commander Tennison smiled inwardly at the order. He and Lieutenant Soloman had been selected to physically board the *Nowrimo's Revenge* and take possession of the Son of God. It was only minutes now to the moment he had been obsessing over for the past day. If all went according to plan, the *Censer* and *Lillian* would secure the area, the *Alaurian Spirit* would approach and dock with the fugitive frigate, and the actual transfer would take all of ten minutes. The excited voice of the sensor officer broke into his thoughts.

"Captain, the *Guardian's Gate* is powering up weapons!"

Sergeant Aedge Faerre and his soldiers led Secael and Athes in a slightly different direction than what they had been traveling in. The rain had stopped, but the sky remained cloudy, keeping the many moons of Je-Fin out of view. After about an hour of snaking through dense underbrush and trees, they came upon a narrow trail and followed it for another quarter of an hour. Soon they could see the glow above the trees from ground lights at the base Faerre had mentioned. Shortly after he stopped the group and approached Secael and Athes.

"This is a sub-orbital base only, so we'll have to use one of the transports to get to a civilian space port. The two of you will wait here with me while a few of my guys go get a transport. We already signed one out for tonight, just in case the boys wanted to go out for some fun. It's about a five minute flight to the space port from here. Once there, we will walk to the assigned port." Aedge turned to the soldier that had come to stand next to him. "Broder, do you have the space port logs yet?"

"Yes sir. Right here," he replied, and handed something to Aedge. The sergeant rubbed his thumb over the device, and a holoprojection of a terminal screen appeared. Aedge manipulated the image until he pulled up the data he needed, including a layout of the space port.

"We'll be looking for this area here," Aedge said, highlighting docking port 5-B with the tip of his finger. "We have a ship and pilot arranged for us." Athes looked up at him in surprise. "As I said, I was going with or without you," Aedge said, responding to Athes' expression. "Once we're in the ship, we'll be catching the first thread out of the system, whatever comes up first. We'll figure out a course from there. Any questions?" Neither had any for the Fe-Ruqian soldier, so he issued orders for his men to move out and retrieve the transport. Fifteen minutes later the three of them were in the air.

The trip was a little longer than five minutes, but it ended quickly enough for Secael and Athes. The transport settled down onto a public tarmac, landing lights bathing the ground in a bright white. As soon as the transport door slid open, the three jumped out and looked around.

The tarmac itself was relatively empty, but the covered walkways leading to the docking wells appeared busy. Aedge led the way, walking briskly towards the far walkway. The Shalothans went relatively unnoticed in the dark on the tarmac, but once they were in the covered walkways, they began drawing stares. Secael looked at Athes and saw how terrible he looked, and realized that he must look as bad. Both were covered in dirt and mud, and Athes' arm still showed the wound. Both wore their weapons prominently, and their natural height tended to draw attention to them.

"I don't think we have gone unnoticed," Athes said under his breath.

"We can't be far from the docking location," Secael whispered, nodding at a passerby.

"Uh oh, heads up," Aedge said. "Four port police are headed straight for us. Someone must have alerted the port authority to your presence."

Secael looked around to get a bearing on his location. Dock 2-A read the sign on the dock entrance further up. He realized the port police would meet them before they reached their destination.

"Are you committed to finding your answers?" Secael asked of Aedge. The soldier glanced over his shoulder and gave Secael a questioning look. Secael and Athes responded by slapping their wrist sheaths simultaneously, activating the weapon. Aedge understood, and slid the rifle off of his shoulder. The original group of port police were joined by another two from a dock entrance that opened as they passed.

"Staff only, if you can help it Secael," Athes suggested. Secael looked to Athes and hefted his staff in one hand, and brought his sheathed arm up to his chest. Aedge brought his rifle up to a semi-ready position, searching for another route. He pushed an area of skin just below his ear and started speaking.

"Broder, this is Faerre. We've run into some trouble. Any other route to the assigned location other than the covered walkways?" Aedge apparently received an answer he didn't like, and swore, pulling his rifle up into firing position. The port police took notice, and scrambled to opposite sides of the covered walkway to take up positions. Aedge fired a few shots above the heads of the three that were on the right side, causing them to duck and crawl into the alcove of a docking well entrance. As soon as the weapons fire rang out, pandemonium broke loose as civilians ran full speed trying to get out of the area. Secael fired off a few quick shots at the group to the left, causing them to backtrack down the walkway. Secael stepped to that side of the walkway, and took up a position just inside of the alcove entrance to docking well 3-A. Aedge moved to the opposite side, sliding into the alcove for 3-B. Athes stepped in right behind him.

Aedge leaned back to speak to Athes, "We have about five minutes before soldiers arrive to support the port police. They're probably scrambling sub-o's already. Do you happen to know how to fly?" Aedge fired off a few bursts at the group on the opposite side of the corridor.

"Both of us do, but it won't do us any good if the pre-flight sequence isn't already in progress. The sub-orbitals will be here before we can depart if we use another craft."

Aedge nodded, then whistled across the walkway at Secael. He pointed at him, then pointed down the walkway at the group pinned down from the last burst of fire from Aedge. Secael nodded, jumped up, and sprinted towards the group. Aedge and Athes laid down suppressing fire towards both groups to support Secael's advance. Secael fired off a burst towards the three on his side of the walkway, sending them back into the alcove for 4-A. Aedge and Athes took the opportunity to slide step out of their spot, and kept the other group in check by pinning them in the 4-B alcove with sporadic bursts.

Secael slowed as he reached the entrance, and pushed himself up against the wall, sliding forward towards the opening. He held his staff like a spear, with his other arm free to fire his weapon. One of the three stepped out of the alcove, firing blindly down the walkway. Secael brought the tip of his staff squarely into the man's right temple, dropping him to the floor. Another started to step out into the walkway, and Secael brought his staff down, lodging the tip in the crook where the floor and wall met. He pushed off and swung his body through the air, using the staff as a pivot. His heels caught the port police officer in the chest, sending him flying backwards onto the floor, his weapon clattering away from him. He had barely hit the ground when he brought up his firing arm and let loose a quick burst into the chest of the remaining officer. The second guard started to get up, but Secael shifted his aim and neatly put him down for good. Aedge and Athes kept the other three pinned in the alcove and moved up to join Secael.

"Nice work," Aedge commented, taking in the scene. Athes motioned towards the next set of entrances, and fired a few more bursts back towards the group at 4-B to ensure they stayed pinned in. Moments later, Secael, Athes, and Aedge slid through the entrance to 5-A and quickly boarded the ship.

"Strap in. We're locked in for departure," a voice said over the intraship comm system. The three quickly found seats in the passenger hold and strapped in. They had barely finished when the ship rocketed upwards, pushing all three deep into their jump seats.

CHAPTER XVII

"Captain, shots fired!"

"Report."

"Captain, sensors have detected multiple ship implosions. The system has lost transponder transmissions from the *Censer* and the *Lillian.* Origination of weapons fire appears to be from the *Nowrimo's Revenge.* The Shalothan vessel *Guardian's Gate* is moving into an intercept position with the *Revenge.*"

Captain Pollard glanced over at Commander Tennison and raised a questioning eyebrow. The *Revenge* was carrying what was supposed to be a peaceful crew, willing to surrender to avoid creating a larger conflict. But all assumptions were now out of the picture as the *Nowrimo's Revenge* had engaged in combat after seemingly powering down and preparing to be boarded. As the Fe-Ruq military ships *Censer* and *Lillian* approached to secure the immediate area and encircle the fugitive vessel, their quarry had hit both with a surprise.

"Lieutenant, do you have that encoded message for us yet?" Captain Pollard asked with a hint of desperation in her voice. The navigation officer pushed a control button and the content of the message was sent to the control panel on Captain Pollard's command chair. She glanced at it quickly, then motioned for

Commander Tennison to review it. He raised his eyebrows in surprise, then cast a glance forward at the scene playing out before them. It all suddenly made sense.

Captain Pollard didn't waste much time. The situation was about to deteriorate quickly, and she needed to make sure that her ship and crew were either safely out of harms way, or prepared to defend against harm.

"Ensign Roach, plot a vector for us above and behind the *Revenge*." Pollard pushed a button on the armrest of her chair, opening an all-ship communication channel. "All hands to battle stations. Ensign House and Ensign Kramer, prepare the MCAC for operation. Ensign Theore, power up the MERL." She pushed another button and triggered the klaxon alarms throughout the ship, dimming the deck overhead lights and moving the physical forward shields into position over the forward view-shield.

"Captain, two ships are arriving from a thread. Sensors have them as the USF vessels *Seraphim* and *Eccentric.*

" What?" Captain Pollard was genuinely startled to hear that her former ship, and the former ship of her replacement, Captain Nicolai, had suddenly appeared at what was supposed to be an undisclosed location for the handover.

The communication console on her armrest beeped, and Pollard touched the button and listened.

"Captain, MCAC and MERL systems are on stand-by."

"Captain, the *Seraphim* is trying to contact us. Do you want me to patch them through?" Lieutenant JG Dalton asked, looking over his shoulder at his commanding officer. The captain voiced an affirmative and waited for the inter-ship communication channel to open.

"Captain Pollard, this is Captain Nicolai of the USF *Seraphim*. On behalf of Admiral Caturorglimi, I'm ordering you to stand down at once. You are ordered to return to the orbiting dock at the moon of Ru-Nula and await further orders.

"Captain, *Nowrimo's Revenge* is turning towards the *Seraphim* and *Eccentric*," Ensign Cummings called out.

"Captain Nicolai, I will request that you transmit his orders directly. I see no need for you to tie up our communications lines during battle for something that could so easily be sent." With that, Captain Pollard touched a button on the communication board and returned her attention to the developing battle.

The Seraphim and *The Eccentric* were quickly moving on vectors that would place them on opposite sides of the *Revenge*, catching the ship in cross fire. The *Guardian's Gate* was seemingly doing nothing, content to be face-to-face with the *Revenge*. Looking at his battle screen, Commander Tennison suddenly noticed that the *Guardian's Gate* was no longer moving to intercept. Just as he was about to point this out to the captain, Ensign Roach called out the arrival of a new ship. The *Rebellious God*, a massive Shalothan battle cruiser, had arrived from a thread just above and behind the USF vessels. Before anyone could say anything, the *Rebellious God* unleashed a massive salvo of missiles and beam weaponry towards the *Seraphim* and *Eccentric*. Both ships already had their energy shields up, but the physical shield arrays were protecting the forward portions of both ships as they approached the enemy, and were not prepared for an attack from behind. Each ship's energy shields began to fade quickly under the onslaught, as the *Rebellious God* continued firing beam weapons to drain their shields.

Captain Pollard could feel a trap. The *Rebellious God* had arrived too closely behind the USF vessels for it to be a coincidence. Regardless, they would have to fight their own battles with the ships directly in front of them. The *Spirit* would have to do what it could to lessen the impact of the *Rebellious God*.

"Lieutenant Daniels, target the *Rebellious God*'s shields with the MERL using tight beam dispersion. Fire at will. MCAC command, target their bridge. As soon as the MERL breaks through their shield arrays, fire two MCAC volleys."

Looking back at her battle screen, she could see that the *Guardian's Gate* and *Nowrimo's Revenge* were moving to engage the two USF vessels under attack from the *Rebellious God*. Both USF ships were maneuvering to get out of the direct line of fire and position themselves better for battle with the Shalothan battle cruiser.

Commander Tennison could feel the anxiety in his chest. It was all well and good to be observing a prisoner swap from afar in a scout ship. It was something totally different to be the smallest ship in a six-ship battle, especially when the largest ship was a Shalothan battle cruiser. Even without the battle cruiser, the two USF ships and the *Spirit* had their hands full. With the arrival of the battle cruiser, the outcome was almost predetermined.

"Captain, we must get out of here now. Send a message to the *Seraphim* and *Eccentric* and let's go. We can't win against that battle cruiser."

Ensign Roach called out more ship arrivals. "Three

ships arriving from a thread on the other side of the planet. Sensors indicate Shalothan vessels. No further identification at this time."

Captain Pollard looked over at Commander Tennison and bit the inside of her lip. She *knew* what the *Seraphim* was capable of. Under *her* control, that ship could take on the battle cruiser. Maybe this Captain Nicolai could coax the same type of performance out of her. And with the *Eccentric* flying cover, the two ships would have a very good chance. That left the *Alaurian Spirit* with the *Nowrimo's Revenge* and *Guardian's Gate.*

"MERL and MCAC commands, switch targeting systems to the *Guardian's Gate.* Immobilize that ship so we can get at the *Revenge.* Commander Tennison, send a message to Captain Nicolai letting him know that we're switching our targets, and that we appreciate the *Seraphim's* and *Eccentric's* assistance by attacking the *Rebellious God.* Ensign Cummings, send an urgent distress call out for a hospital ship and recovery ship. I have a feeling we're going to need them at some point.

"Captain, this is MERL command. We're engaging." The MERL device hummed with a tight-beam dispersion, aimed at their target. The *Guardian's Gate* lit up where the beam had burned through their energy shields, and several communication nodes disintegrated into space.

"Captain, this is MCAC command. We're engaging." Almost instantaneously the ship shuddered violently, and the emergency sirens signaling depressurization began to sound. A horrible sound of metal being wrenched apart echoed through the ship, and alarms across the systems control panel began flashing.

"Catastrophic depressurization in the MCAC command cell! Blast doors have sealed the bulkhead," Ensign Sears reported. Captain Pollard sat in her chair, still following the battle screen while listening to the damage reports.

"Captain, we have a pressurization leak. One of the blast doors did not seal properly. It's a matter of time before total ship depressurization…" Captain Pollard could not see who was reporting the damage, and the voice faded as realization quickly came to everyone; the ship was doomed unless they could land somewhere. Captain Pollard reacted without having to think. She had been through drills like this numerous times, and the procedures were now indelibly imprinted in her brain. The last thing she wanted to do was lose her crew.

"Roach, Cummings, plot the most direct course to get us down to the planet's surface. Fire the emergency beacons, and send out a request for the PLD satellite ship.

"Captain, the most direct course takes us through the line of fire between the *Seraphim* and the *Rebellious God*," Roach responded within seconds.

"Do it. We don't have much time." Captain Pollard pulled up weapons and shield statuses from her console. The MERL was showing active, but all MCAC units were offline. The energy shields were down, but the physical shield array remained intact.

"Captain, the *Nowrimo's Revenge* is on an intercept course with us," Ensign Cummings reported.

"Do not evade." Pollard clicked the all-ship communication button. "MERL command, switch targeting to the *Nowrimo's Revenge*. Engage at will with broad beam dispersion.

The ship shuddered as the engines increased thrust. The *Spirit* was venting gases as metal near the blast point on the hull continued to tear away. Commander Tennison had situated himself near the systems control panel, and was monitoring the damage reports as the various onboard sensors reported or failed. On the screen a new pressurization failure alarm appeared, indicating a leak near the MERL command deck blast door.

Tennison pushed the all-ship communication button, but the relay systems failed, shutting down the transmission before he could speak. He swiveled around to alert Captain Pollard as he made his way towards the bridge door.

"Captain, there's another pressurization leak – the MERL deck," he stated. "The communication system has failed – they don't know they're about to lose pressure.

"Commander, take the bridge. Daniels, Barry, you're with me. Grab one of the hull kits on our way down. We might be able to seal the leak if it's small enough."

The *Revenge* opened fire on the *Spirit* with a particle beam weapon, hitting the forward shields. The ship began shuddering more violently, seemingly intent to rip itself apart at the seams. Commander Tennison began barking out orders for the pilots, directing them to continue towards the planet's surface. He hoped the *Seraphim* and *Eccentric* would time their weapons to let the wounded ship pass without getting caught by their friendly fire. It was only a matter of seconds before they would pass the *Eccentric*, and then the *Seraphim*. The *Rebellious God* hadn't targeted the *Spirit* yet, but flying directly in their line of fire would assuredly give them a few shots without having to take any pressure off the other two ships.

The *Revenge* was still bearing down on the *Spirit*, and it was a race to see which ship they passed first – them or the *Eccentric*. Just as it looked like they would get past the *Revenge*, and head in front of the *Eccentric*, the USF vessel's bridge exploded from an apparent missile hit from the *Rebellious God*. The disintegrating superstructure disgorged its contents, spilling crew and anything else not bolted down out the large hole where the bridge used to be. Several of the crew on the *Spirit* gasped as they watched the ship continue to take direct hits from particle beams on the *Rebellious God*. It wasn't until Tennison had stared at the ship for a few heartbeats that he realized his ship was about to cross directly into the onslaught of firepower that had just effectively killed the *Eccentric*.

"Evasive maneuvers! Roach, swing us up and around the *Eccentric*. Use what's left of their ship as a shield."

The pilots responded immediately, taking manual control back from the navigation system. The ship was smaller than any of the others in the battle save for the *Revenge*, but the ship was still large enough to be bulking and sluggish when turning. The damage already incurred did nothing to help the performance of the ship.

"Parsons, transfer maximum shield strength to port side. Keep the wreckage on our starboard side as long as you can." Tennison hoped that his gambit would work. By reallocating all remaining shield strength to the port side of the ship, the heavier damaged areas of the ship would be protected from the oncoming *Revenge*, and the *Guardian's Gate*, wherever it was.

With the *Rebellious God* still firing at both USF vessels, keeping the disintegrating *Eccentric* hull between their starboard side and the weapons ports of the *Rebellious God* effectively gave them a physical shield for that side of the ship. At least for a few moments.

"Commander, *Guardian's Gate* is engaging the *Seraphim*," Lieutenant Parsons reported. Tennison looked at his battle-screen to see exactly what was happening. Quickly taking in the positions of all ships, he realized that they were almost safely out of the battle zone. The *Seraphim* was above them and to their starboard side. *Nowrimo's Revenge* had looped away from the *Alaurian Spirit* once they put themselves in the *Rebellious God's* line of fire. They were currently swinging back around to attack the *Spirit*, probably the port side of the ship Tennison surmised. *Guardian's Gate* was almost directly behind the *Seraphim*, unleashing every weapon available in their arsenal as their quarry desperately tried to evade them. With the *Seraphim* moving away and taking *Guardian's Gate* with them, the *Spirit's* initial vector to the planet surface was open.

The ship suddenly shook in a pronounced fashion, and the bridge lights flickered before going out.

"Commander, that was the *Revenge*. She fired multiple shots at us; they all hit in about the same spot. Port shield integrity is stable, but we won't be able to take much more." There was a short pause from Parsons before he spoke again. This time, his voice was filled with incredulousness as he reported what he saw. "Commander, the *Seraphim* is *attacking* the *Rebellious God*. They are on an attack vector that will take them underneath the battle cruiser."

Commander Tennison allowed himself a smirk as he realized what Captain Nicolai was doing. The esteemed captain was drawing his trailing attacker into the *Rebellious God's* line of fire. It was risky for the *Seraphim*, but both of their attackers would need to weigh risks also. The *Guardian's Gate* could continue trailing, but risked being hit with friendly fire from the *Rebellious God*. They also risked hitting their ally with an errant shot. The same decision was being made aboard the *Rebellious God*, as their captain had to decide whether to continue firing or break off their attack and let the *Guardian's Gate* chase and attack. The captain of the *Rebellious God* would have to decide whether the S*eraphim* was capable of a suicide attack, which would also severely damage the *God*.

The *Rebellious God* took the lead in the decision, deciding to continue its salvo against the *Seraphim* as their attacker pressed towards them. As the two smaller ships approached the battle cruiser, the salvo was halved, and restricted to only beam weapons, which allowed for a higher percentage of accuracy.

Tennison focused back on his own ship, now with a clear path to the planet surface. The *Revenge* was still chasing, and he assumed they were lining the *Spirit* up for another round of weapons fire.

"Reallocate the remaining shields. Fifty-fifty split on the stern and the port sides." Marshall assumed the *Revenge* would either continue to target the existing damage or attempt to knock out their engines, resulting in an easy kill.

The lights on the bridge control panels lit up the faces of the remaining officers on the bridge. Tennison looked briefly at each one as the ship plummeted towards the atmosphere. *How many would survive this landing? Would they even make it to the surface?*

The Commander's thoughts were interrupted by a shout, almost in glee, from one of his officers.

"Commander, the MERL device has just fired on the *Revenge!*"

The *Alaurian Spirit* flew ahead of the *Nowrimo's Revenge*, just to the starboard side. Commander Reaz Apxlus could feel elation coming on. His day was going very well. He had already sent two sinner ships to their deaths with his unexpected attack. Now, the other sinners would die as well. They would not take his Savior from his people. He would destroy his own ship before allowing them to capture the Son of God. His clan would be well remembered on this day, regardless of the outcome.

"Warrior Moak, engage the *Alaurian Spirit*. Focus all weapons on their damage. Use a variable phase beam to defeat their shield grids, then follow with a concentrated blast at the hole on their hull."

The Shalothan warrior stationed at the weapons console nodded his reply, and programmed in the exotic settings for the weapons choice of his commander. The *Nowrimo's Revenge* was not heavily armed, but the weapons available were certainly deadly. The particle beam weapon favored by Commander Apxlus was military-grade, and capable of numerous functions. The missiles were very powerful, although any distance other than a few kilometers rendered them almost useless due to their inaccuracy.

As Moak readied the beam weapon, the *Spirit* opened fire on the *Revenge*, using its own beam weapon on the craft. The vessel was jolted by the hit, but the beam didn't seem to be concentrated enough to cause major damage. The forward shields on the *Revenge* absorbed the entire blow, leaving the integrity of the hull intact.

"All Honor and Glory is Yours, Almighty God!" Moak called out as he fired the *Revenge's* beam weapon. The bright blue beam stuttered against the shields of the *Spirit*, continually draining the remaining energy of the modified frigate. Once the weapons system in front of Anacen alerted him to loss of shields on the *Spirit*, he switched to a concentrated beam directed at the gaping blast hole in the side of the hull. The beam sliced a gash along the horizontal axis of the ship, opening up what appeared to be several isolated container holds. It was the last area that the beam hit that proved to be the most successful. The *Spirit* glowed from the inside near the edge of the beam, and then a large piece of the hull spun away, allowing several items to float out of the ship. As the *Revenge* continued to chase, the items that had come out of the *Spirit* zipped by. Commander Apxlus watched out the forward viewshield as the items grew in size and then passed the ship. The body of one of the crewmembers sailed by, burned from the beam and partially severed in half from being ripped out of the ship into space. The commander bowed his head briefly to honor the fallen soldier, made the sign of the cross with his right hand, then returned his focus to the wounded ship.

The ship in front of him had begun to slowly spiral as it plummeted towards the atmosphere. A faint glow began to appear around the edges of the craft as it entered the planet's atmosphere. Suspecting he was watching the ship in its death throes, Commander Apxlus called off the chase and directed his pilot to return them to the battle with the *Seraphim*.

CHAPTER XVIII

"Commander, I have the initial casualty report."

"Go ahead Ensign." Commander Marshall Tennison didn't look up at the soldier as she gathered her information together. He continued packing weapons and food into a rucksack, neatly organizing food and ammunition together.

"I have the list organized by rank, sir. Confirmed deaths include Captain Angelina Pollard, Lieutenant Louis Daniels, Lieutenant Junior Grade Barry Guy, Clone Angelina Pollard, and Clone Marshall Tennison. The following are Missing In Action, Presumed Dead; Ensign Jason House, Ensign Omer Kramer, Ensign Kevin Theore, and Clone Daniels. Lieutenant Parsons was critically injured, but the ERCs harvested his clone and stabilized him. It appears that the injuries are listed as amputation to the right arm and right leg. He's been heavily sedated, and wrapped in a bio-blanket. His clone has been put into stasis and will be re-evaluated when we return back to base.

"Thank you Ensign Sears. Pass the word for everyone to pack up a rucksack with ammo and food." Ensign Aileen Sears audibly confirmed and turned on her heel to follow her orders. So this is what it had come to. Commander Tennison was now the ranking officer of the crew. Or rather, what remained of the officer crew. Eighteen officers strong at the start of their mission, they had lost two thirds of the roster to casualties. The observation mission was not going well.

Marshall glanced at his PLD one last time before shoving it in with his field gear. With no signal, the group would have to manually track their quarry. He glanced back up at the *Alaurian Spirit* and took in the damage once more. Almost two hundred meters long from bow to stern, and over six stories high, it was a testament to Ensign Roach's piloting skills that he was able to bring the wounded and dying ship into atmosphere without burning up or crash landing. The acrid smell of burned flesh, simmering wiring, overheated titanium, spilled coolant, and now, flame-retardants mixed in the air with the smells of the planet's atmosphere. Four ERCs were securing what missiles were left in the remains of the MCAC system to prevent manual removal. Others flitted about securing air locks, transporting supplies out of the ship, or working with the sentry droids to set up the security perimeter around the ship.

The hole in the starboard side of the ship ran almost a full third of the way along the length, with a large blast hole slightly forward of the half distance mark of the gash. The commander correctly surmised that the attack had hit an MCAC well as it was opening to fire, triggering an internal explosion that gutted the ship along the bisecting bulkhead. The ship's system slammed the blast doors down on either side of the section to limit the blast fire, trapping any crewmembers that may have been in that particular cell. Ensigns Jason House and Omer Kramer were the only MCAC techs on the ship, and they both just happened to be listed as Missing in Action. Marshall hoped they didn't survive the blast; death in the cold void of space was not as quick and painless as one would think.

The rest of the ship looked fairly intact, with the exception of a rear stabilizer and the aft shield arrays. If help didn't contact his crew or arrive planet-side within the next 24 hours, he'd have to abandon the search and order everyone to return back to the ship's secured perimeter zone. It would certainly be a devastating blow, especially after coming so close to retrieving Him.

As he was finishing his thought, a sonic boom surprised him, causing him to reach for his rifle and seek cover. Searching the hazy sky above, Marshall could pick out the billowing contrails of an inbound orbital ship. From initial inspection, it looked strikingly similar to the *Nowrimo's Revenge.* Moving away from the *Spirit*'s landing site and heading south, the ship appeared to be on a steep descent trajectory.

"Solomon, get a bead on that inbound! Roach, can you get vector?" Marshall's commands were no sooner out of his mouth than his crew was acting upon them. Lieutenant Soloman had one of the Personal Missile Systems activated and tracking the unit. Ensign Claude Roach raced his fingers across his data-tablet, utilizing the remote features within the ship's tracking system to determine the course for the bogey.

"It's a distressed flight path, sir," Soloman called out. Marshall tapped the side of his visor to bring up the binocular function. Squinting into the lens resulted in the optical sensor within the visor to polarize the viewfinder and automatically adjust the magnification based on the amount that the person squinted.

He could see the billowing contrails were actually smoke escaping from a damaged engine and, from the distance they were at, possibly the forward bridge.

"It's on a steep descent. The long-range scopes are picking up reverse thruster action, but it doesn't appear to be working. She's going to impact in about twenty seconds at this rate." Ensign Roach continued tracking the surface-bound ship through his tablet, while the rest of the crew watched its descent into the horizon. Eighteen seconds later, a flash was seen on the horizon, followed by a mushroom cloud moments later.

"Commander, we were able to get ship data from their transponder. It's a Shalothan Planetary Dropship. Registered under the name *The Insanity Savior.* It was sending out a distress signal upon atmospheric entry. The system wasn't able to pull crew rosters, manifests, or damage logs in time. Signal was terminated at impact.

The Shalothan sector had been the primary antagonist at the start of the inter-sector wars. Historically, they were a vicious inner-sector technocracy that was known for their advanced planetary and orbital ship architecture. Civil war destroyed the planet, but the manufacturing plants survived intact. Fueled by anger from the perceived lack of assistance from neighboring systems, the Shalothans finally ended their civil war, only to wage an inter-sector war against the Fe-Ruq, Otine, and Aormy systems. Strengthened by their superior vessels, they decimated most of the Otine and Aormy systems before meeting any real resistance in the Fe-Ruq sector. For a Shalothan ship to plummet out of space, it usually meant it had been outnumbered and outgunned in a battle; one-on-one battles typically fell in favor of the Shalothan vessels.

"All right, it doesn't concern us right now. The

battle is obviously still going on, so we have a small window of opportunity to capture our target before the rescue crews come and get us. Clone Theore, grab a rifle; you're on point first. Dalton, you're bringing up the rear. Roach, Cummings, sit tight and stay with the ship. Inform me immediately if any contact is made either with any of the crew of the *Nowrimo's Revenge* or any recovery crews.

Tennison took a last look back at the *Alaurian Spirit*, then turned and queued up behind Theore and Soloman as they began their hike towards the Son of God.

CHAPTER XIX

"Commander Apxlus, three Shalothan vessels have arrived in-system. Sensors indicate that it's *The Insanity Savior*, *The Exodus*, and *The Savior's Clay*."

Reaz Apxlus looked over at the warrior that had spoken, dismayed to learn of the additional vessels. He said nothing, but nodded slightly at the warrior to signal his acknowledgment of the report.

The arrival of the *Exodus*, a Heavy Infiltrator-class warship, could only mean that the supposedly secret transfer location was anything but. He briefly wondered why General Tesuh's flagship was in the area, but pushed the thought out of his mind and returned his attention to the battle at hand.

"Prepare to reengage." Apxlus looked through the viewshield, and pointed at the damaged *Eccentric*, slowly making its way out of the theater of battle, presumably towards an exit vector to get them out-system. Peering into the gaping hole that was previously part of the bridge of the *Eccentric*, Apxlus guessed the ship was being controlled from an auxiliary bridge, possibly from some type of engineering station in the bowels of the ship.

"Move us within missile range and target that vessel's engine cluster." Warrior Anacen clicked in acknowledgment, and responded with a quick adjustment on his control board. The *Nowrimo's*

Revenge accelerated quickly, drawing the *Eccentric* close enough until the image filled the entire viewshield.

"Fire at will."

The missiles shot out from the weapons package attached to the hull of the *Revenge*. Traveling at sub-lightspeed, the impact occurred a millisecond after the launch. The general area of space that had been occupied by the *Eccentric* engines quickly gave way to emptiness, spreading shards of superheated hull in every direction.

The vessel continued to drift on its original vector, unhindered by the vacuum of space. Smaller secondary explosions erupted in portions of the hull adjacent to the destroyed engine compartments. Seeing that the vessel was adrift, Apxlus directed his crew to change vectors and engage the *Seraphim*.

Aboard the *Seraphim,* Captain Nicolai barked out orders to his weapons officer, directing her to alternate which weapons were being fired at the massive Shalothan battle cruiser.

The arrival of three additional Shalothan vessels was barely noticed by the young captain. His attention was focused on keeping his crew alive, and he was doing everything he could think of to disrupt the usual tactics of his Shalothan opponents.

The *Rebellious God* had stopped its salvo temporarily as the *Seraphim* traveled perilously close to her hull, but the pursuing *Guardian's Gate* continued to batter the aft shields of the enemy vessel. Shields were continually reported as failing, with each thirty second update showing incremental percentage loss. The weapons fire directed at the *Rebellious God* was insignificant at best, but provided Captain Nicolai and his crew with a sense of fighting back.

His officers continued to call out the location of the various Shalothan vessels. The *Nowrimo's Revenge* was attacking the *Eccentric*, and apparently succeeding, based on the frantic pleas for assistance that were coming from the damaged vessel. The three late arriving Shalothan vessels were almost dead ahead, gliding over the cusp of the moon's terminator line.

"Captain, we have an exit vector," the navigation officer reported. Captain Nicolai glanced at his battle screen, gripping the armrests of his command chair with both hands. His data display revealed the arriving Shalothan vessels were coming up on the *Seraphim's* position quickly, with the *Guardian's Gate* relatively close in pursuit. The goliath battle cruiser *Rebellious God* was slowly maneuvering around to bring up the rear of the newly forming flank.

Assessing the situation quickly, Nicolai could see that one of the inbound ships, the *Insanity Savior*, was beginning to break formation and head for the outer edges of the atmosphere. The *Exodus* and the *Savior's Clay* opened up with long-range beam weapons to provide a covering fire for the *Insanity Savior*. The situation was quickly deteriorating, and the odds of survival were quickly falling to zero.

"Weapons command, target all long-range weapons on the transport ship. Do not let her make atmospheric entry!" Captain Nicolai quickly surmised what had happened. The Shalothans, a species that Captain Nicolai viewed as untrustworthy, must have had the three ships lying in wait only moments away by thread travel. The *Insanity Savior*, a Shalothan military dropship, was descending to the surface for what Nicolai could only guess was a retrieval mission targeting the Son of God.

The crew watched as the *Seraphim's* complete assortment of long-range beam weapons opened up simultaneously on the dropship, silently slicing through space to pound her shield arrays until they flared and dissipated into space.

"Continue firing phased blasts until we penetrate their shields."

The straight line weapons fire almost instantly morphed into stuttering blasts, cycling in a rotation among all the beam ports. The beam blasts rained down on the descending ship, overwhelming the shield capacity of the vessel. Captain Nicolai glanced at his own readouts, silently holding his breath that the *Seraphim's* shields would hold out longer than the military transport's. Each bombardment by the oncoming vessels, as well as the continuing rear action from the *Guardian's Gate* drained precious shield strength. The last report had listed the shields at ten percent, but that wouldn't last another minute. Nicolai made his decision.

"Launch all concussion torpedoes at the target" Nicolai paused to ensure the order was carried out. "Navigation, get us out of here *now*."

With a short confirmation, the *Seraphim* turned to port slightly and increased velocity to hit the thread opening. The ship shuddered as the shields finally failed and allowed the beam blasts to penetrate through to their hull. System warning alarms began sounding out throughout the bridge, signaling the loss of some vital function or another. Captain Nicolai leaned forward in his command chair, almost certain he was about to meet his death. He glanced down at his tactical display and saw that the torpedoes had not destroyed the *Insanity Savior*; it merely damaged the craft enough to send it plummeting helplessly into the upper atmosphere. He looked up through the viewshield, and the last thing he saw was the bright flash of a beam weapon filling his field of vision as it hit a forward portion of his ship.

General Landiz Tesuh didn't just glower *at* the warriors stationed on the command deck of the *Exodus*. He glowered *down* at them, even when they all stood at attention within his presence. Easily one of the tallest in the warrior caste to serve Shalotha, General Tesuh stood a full head taller than the next tallest warrior, and typically was two heads taller than the average warrior. His body was larger than the typical Shalothan in just about every aspect. From the thick cranial ridges atop his head, to the long keratin horns protruding from his shoulders, to the muscular development and thickness of the keratin plates covering his body. His anger at the perceived defeat by the infidel forces did nothing to soften his demeanor.

The assembled warriors had not seen nor heard from General Tesuh since he arrived on board at the start of the journey. Although a disciplined species, the warriors aboard the *Exodus* were not immune to pondering the meaning of his notable absence from the command deck. As his flagship, it was the General's right to station himself anywhere he saw fit. Most high-ranking officials with their own assigned flagship typically made a point of being on the command deck throughout the trip, if only for reinforcement of their command by visual representation. Tesuh's lack of presence in the most important area of the vessel spawned questions among the warrior-officers.

The past two wake periods had not gone well for the triad of vessels that had been dispatched with General Tesuh. From the moment he descended the shuttle ramp onto the flight deck while in orbit high above Shalotha, tensions had run high. His arrival predicated a swift departure from orbit, with a slight delay near the outer edge of the system to await the arrival of a battalion of warriors that had been ordered to rendezvous with the military dropship that accompanied the *Exodus*, the *Insanity Savior*.

On station for barely half of a wake period, the General had received an urgent communication from Shalotha, resulting in a change of orders. Soon thereafter, General Tesuh had the vessels powering towards the Fe-Ruq system, with Jethl as their final destination. Their arrival at Jethl had been successful only by traveling through relatively unoccupied space, away from the mapped threads and millennia-old trade routes. It was safer in respect to the Fe-Ruq force that they would have faced on the known routes, but unknown space was just as dangerous. Free-floating debris and unknown obstacles could disable a ship just as easily as a successful attack. The difference was that in unknown space, there were no planets or moons nearby for the escape boats to land on, nor any orbital docks to respond to their distress calls. It could be a very deadly place indeed.

Despite all of the potential opportunities for disaster, Tesuh's group had arrived on the dark side of the Jethl moon free of damage. It wasn't until they had swept across the terminator line that danger greeted them.

Immediately upon entering sensor range of the USF vessels, the triad had been fired upon. Minutes later, their attackers had fled to deep space on a thread, and the dropship containing the Nihon Regiment ground warriors had presumably crashed into the mottled green and gray surface of the foreign moon.

It was for this perceived disgrace that the Shalothan General of the Armies stood wordlessly, glaring not just at the warriors, but through them. In his eyes, one could see the utter look of contempt for the failure.

The *Exodus* and the *Savior's Clay* drifted high above the moon of Jethl, settling into parallel orbits. The only operational vessels left in the immediate vacuum of space around the moon belonged to the Shalothan Imperium. However, even with the departure of the *Seraphim*, the immediate danger to General Tesuh had not dissipated, and he was fully aware of it.

Striding over to the communications station, General Tesuh shoved aside the young warrior and jabbed at the controls, hailing the *Nowrimo's Revenge*. Within seconds, a small hologram of Reaz Apxlus appeared over the console.

"Warrior Apxlus, this is General Tesuh. On orders of the Primary, you are ordered to surrender your prisoner to me immediately." He stared stonily at the vision floating in front of him, waiting for some type of response.

"General Tesuh, you honor me with your presence. Is there any indication that any of the warriors aboard the *Insanity Savior* have survived the impact?" The image of Reaz Apxlus bowed his head slightly.

"You will surrender the prisoner to me at once, or prepare to be boarded, Apxlus."

"General Tesuh, have you no concern for our

brethren? How many were aboard that ship?" The voice scolded the General, fanning his anger.

"Reaz Apxlus, surrender your prisoner. I will not ask again." His tone rose slightly, and the words became more pronounced. Tesuh clicked in his throat at the end of the statement.

"General Tesuh, I cannot relinquish a prisoner to you. There is no prisoner aboard this ship for me to give. Board us if you so desire."

Tesuh made a slashing motion with his hand.

"Enough of this Apxlus. You are escorting the Son of God. Do you think I am here by chance? Primary Radael has ordered your arrest for the unauthorized attack on Je-Fin. You have provoked the Fe-Ruqians to the point of war, Apxlus. You have threatened all of Shalotha with your actions." He paused, considering his next statement. "We must return him to the Fe-Ruqians in order to avoid conflict. If He truly is Christ, then He will still reign in His Kingdom, regardless of who claims Him as a prisoner."

"General Tesuh, did you bring your most treasured possession with you into battle?"

General Tesuh visibly pulled his head back, as if stunned by the question. Realizing an immediate response was not forthcoming, Apxlus asked again.

Apxlus' superior commanding officer finally responded.

"Of course not. Only a fool brings that which he values most into a conflict. My possessions are of no concern to you at this moment, Apxlus. Stop prolonging the inevitable."

"Understand then, General, that you have no need to board us." With that, the image of Apxlus faded away, leaving General Tesuh to glare at empty space.

Apxlus flicked his hand over a control on his communications board, and the image of General Tesuh faded.

"Moak, did the *Guardian's Gate* and *Rebellious God* receive the transmission?" Apxlus looked over at Moak, who was still engrossed in a function at his console. He answered back without facing Apxlus.

"They missed the first ten to fifteen seconds of the conversation with General Tesuh, but *Guardian's Gate* has confirmed receipt of the surface coordinates of our Lord and the encoded message regarding our mission. Both commanders are hailing you now."

Greeting both commanding warriors of the vessels, Apxlus inquired about what they had just witnessed, and listened to both warriors' interpretations. Understanding their concerns, Apxlus began his own explanation.

"Warriors of Shalotha, we are being faced with a test. Do we worship our government as a false idol, or do we protect our Lord? What true follower of Christ would turn Him over to the hands of His enemies? What true follower of Christ would follow those orders? Our General has decreed his loyalty clearly. Undeterred, he would readily assume the role of Judas and condemn our Lord to an unknown fate in the hands of the Fe-Ruqians. I tell you now, my ship will not allow our Lord to be returned to the Fe-Ruqians as a political prisoner. We will become martyrs for His cause, should General Tesuh persist in blindly following these supposed orders. Perhaps General Tesuh speaks on behalf of the Beast. I ask each of you to consider where your loyalties lie – to your government, or to your Lord. If it is the former, then fire at your leisure and destroy our Christ with this ship, for He will have no meaning to you." Apxlus paused for a moment before finishing his statement. "Otherwise, hold General Tesuh in the same regard as you would an enemy of Christ." Apxlus bowed his head towards the junior warriors, and ended the communication.

"Moak, has there been any contact from Naoh or Anacen?" Apxlus leaned back in the command chair, rubbing the side of his hand ridge. The warriors had been left on the surface of the moon of Jethl as escorts and protectors to the Son of God. The location of the two warriors, as well as the location of their Lord, was the content of the encoded message that Apxlus had transmitted to the *Guardian's Gate* as they arrived in orbit. He had not provided precise coordinates however; only a cryptic message alluding to the general location of the trio. He had done so as a deterrent to firing upon the *Nowrimo's Revenge*. Apxlus had prayed that the commander of the *Guardian's Gate* would refrain from destroying the *Revenge* since only they had the true location. So far, the ruse had worked well.

"The last transmission was a pre-programmed beacon emission from Naoh, approximately an hour ago. Nothing further." Apxlus nodded at the information. He had time to wait, and suspected that General Tesuh did not. It was unfortunate, but Apxlus surmised that the General of the Armies would meet his death in the near future. He prayed that the other commanders' faith was as strong as his own.

General Tesuh did not make Apxlus wait long for an indication as to what the General of the Armies was going to do. It was less than ten minutes before *The Exodus* began to maneuver closer to the *Nowrimo's*

Revenge in an attempt to board the smaller frigate. Apxlus watched on the sensors as the Shalothan vessel drifted closer to their position.

"Fire a warning shot at *The Exodus*," Apxlus calmly ordered. Moak enacted the order, sending a burst of energy flashing past the oncoming ship. The vessel did not slow. Apxlus rubbed the keratin ridge on the back of his hand thoughtfully, trying to calculate their chances of escape. "Fire another burst," he ordered. Moak fired again, this time sending the burst closer to the growing image of the vessel.

"Moak, it is time for us to place our survival in the hands of God. Find a thread and plot a vector, quickly," Apxlus said in a low voice. Moak looked up at his commander questioningly.

"You intend to leave them behind," Moak stated. He jabbed at the control console, pulling up the mathematical data needed to create a course projection.

"For now, yes. We must be alive in order to return our Lord to Shalotha. Dying at the hands of our brethren does not accomplish our mission." He looked at Moak and held the warrior's gaze for a heartbeat. Flashes of light outside the ship caught the attention of both warriors.

"What was that," Apxlus asked, moving to the command chair. More flashes filled their view.

"Weapons fire detected. Originating from *Rebellious God*. It appears it's directed at *The Exodus*." More bursts of energy flashed through space, this time from a different direction. "*The Exodus* is taking fire from *Savior's Clay* and *Guardian's Gate* as well. Orders?" Moak held his hand over the navigation board, awaiting his commander's order.

"Our brethren have made their choice. Support the

attack with our entire arsenal."

Moak quickly glanced at Apxlus and bared his teeth in the approximation of a Shalothan grin. Quickly activating the targeting systems, he began cycling through the weapons package, firing each in a rotating cycle. *The Exodus* began returning fire at all four attacking vessels while maneuvering in an attempt to get out of the line of fire. Flashes of energy continued to fill the space between the attackers and their prey as the two warriors watched in silence.

The Exodus swung upwards and over the *Revenge*, focusing on the three larger Shalothan vessels that were attacking it. One of the vessels moved in closer, and Moak identified it as the *Savior's Clay* – the ship that had arrived with *The Exodus*. Apxlus watched as it emptied its entire arsenal during one massive salvo aimed at the fleeing ship. The energy overload caused the shields on *The Exodus* to abruptly fail, allowing all four attacking ships unhindered access to the hull. Within thirty seconds General Tesuh's vessel was disgorging its contents into space, broken in half from the concentrated weapons fire. Apxlus and Moak bowed their heads in prayer for the hundreds of Shalothans that had just been flash frozen and sent to their deaths.

"Apxlus, the other ships have sent a message."

"What does it say?"

"We consecrate our vessels to the service of our Lord. Awaiting orders."

CHAPTER XX

They had been on the surface of the planet for about twelve standard hours, with the midnight sky giving way to early morning before they had actually left the landing site. The sun was high, and the temperature was rapidly rising. Commander Tennison surveyed the landscape as he and his team trekked through the mountainous region. Roach and Cummings had brought the *Alaurian Spirit* down safely on a plateau near a small ridge. To the magnetic north was flatter terrain that appeared to be heavily forested, from their unaided observations. To the east of the landing site was more forest area, but thinned out by what appeared to a swampy region that was overtaking the dense tree growth. To the south were smaller ridges, with what appeared to be grassy areas intermingled among bunches of trees. To the west, in the direction they were heading, was the ridge. Beyond that, they had to rely on the last readings from the sensor package onboard the *Spirit*.

The map that Lieutenant JG Buck Dalton had pulled up showed a much larger mountainous region about fifty kilometers to the west, with intermediate hills and peaks between their current location and the tallest set of peaks within the range. During their initial hours on the surface, Tennison had put Dalton on the task of gathering as much intelligence information as possible from the sensors on the ship before they shut down. The terrain map generated by the sensors was limited at best, with a small radius of about two hundred kilometers from the ship. Even though Roach and Cummings attempted to pilot the ship down to the general location where they thought He had been left, they couldn't be sure they were even within several hundred kilometers of the correct location. The information they had to work with had been very limited, and the Commander had taken it upon himself to decide it would most likely be a mountainous area they would need to search for Him in.

Marshall recalled that many of the ancient teachings had described the Son of God going up onto a mountain or hill during critical points in His life. He assumed that the Second Coming of Christ qualified as another critical point in the history of civilization. For no other reason than his instinct, he and the remainder of his crew were hiking through hilly terrain on a planet that no one had cared to colonize yet. *No, not even a planet,* Marshall thought. *It's just a moon.*

The path wasn't as much a trail as it was an eroded gulley from some type of liquid run-off. There wasn't much else in the way of a trail once they had started ascending the nearest mountain, so they continued to follow the path. The crew seemed in poor spirits, and Marshall wasn't sure if it was only because they had effectively lost the battle, or because Captain Pollard was dead and he was now their commanding officer. He could understand the first reason, but the second reason would be totally unacceptable to him. If that's the case, he thought, then I'm better off without them.

The group trekked through the vegetation, unsure as to where they were going. None of the crew talked, and even Marshall began to feel despair as they seemed to be headed towards the middle of nowhere. The thought of his clone dying presented itself in his mind. Unsettling, yet somewhat satisfying, the thought lingered enough for him to begin to dwell on it. How had his clone actually died? He wasn't sure. For that matter, was his clone actually dead? What if the report was wrong? It's possible that the bodies of the clones were confused after the battle, and his was still in the medical capsule, awaiting a release from hibernation. If it were alive, what help could it possibly provide now, other than being used as harvest material? If he had brought the clone with him, he'd have to feed it, watch out for it, possibly even attempt to train it to defend itself in battle. It could attack one of his crew members, attempting to defend itself and hurting someone in the process. It wasn't worth it, he decided. Yet, once again he felt a slight pang of jealousy toward the clone. It hadn't even known that it was about to die. It didn't suffer from the wounds of battle, and wouldn't feel the pain and exhaustion of marching dozens of kilometers in the heat of a foreign planet to find their target.

Their target. The words sliced through his revelry and jolted him back to the present. Their target was presumably alone, stranded on the same moon. He was confident they would reach the target within a few days, provided He didn't move from the last known whereabouts. *But then what*, he wondered. Calculating the food rations, he figured that almost everyone would be out within a few days. That left them with enough food for half of the trip; they would have to gather food from the wilderness on the way back.

Another thought intruded on his mind. *How am I going to get Him off-world*, he wondered. Lieutenant

Dalton slipped on some loose gravel, sending stones sliding down towards Marshall. He sidestepped them and glanced up at the officer. He thought again about their predicament. Assuming the personal locator system was still not functioning, any rescue and recovery team would start at the landing zone, and begin a search there. That would leave them a day behind in trying to catch up, without really understanding exactly where the survivors were.

He marched on in mental silence for a while, listening to the heavy breathing coming from some of the officers. He tried to control his own breathing, measuring each breath as they continued along the path. Glancing off to the horizon, he could see bands of low clouds gathering in the distance. He wasn't sure what the weather pattern was on this particular celestial body, but he hoped it was going the other way. They didn't need poor weather to add to their misery.

The weather hadn't held out. Commander Tennison's crew had been marching for a day and a half, based on the moon's rotation and the position of the sun and mother planet in the sky above them. The rain clouds that had gathered on the horizon quickly filled the sky above, and had accompanied them for the remainder of the day. After a restless night for the entire crew, Marshall had them continue their trek before the sun was fully in the sky. The rain the day before had made the trip much more dangerous, as the terrain had degraded from loose clumps of soil to slick mud. The upward path they had been following continued to climb steeper, and the footing became more treacherous. Several times a member of the crew would slip and fall, sliding down towards the bottom of the path. Most of the falls had resulted in some bruises, a cut here or there. It was the last fall that reminded Commander Tennison they were in dangerous territory.

The group had been following the trail to the left, which was butting up against the wall of a steep bluff on the left, and featured a steep drop on the right. Until they had reached this part of the trail, the crew had seen rare glimpses of the wildlife on the moon; an avian creature winging through the low clouds, or a rodent scurrying across the trail ahead of them. It wasn't until the trail widened at the base of the bluff they discovered that there were much more dangerous predators on the moon.

Ensign Sears was leading the march at that particular moment, clawing and grabbing at the rock face to help pull her along the trail. The trail was only a meter wide in this area, and the mud had made it almost impossible to use. Commander Tennison was behind her, wary of the loose ground and the potential for a fall. Lieutenant Soloman, Lieutenant Buck Dalton, and the clone of Ensign Kevin Theore followed, slowly picking their handholds to advance with.

Tennison looked out over the area to his right. Fifty meters below, the dense foliage was shrouded in a morning mist, and small creatures flitted through the sky in the early morning light. Above them the bluff wall slowly curved up and away to the left, hiding its crest from view. Tennison was actually enjoying the difficulty of the trail, reminding him of days spent rock climbing in his youth. He stopped for a moment to drink some water, when Ensign Sears yelled out.

Marshall quickly brought his blaster rifle to bear in the general direction of Ensign Sears. She was flailing her arms above her head, shaking and waving them at some unseen attacker. Moving as quickly as possible, Marshall pushed himself up against the rock for stability and side stepped along the trail while holding onto his weapon. About two meters from his crew member he finally saw what was wrong. From his distance, it appeared that a black film was quickly enveloping her, starting at her feet and moving upwards. As he looked closer, he could see that the film wasn't a liquid at all, but the constant movement of thousands, if not tens of thousands of black insects. They were swarming out of a tiny hole in the ground near the base of the bluff where it met the trail.

"Help! They're biting me!" Ensign Sears screamed. She continued to flail around, swatting at the insects that had now covered her from her waist down. Commander Tennison didn't move, watching the scene unfold. Within seconds, droplets of blood seeped out of the blanket of insects, running down and beginning to pool on the ground. It took another moment before Tennison realized what was happening. The creatures were eating her alive right in front of him.

Sears stumbled back down the trail towards Marshall, flailing at the insects with what remained of her hands as the living blanket continued above her shoulders and crept up her neck. Marshall stared in horror as Sears neared him.

"Get back!" Marshall screamed at her. Panic filled him as he watched. He couldn't believe how quickly the insects were growing in size until he realized that they weren't maturing in size, but rather they were gorging themselves on her blood and skin so quickly that they were bloating. She fell against the bluff wall, and started to slide towards him. The creatures had now swarmed above her neck and coated her head, leaving only the very top of her forehead visible.

Marshall slid backwards from Ensign Sears, yelling back at the rest of the crew to move back down the trail. He faced the insect encrusted officer again, pleading with her to get away from him. The distance between the two quickly closed as the screaming officer continued moving without caution on the path. Marshall backed into something or someone, and came to a stop. Before he could look behind him to see what he had backed into, the muzzle of a blaster rifle whipped up and over his shoulder, firing several short blasts into Ensign Sears.

The insect-infested body of Ensign Sears buckled under the blaster shots and fell off the trail into the mists below, taking most of the blood bugs with it. Only bloody footsteps remained in the mud, with a few of the engorged insects scattered about the path. Marshall leaned back against the rock, and looked to his right at the shooter. Ernie Soloman was still in the same position, rifle held up in a classic shooter's pose, scanning the rock and path ahead for more of the insects. She glanced at Marshall briefly and gave him a severe look, and then motioned with her rifle to encourage him to move forward on the path. Filled with shame for not acting as quickly as his lieutenant, Marshall glanced sheepishly at Soloman and inched his way forward along the trail, apprehensive about disturbing more of the insects.

In the aftermath of the horrific scene that had played out before them, Marshall and his crew set about determining what had happened to Ensign Sears. No one said a word, but the shock was evident on each face of the crew. Silently Lieutenant Soloman stood and gazed at the sullen faces before her.

"Let's go," she said, surprisingly without emotion. "Theore, move up and search for more of these nests. Parsons, keep our backs covered – watch for any sign of other predators that may have been alerted or drawn to the screaming. We don't know enough about this ecology to understand what else we may have disturbed."

As they searched the trail, Clone Theore pointed out to everyone that Ensign Sears had stepped directly into the nest or hive of the insects. The soft, muddy ground had made it that much easier for her foot to break through the thin dirt covering that protected the opening from the insects' natural predators. Her actions had merely provoked the insects' natural survival instincts. It appeared that this unfortunate event had been an accident. They would all have to be more careful of where they stepped and what they grabbed a hold of.

Marshall cursed himself as they continued on. He replayed the scene through his mind, evaluating how he had reacted. Or rather, how he had failed to react. In a crisis moment, his first as the highest commanding officer of the crew, he had frozen when they needed him most. He had panicked when they could afford it least. What would he do the next time they found themselves faced with a dangerous situation? He continued his self-flagellation as they marched on through the morning.

The morning turned into afternoon, and afternoon faded into evening. The path had finally leveled off, and had opened up on to a fairly flat area of the mountain. The crew traversed the remainder of the narrow bluff-path without further incident, but the loss of Ensign Sears had shaken the crew. None of the others had actually witnessed the attack, but each of them heard her screams echoing off the rock face, and the high-pitched whine of the blaster rifle as it had pierced the air. Each of them took more time to plan their steps and watch where they placed their hands. The inevitable result was a slower pace, leaving them further away from the target destination than they would have liked.

Once they reached the open area, Marshall directed the crew to stop and rest. Lieutenant Soloman and Marshall took up points at the front and rear of the group respectively, guarding their position while the others rested. Marshall kept his rifle loose in his hand, ready for any surprises. He looked back towards the group, spread out in the open area, and then past them, towards the dark shadow of Ernie Soloman standing at the ready, rifle cradled in her arms. He couldn't see her face in the shadows, but he could sense anger and hostility from her rigid posture. He assumed it was directed at him.

Marshall stepped down off the rock that he was standing on, and walked towards the Lieutenant. As he passed the group, Marshall couldn't discern what their low voices were saying, but he feared that it wasn't anything positive. Lieutenant Dalton looked up at him expectantly as he stepped past him, and Marshall patted him on the shoulder, not saying a word.

Ernie turned towards him as he approached, and Marshall flipped his free hand up to give a halfhearted wave. He couldn't see the expression on her face, but he didn't see any motion of response from her either.

"Lieutenant Soloman, how does it look over here," Marshall asked with a low voice, suddenly uncomfortable even approaching her. She paused for a moment before answering.

"Nothing in sight. Not that it means anything to us."

"Listen, Lieutenant, I wanted to thank you back there for doing what you did. I'm not sure what happened, uh, or why I didn't react quic-."

Soloman cut him off sharply, "Well, you better figure it out pretty damn quick, don't you think *Commander*?" Her sarcastic tone on the last word stung Marshall, more than he thought it would. "If you can't handle this, then step out of the way and I'll take it from here. You can march your ass back to the ship for all I care. We have a mission, Commander. A mission. This isn't the time for you to be figuring out if you can play captain or not. If this is how you led in your other commands, then it's probably why you weren't made a captain of a ship yet. It's obvious to everyone here that you're not even sure about the orders you've given us. Why are you marching us out to God knows where to search for someone that's claiming to be the Son of God? Why didn't we just stay with our ship, where we were protected, where we had our communications, where we're most likely to be found? Why endanger your entire crew to go after this one man? Are you even sure that He's the Son of God? Or is that just your wishful thinking? Is this your way of trying to prove that you're worthy of being a captain? Did it ever occur to you that He probably wasn't dropped off on this rock by Himself? That maybe, just maybe, the Shalothans left some of their soldiers - or warriors, or whatever the hell they call themselves – behind to protect their Savior until the cavalry comes? Did you happen to notice that we were a bit outnumbered up there, and chances are they were all there for one person? The same person that you have us going after? Commander, do you even realize that you're leading us to certain death if we continue? What did you have planned for when we finally meet up with the Shalothans, be it a platoon or a battalion? Do you happen to have a regiment of hover tanks in your back pocket that you can whip out to give us some support? Perhaps some fighter craft that you packed in your rucksack?" Lieutenant Soloman snorted in disgust.

Marshall's mouth hung slightly open, and he involuntarily took a step backward. He gripped his rifle hard, trying to control the anger that welled up within him and threatened his ability to keep his composure. He thought of an angry response, tried it in his mind, didn't like it, and thought of different, calmer response.

"Lieutenant Soloman, whether you like it or not, I'm the commanding officer of the crew now. As you said, we have a mission - a mission to transfer this prisoner back to the Fe-Ruqians. That means we need to recapture Him so that when the extraction ship comes, we can take Him with us. Staying near a damaged frigate on an uninhabited moon while the target is free on the same moon does not seem to be the best way to accomplish our mission objectives, wouldn't you agree? We can't leave Him here. The rescue ship will wait for us, especially once Ensigns Roach and Cummings explain where we went. They'll probably send reinforcements to assist if we're not back by the time they arrive. Either way, we still need to capture the target and hold Him until we can get off this moon."

Marshall paused to wait for a response from Soloman. She had stood her ground even though his voice had risen while he was talking, and he feared the others were now listening to their conversation. She was glaring at him, almost defiantly. Quickly sneaking a glance back at the group, he was relieved to see that neither of the other officers had turned their attention to him. In the fading light he could see Dalton and Clone Theore sitting next to each other, quietly eating. The last rays of light were quickly disappearing as the sun drifted below the mountaintops piercing the sky ahead of them. Marshall decided he didn't want to continue any further at night.

"Lieutenant, inform the others that we're going to make camp here. It's getting too dark to travel, and I don't want to risk walking into another nest of those things. And, since you're so concerned about our safety, you have first watch, Lieutenant."

Lieutenant Soloman acknowledged the order and continued to glare at Marshall for a moment before brushing past him and walking over to the other two officers. Marshall watched her walk and absently fingered the trigger on his weapon.

First light came early, with a clear sky brightening quickly with the rising sun. Soloman had finished the first watch, and Marshall had taken the second shift leading into daybreak. The night had been uneventful; only the sporadic sounds of indigenous creatures broke the silence of the darkness. But the solitude had given him time to think. Rather, it gave him time to think about Lieutenant Soloman.

He had been angered by the disrespectful manner in which she addressed him. His mind raced through different possible explanations for her outburst.

He wondered if she was planning to organize a mutiny. Three against one weren't outrageous odds, but it was enough to concern him. He didn't really understand how the other officers felt, but he wouldn't have been surprised to learn that they felt the same as the disrespectful Lieutenant Soloman. If she were to refuse his orders, he wondered if Dalton would do the same. He didn't care what Clone Theore thought; in his mind he was just a clone after all, not worthy of opinion. Still, it was a clone with a weapon. It was an unknown. *He probably wouldn't act without orders from me*, he thought. In any event, his safety was becoming a concern.

His mind shifted through his recent experiences, and it came to one question. *Why was Lieutenant Soloman so afraid to retrieve the Son of God?* Various thoughts flooded his mind. *Perhaps she had some great sin in her past, and was afraid to face Him. Maybe she was just afraid of running into another one of those nests that had killed Ensign Sears. Perhaps she's not Christian.*

That was it, he convinced himself. *She isn't a Christian. Which makes her, what? An atheist? A Satanist? A believer of some other type of religious order?*

What if she's on this mission to kill the Son of God? An assassin, sent by the Fe-Ruqians. Of course, how could I not have seen it before. The way she handled the nest situation. She had fired without a trace of remorse, killing Ensign Sears.

Wait, if she killed Ensign Sears, then she's a murderer. If she's willing to kill part of her own crew, then she's definitely capable of mutiny. I don't have a choice.

Commander Tennison had the same conversation with himself throughout his watch, and each time he came to the same conclusion.

Lieutenant Soloman was dangerous.
Lieutenant Soloman must die.

Marshall stepped lightly across the patches of moss that carpeted the ground, searching for any signs that his crew had noticed his absence in the early morning light. Seeing no sign of fresh footprints in the dirt he had smoothed flat out around each of them, he slowly stepped towards the three as they lay in various positions of sleep. Coming to the sleeping member of the crew, he sat down next to Lieutenant Soloman and nudged her with the butt of his weapon.

"Wake up," he said, glancing over at the other two officers. Her eye's fluttered open, and seeing Marshall so close, she leaned away from him and reached for her weapon.

"Don't worry, nothing's wrong. It's just time to move," he said, smirking slightly at her reaction. He twisted himself up and walked over to the other two officers and nudged them with his boot to wake them. Both awoke and began to pull themselves off of the ground. He watched the three in silence as they mumbled 'good mornings' to one another, each quickly gathering his or her belongings in the faint light.

Within ten minutes, the group was on their way, leaving the makeshift campsite and trudging towards a destination unknown. Marshall started on point, with Lieutenant Soloman bringing up the rear. Thirty minutes into the hike, the natural trail that they had been following came to an abrupt end at a large cluster of dense tree-like vegetation. Marshall indicated for the group to stop, and backtracked towards the other three.

"I can't see far into the vegetation, but it looks like we may be able to pick up this trail, or even a new one, on the other side. We're getting close to His suspected location, based on my calculations, so I'm thinking this is a perfect spot for an ambush or defensive perimeter. Ensign Theore, you'll take point, and head directly into the vegetation. Lieutenant Dalton, you're up next after he gives us the all clear. Lieutenant Soloman, you'll bring up the rear once we've made it through." Marshall looked at each to make sure they understood. Soloman held his gaze longer than the others, and for a moment he thought he detected a hint of suspicion in her expression.

The clone of Ensign Theore moved slowly forward from their position, rifle held up in a defensive firing position as he walked towards the thick vegetation. Dalton scurried across the trail behind him and set himself up in a covering position near some small outcroppings of rock. Marshall and Soloman stayed back, keeping off the trail and out of sight of the advancing Clone Theore.

Marshall listened for any indication of an ambush. Soloman did the same, but continued to glance over at him as if expecting him to say something. The minutes passed, and nothing happened. Marshall nodded at Soloman, and eased himself out onto the trail to see where Ensign Theore was. The clone was just inside the edge of the vegetation, searching for any signs of a trap or ambush. Marshall glanced over at Lieutenant Dalton and whistled, who waved back and started forward towards the vegetation. Marshall was just starting to back off the trail when a hand pushed up against his back, stopping him in place.

"If you're sending Dalton in, you or I need to take his covering position, Commander." Soloman's words were just a whisper in his ear, but firm enough that he didn't even bother looking at her to see her expression. He nodded without looking at her, and scampered across the open area between his current position and Dalton's former one. He knelt into position behind the rock outcropping, never taking his eyes off the back of Lieutenant Dalton. The officer was quickly working his way towards the point of entry that Clone Theore had used. Marshall grimaced as the officer disappeared into the vegetation. Seconds later the scene in front of Marshall exploded noisily into a miasma of flames, smoke, and flying debris.

CHAPTER XXI

The ship lurched back into realspace from the thread, admitting its ancient history. Athes stumbled slightly as the power grid flickered, momentarily cutting the power to the artificial gravity generator. He looked over at Secael, who was seated with eyes shut, still strapped into his jump seat. Glancing at Aedge, he could see the Fe-Ruq soldier had taken to moving about the hold and inspecting star charts on the wall, but didn't seem to mind the sudden end of the thread jump.

Looking around the hold, Athes tried to decipher the class type of the ship they were on. He didn't remember the Fe-Ruqian giving the information out at any point, nor did he remember to search for any information as to what was in the docking well when he had the chance. He couldn't help but feel they had made a mistake in agreeing to this trip. He was having second thoughts, and strongly felt they may have had more control of their destiny without placing their trust in a soldier of the enemy, regardless of what he had said.

By Athes' internal clock, the trip had been a little less than five hours, from departure until now. He could only guess at when they had jumped on a thread by the physical stresses that were evident at the time of the event. Much like when re-entering realspace, the ship had shuddered and the lights dimmed slightly as power was diverted to the equipment necessary to propel the vessel onto a thread. As well as he could tell, they had jumped about thirty minutes into their trip. Even if he was wrong, there was no way he could guess their current location or vector without being on the bridge.

Sergeant Faerre's voice interrupted his musings.

"You never gave me your name." He looked directly at Athes with an expression that indicated it was more than just a statement. Athes glanced up at him, mildly surprised to hear the soldier speak.

"I did not," Athes replied, turning to look at a section of conduit running along the wall. He picked at a piece of ancient insulation flaking off the section in front of him. He followed the piping along the wall with his eyes, and saw that it wrapped around the room and connected to a box built onto a wall near the ceiling.

The hold itself wasn't that large. Athes estimated it was ten meters by ten meters, give or take a meter each way. There were two rows of jump seats, one opposite of the other on either side of the hold. A entrance to the airlock was the main focal point of one of the remaining walls, and an entrance to the remainder of the ship, currently closed, was opposite of the airlock. Athes swiveled in place as he followed more conduit around the room, stopping when his gaze was interrupted by the sight of Aedge staring at him with a frown from across the hold.

"So, are you going to tell me your names or not?" he asked slowly, holding his hands out as if waiting to be given something.

"No," Athes replied, returning the human's gaze. "It is not information that you need to have at this time."

Aedge looked at him incredulously. "I just got you

and your friend here off an enemy world. I think that earns your names," he replied, thumbing a finger towards Secael.

"It is true that you assisted us off-world, however your means are less than honorable, as I understand it. Perhaps you forgot that you essentially threatened us with capture had we not cooperated. I don't view your tactic as honorable, nor deserving of any additional information. I believe our agreement was that we would assist you in reaching our Lord, in exchange for you providing access to a method of departure. We are on our way to help Him, are we not? If so, that should be sufficient for your needs at this point. If so, I believe that we are upholding our end of the agreement, which means you have earned no further information from us. You are still an enemy soldier in our eyes, until you have proven your belief." With that, Athes turned his back on Aedge, half expecting a verbal attack at the least, if not a physical one. The room went silent, and Athes assumed the soldier had given up for now.

"My name is Zenaztalon Secael, son of Rernihaat," the other Shalothan warrior spoke into the silence. "And I am a warrior of God." Athes swung around at the sound of the voice, both surprised and angered by his admission. He clicked loudly in the back of his throat, showing his anger at Secael's willingness to give his name.

Aedge took a step forward towards the still-seated Secael, caught a glance from Athes with his teeth bared, and thought better of it. He nodded instead, and waited for further introductions. Both Secael and he looked to Athes, expecting the second half of the pair's names.

"I am Ronoson Athes, son of Malan. I too am a

warrior of God." He bowed his head slightly towards Aedge, never taking his eyes off the soldier.

"You may call us Athes and Secael. Speak them sparingly." It was Secael who had added this last part, drawing attention back to himself. Aedge only nodded again in response. He turned to Athes and smiled.

"That wasn't so difficult, now was it?" Aedge had barely uttered the words before Athes was upon him, clutching him with one hand and pushing back and up against the nearest wall. Athes slowly pushed the soldier upwards along the wall, until his feet dangled a few centimeters from the floor. Aedge grabbed at the warrior's hand pushing into his chest, failing to relieve the pressure.

"Do not think that you can speak so freely among us, Fe-Ruqian. I would sooner rid myself of your nuisance, however we have an agreement. Be mindful – that agreement does not give you any freedoms or liberties with us. We will take you with us, but we act only as a nazodak herding a jettalon from the field, not as if you are one of our brothers." Athes held him for a few seconds longer, waiting for Aedge to speak. Seeing he wasn't able to breath with the force of his hand on his chest, he let the soldier slide back to the ground.

"Understood," Aedge managed to breath, and stumbled over to the nearest seat, rubbing his chest. Athes walked over to the seat next to Secael and sat down.

"Call the pilot, and have him update us as to our position. We need to begin planning our approach for safe entry into the Shalotha system," Secael ordered. Aedge waited a few moments before moving, then walked towards the entrance to the rest of the ship. The door did not open when he walked up to it.

"Sensors must be down," he muttered to himself. He stepped backwards, then moved towards the door again, but the door did not move. Searching the walls on either side, he saw that there was an old communications interface built into the wall to the right of the door. Stepping up to the unit, he ran his fingers over the interface, seeing how it operated.

"Back away from the door," a voice said over the overhead comm. system. Athes and Secael stood up immediately, looking around for something that could be monitoring them. Aedge backed away from the door, and turned to grab his weapon, stowed under his seat. Secael and Athes each activated their wrist sheaths upon seeing Aedge reach for his weapon.

"Please put your weapons away," the voice overhead said. Secael realized for the first time that the voice was being disguised through distortion. None of the three made a move to disengage their weapons.

"Once you've deactivated your weapons, we can discuss our flight plan," the voice stated. "I will not ask again about the weapons."

Athes suddenly realized what the long conduit was encircling the room. He reached over and slapped his wrist sheath, deactivating it. Secael noticed his actions and did the same. Athes stepped forward and ripped the rifle out of Aedge's hand, and laid it on the ground.

"Thank you. You're either very reasonable, or you see that the hold you're in is configured with a shock ring designed to fell large predators. I didn't anticipate having to use it, then again, I didn't anticipate having Shalothan warriors aboard. Aedge, you will step forward alone and pass through the door. The two Shalothans will sit down. Do it now. Now."

Aedge looked backed at the two Shalothans and

shrugged, then moved forward towards the door. Secael and Athes sat down and watched. The door slid to the side for Aedge as he approached, and quickly shut behind him. Once they were alone, Athes turned to face Secael.

"We are in a trap," Athes whispered.

"How do you know?"

"The shock ring is an old technology used in species transports. Species transports weren't typically fast. I doubt that the Fe-Ruqian would have selected this type of ship for his journey to see our Lord."

"Unless he was planning on capturing Him and keeping him secured in here until he could return Him to Fe-Ruqian space. Or perhaps the Fe-Ruqian is planning on keeping us secure on our trip."

"Either way, our situation has not improved much from Je-Fin. Suggestions?"

"We wait."

Marshall looked up at the figure looming over him. His field of vision was obscured by the face contorted into a mask of horror, soundlessly mouthing something at him while the smoke swirled around in his peripheral vision. He blinked hard a few times, trying to clear his head of the silence. Gradually, sound returned.

"-mmander, are you injured? Commander Tennison, can you hear me! Are you injured? Say something." Marshall realized he was on his back, looking up at his second in command. The visage of Lieutenant Soloman filled his view, but she suddenly began to retreat slowly in size as she pulled away from him and directed her attention towards something further away from them. He tried to roll over to get up, only to be met with Soloman's hand shoving him back to the ground. He glanced up, and saw Soloman bringing her weapon up to bear on an unseen target.

He felt around with his hands splayed to his sides, trying to find his own weapon. Soloman stalked forward out of his view, leaving him with the opportunity to get up off the ground. He rolled over and steadied himself, bracing his arm against the side of the rock outcropping that he had been positioned behind. His weapon lay a few meters away. Marshall looked around to see what Soloman had gone after. She was just entering the gaping hole in the vegetation cluster where the other two officers had been moments earlier.

Staggering to his feet, Marshall gathered up his weapon and followed after Soloman. She had stopped just inside the edge of the blast radius, and was searching the area before moving forward.

He touched his head, and found his hand covered with blood from a wound. He shoulder ached, and a quick look down showed why – debris had flown into his shoulder, puncturing his uniform and cutting the skin.

"Soloman, stop!" Marshall tried to yell, only to have his voice crack. He stumbled forward, quickly regaining his sense of balance with each step he took. He didn't see any sign of the remains of Dalton or Theore, but he surmised that the explosion had spread bits and pieces of them everywhere.

Soloman edged slowly forward. Marshall was just a few meters behind her now, and he himself was now entering the blast area. The fireball created from the explosion had removed much of the organic material from the vegetative cluster. On the fringes of the blast zone, remnants smoked and smoldered, or hung in place, blackened by the blast. The area on the other side of the cluster could be seen now, revealing the trail as it continued to wind up through the crevices of the mountain they were on.

Marshall came to a stop next to Lieutenant Soloman. She was still searching the area around her and ahead on the trail, scanning for something he hadn't seen.

"What is it? What did you see?" he asked. She glanced at him out of the corner of her eye without moving her head. She nodded forward, then hefted her weapon to indicate she wanted him to do the same. He raised his own, not knowing what he was defending himself against. She motioned for him to move away from her as she slowly sidestepped to her left. He moved to his right, leaving a gap of a few meters between them. He watched as she inched forward towards the opposite edge of the cluster. He did the same, assuming that whatever it was that she was tracking was just ahead of them, hiding unseen on the trail.

She knelt down into a firing position just inside the outer edge of the cluster, and trained her weapon on a spot up the trail from where they were situated. Playing along, Marshall did the same on his side of the cluster. Once in position they waited. To Marshall, it seemed hours had passed before Soloman finally lowered her weapon and backed away from the edge of the cluster, retreating to the rock outcropping on the side of the trail. Marshall followed as she silently sat down and leaned back against the rock. Taking a quick look around before seating himself, Marshall leaned his weapon against the rock.

"Care to tell me what you saw?"

Lieutenant Soloman bowed her head forward, then reached for her water supply. She swigged a drink, pausing for a moment before speaking.

"I thought I saw a Shalothan warrior on the other side of the blast. I couldn't make anything out for sure, but it wouldn't have surprised me. They wait to confirm their kills, or so I'm told."

Marshall smiled inwardly at her statement.

"So, did you actually see something, or was it just blowing smoke?" he asked in a joking manner. She snapped her head up and glared at him.

"Do you not realize that you were almost killed? Remember what I said about Shalothans probably being on-world to defend Him? They'll defend Him at all costs. I'm surprised that this little ambush is all we've seen so far. I would have assumed they would have tried to stop us prior to now. We must be getting pretty close to the location."

"Maybe they're only going to defend an attack on Him. I doubt He would have them attack us."

"Sending two armed soldiers up a trail towards Him could be interpreted as advancing on their position, wouldn't you agree? Regardless, we need to figure out how we're going to continue, if that's what you're determined to do."

"We need to capture our target. What other choice do we have? Go back to the *Alaurian Spirit*? Sit here until He decides to come down and see if the ambush worked? We can rest a few minutes more, then we continue on. At least with just the two of us, we're more likely to sneak up on them."

Lieutenant Soloman looked at him silently for a few heartbeats.

"It makes sense now," she said matter-of-fact.

"What makes sense?"

"You. Your decisions. Your thought process. You're flawed."

"What the hell are you talking about Lieutenant?"

"Captain Pollard never got the chance to tell you, did she? Hmmm. This should be interesting. What did you think about your clone?"

Marshall didn't answer. He just stared into Soloman's face, searching for the reasons behind her question.

"Captain Pollard ordered testing done on the clones as soon as we returned, mostly as a precautionary measure due to the nature of the acquisitions. Do you know what the testing encompasses, Commander?"

Marshall shook his head, wondering where she was going with this.

"The tests that were conducted were supposed to verify that we had taken the right clones, and that they weren't contaminated. As I'm sure you're aware, having a bad match isn't the most optimal solution for the purposes that we would have used them for. During the tests, some interesting information came out." She stopped and took another drink of water.

"The med droids processed your bio-info and compared it to that of your supposed clone. Guess what? It didn't match."

"How did we target the wrong clone?" Marshall asked incredulously.

"We didn't. The genetic sequencing of the clone and you are identical. Problem is, your genetic sequencing had the same additional gene key in your DNA as your clone."

Marshall looked puzzled, not understanding for a

moment what she meant. She watched him as he began to comprehend the meaning.

"That's right *Marshall*, you're not the master copy. You have the clone ID key in your DNA. You're just a clone, same as the poor soul that we picked up."

It had been an hour since Aedge had left when a voice piped in overhead.

"Please remain seated as the other passenger returns." The door opened, and Aedge walked in, smiling.

"Seems we have a bit of a problem," he began, taking a seat next to Secael. "My pilot wasn't aware that I was going to bring Shalothans on board. She thought I was going alone, so having three on board is making her a bit nervous. Because of that, you guys will be staying here for the rest of the trip." He looked from one to the other, then back to Secael.

"Where are we now?" Secael asked.

"We're on a trade route headed towards the Aormy sector. We'll divert from there on a thread into the Shalothan sector. I assume you'll have to get us clearance in?"

"Why are we going so far out of the way," Athes asked, ignoring the question.

"Apparently there are some military build-ups taking place along the Fe-Ruq borders, and they're monitoring all threads. Our pilot has doubts about being able to get us through without inspection, so we've turned around. We've doubled back, and should be out of Fe-Ruq space in another twelve hours. After that, it'll be a few more days before we reach the Shalothan system. There is one problem." Aedge paused for effect. "My pilot doesn't want to continue on with both of you on board. We're docking at the first chance we get in the Aormy sector, and one of you will be getting off there. She doesn't want two of you together for the rest of the trip, especially after seeing what Athes did to me." He looked over at Athes and smirked. "So figure out which one wants to stay, and let me know."

Athes and Secael glared at him, and Athes began to click slowly in his throat. Secael laid a hand on Athes to quiet him, then dropped his gaze to the floor.

"Athes will be staying," he said. "He can provide the clearance necessary to get you into the system. Will I be permitted access to funds for transport to Shalotha?"

Aedge snorted. "I doubt it. You take only what you brought with you. I didn't plan on having to pay for a second fare to Shalotha, so you're on your own. "

"Do you know what the first available location is?" Secael asked.

"Rdoubhe, or one of her moons, most likely a moon."

"One of the moons is very mountainous. I believe Eurgea is the name. That would be an optimal place to set down and depart without being noticed. Inform your pilot of this moon, and she will see that it would be a safe location."

"How do you know so much about the moons of Rdoubhe?"

"It was a staging point for advancing into Fe-Ruq space during one of the last campaigns that I participated in. I would at least be familiar with the territory and local inhabitants." *And there are ways for me to contact Shalotha from there*, he thought.

"I'll let our pilot know. Until then, sit tight." He stood up to go, and gave each of the warriors a small smile. "Hopefully we'll find your Lord soon enough, so I can start asking my questions." With that he turned and left.

The remainder of the trip out of Fe-Ruq space took longer than expected, and the entry coming off the thread was as rough as it was jumping onto it. Secael and Athes hadn't spoken much since Aedge had informed them of the pilot's acceptance of Secael's request to be left at Eurgea. Both were aware that they were being watched, and neither wanted to give away any more information. In their limited conversation, they had managed to communicate in code with each other and had planned for the landing on Eurgea. They had agreed that when Aedge came to let Secael out, Athes would rush the entrance to the remainder of the ship, and Secael would pull Aedge deeper into the hold. Their plan was to take command of the ship, imprison the pilot and Aedge in the hold, and fly back to Shalothan space direct on a thread.

The overhead voice announced that they were descending for landing, giving Secael and Athes the signal they had been waiting for. Both remained in their seats, but sat at the ready for Aedge to come in.

The ship touched down hard, jarring both in their seats. The lights dimmed for a moment, then came back on full strength. Athes thought through the plan again in his mind, preparing himself for the advance on the pilot. The overhead voice spoke again.

"We have docked on Eurgea. You are now free to stand. Sergeant Faerre will be taking Secael off ship shortly." Mechanisms within the walls clicked and began to hum, setting Athes on edge as he prepared to move.

"I do apologize for not telling you this sooner," the voice continued, "but I will be ensuring that both of you do not escape. I can assure you that the shock is not lethal." Athes and Secael turned to face each other, realizing instantly what the voice had meant. Neither had a chance to move before a large hum filled their ears, and the shock ring activated, pitching them into unconsciousness.

Marshall was paralyzed in thought, staring at his second in command with his mouth gaping open, afraid to repeat what she had stated for fear of making it true. Lieutenant Soloman faced him with a cold look on her face, accented by a smirk forming on her lips.

"You lie," he finally managed, drawing in a breath with his words. She cocked her head and looked back at him.

"Do I, Marshall?"

"Get up Lieutenant," he ordered. He stood up and grabbed his weapon.

"Is that an order, *sir*," she asked with a sneer. She reached for her own weapon while she stood, leaning one hand against the rock for balance. He kicked her weapon away and brought his rifle up to bear on Soloman.

"I get it. Captain Pollard is dead, and I'm next in line? I don't think so. We have a mission to accomplish, and whether you think I'm a clone or not, we, the two of us, have orders from our commanding officers that we need to follow. Should you choose not to follow mine, you'll be in direct violation of a directive from senior USN officers. I warn you now that I will take that as a form of mutiny, and will act accordingly." He held his rifle up at Soloman, keeping her squarely in his sights. She backed up a step and slowly raised her hands.

"Commander Tennison, I am going to slowly turn around and head back to the *Spirit*. I would like you to come with me. We don't have to tell anyone else about the tests."

Tennison was jolted with a thought. *The records are still intact on the Spirit, but Soloman is the only living officer who knows. No one has to know.*

Tennison pulled the trigger and blasted Soloman from less than three meters away as she was turning, knocking her to the ground. Her uniform smoldered around the edges of the wound on her torso, and blood started to seep out where the skin had not been cauterized from the blast. He knelt down to check her pulse, and found her still alive, but unconscious. He grabbed her weapon and took the power pack out, and stuck it in his own pocket. *Better to have extra juice*, he thought.

Tennison turned and began his march up the hill. He didn't look back.

CHAPTER XXII

Blood streamed from the wounds on Marshall's forehead and shoulder, as the Commander of the ill-fated *Alaurian Spirit* strode up the hillside towards the Son of God as He sat under the tree. To his right, the hill slowly rolled into a meadow, with the tall grasses whispering in the breeze. To his left, the hill merged with a rocky outcropping, forming the base of the mountain that rose to an undetermined height. Glancing back, there was still no sign of protectors of the man on the hill. This would be the end, here and now. He would not, could not let this war go on any further. He would make this man understand that He needed to use His power to help them all. To save them all.

At about one hundred meters away, Commander Tennison lifted his rifle with his left hand, and pushed the butt of the weapon into his left shoulder. He cupped his right hand under the barrel, and squinted down the sight, bringing the barrel to bear upon the image on the man in the white clothes. It came naturally to him now, the attack positions. His walk started to slow, his body started to slip closer to the ground. He slid his trigger finger over the mechanism that he had used so many times over the past few days. Too many times it seemed. The man on the hill stood still, gazing down at him.

"Don't move!" Marshall yelled. The order itself

was preposterous, based on who this man was. He could just assuredly go straight up into the heavens before Marshall had time to blink. As he neared the hilltop, he suddenly sensed that this was very familiar to him. The way the man stood below the branches of the tree, the whispering of the wind, the angle of the sun and the shadows it created. It was a perfect example of déjà vu, but the feeling gained strength as he ascended the hill. Almost as quickly as he felt it, Marshall realized it wasn't familiar to *him,* but rather his clone. Fifteen meters out, the man on the hill quickly raised His right hand towards Marshall. Instinctively, Marshall squeezed off a shot that hit the man's raised hand dead center in the palm. The man did not flinch, and Marshall was surprised to see that the man did not make any further movements. He stopped at about seven meters out from the man he was hunting.

"You. Are you really the person everyone thinks you are?" Marshall demanded. As he waited for the answer, he could almost sense a feeling of giddiness and excitement at what the answer would reveal.

"I am who you say I am," the man replied. "What do you say?" The blood from His wound streamed down His hand, now outstretched before Him as if asking Marshall to physically place the answer in His palm.

"I have been told that you are the Son of God, come down from Heaven to save us. Yet, war has consumed us for centuries, and you refused to help until now?" Marshall could feel anger crawling into the back of his throat. He gripped his weapon a bit tighter, and realigned his aim on the man from his chest to his head. "We were near extinction, yet you did NOTHING!

You've let us down every time we needed you the most. You've declined or ignored all of our pleas for help. You were letting us die!"

Marshall could feel his hands starting to tremble with rage. More disconcerting to him was that, despite everything he had believed and thought, he wasn't feeling overcome with awe. He didn't feel warmth in his chest, much like he imagined his mother and father had taught him. He didn't feel reverence for the figure in front of him. Now, at this moment of truth, the moment that he had sought for the past year, the feelings he had for this man were rage and contempt.

"I cannot help you," the man replied to Marshall. "It is as it has always been. Man has brought this destruction upon himself. The warnings have been numerous throughout the ages. And now, the reign of man is nearing its end, with the dawn of a new day at hand. My Kingdom shall rule for one thousand years.

Marshall listened to the words, but something gnawed at his mind. He started to hear words in his head, words that were disturbing to him. *You are not of mankind. You are an abomination. The Grace of God shall never fall upon your shoulders.*

CHAPTER XXIII

The words repeated softly on his head, and he glanced left and right to see if there was someone hidden off to the sides of the hill.

"There is no one here," the Son of God said. "There is no man present on this hill."

Marshall struggled to understand what he meant. How could the two of them be standing here, yet the wording of the statement suggested they were not there?

Marshall took a step closer to the Son of God, and looked into His eyes. Pools of blackness defined them, with softness around the edges and ageless look. It was the first time he had actually *looked* into His eyes.

"I am a man. You cannot deny that. You may be the Son of God, but there is at least one man on this hill." The man in white looked back upon Marshall with a gaze that reflected sadness. The voices in Marshall's head continued repeating, getting louder and more forceful with each repetition.

"What is it you seek of your Lord," the Son of God suddenly asked Marshall. Taken aback at the bluntness of the question, Commander Tennison began to feel words forming in his mouth, words that were not his own.

"I seek the Grace of God, and my place in Heaven," the words in Marshall's mouth came out. Marshall stood slack-jawed, surprised at the admission. He had always been a believer in Christ, and had practiced his faith when he could. The battles he had participated in over the past few years had brought about a renewed faith in Christ, and he had prayed often during battles, praying for deliverance should he die, praying for the souls of those lost in battle. Yet, he couldn't recall ever *stating* that he desired the Grace of God.

"You will be denied the Grace of God," the Son of God said. The statement rocked Marshall, and he felt himself roll back on the heels of his feet. He stared at the being that had uttered the words, and subconsciously lowered his weapon slightly.

"What?" he managed to utter.

"You will be denied the Grace of God. So it has been foretold. You are not man."

"How? Why?" Marshall's questions died off as they came out of his mouth. He suddenly felt very lightheaded.

"Sit down," the man commanded in a soft voice. Marshall complied, slinging his weapon over his shoulder and kneeling down before the Him. The voice in his head stopped, and in its place was the voice of the Son of God.

"The Gates of Heaven permit souls that have been gifted the Grace of God to pass into the eternal paradise. Each man has a soul, and the actions of that man during his life determine how Judgment is passed down on him. You will not receive Judgment.

The voice continued speaking, and as Marshall looked at the Son of God, he realized that the words weren't coming directly out of His mouth. The Son of God continued to look at Marshall with a sad, almost pitiful gaze. The voice in Marshall's mind continued.

"The Grace of God cannot be given to a sin."

Marshall caught himself waiting for the rest of the word *sinner,* yet the voice ended with the word sin. How could he be denied for sinning? Was he such a horrible person as to be banished to hell? The voice answered his unspoken question.

"Neither can you warm yourself on the fires of hell, for you are not man. You are a sin of mankind, the result of sinful devices. You are an abomination to Christ. You were created by man, but not as a man."

No sooner had the voice finished the words when horror washed over Marshall as the meaning of the words became realization. He wasn't being denied the Grace of God because he was a horrible human being. He was being denied because he *wasn't* a human being. He was a clone.

"No. Noooo. NOOOOOOO!" Marshall screamed a guttural cry, animalistic in its purest form, and quickly stood.

"You can't do this to me! It's not my fault! I didn't have a choice! If it's how you say it is, then how can I be denied for something that I never had a chance to change?" Marshall subconsciously raised his weapon and brought it to bear on the Son of God. He did not move, but continued to look on His hunter with pity.

"I am NOT merely a *thing*! I have a soul! I have feelings. I love, I hate. I AM A MAN!" Marshall was screaming the words out now, somehow believing the louder they were, then more likely that this man would believe him. He began to circle to his right, left foot over right, keeping aim at the man's head.

"What happens when I die then?" Marshall asked more quietly. The feeling of dread began to creep into his stomach and chest, tightening the muscles to the point that he began to have a difficult time breathing.

"Nothingness. You will not witness Heaven nor Hell. There will be nothing."

Something snapped inside of Marshall. Not having Heaven was a horror that he suddenly couldn't bear the thought of. But having nothing, just an infinite darkness, brought a terror that welled up in his throat and threatened to strangle him. He fought back tears as he began to tremble.

"This *can't* be," Marshall said, drawing out emphasis on the feeling. Thoughts raced through his mind. His hands trembled as he circled to the back of the Son of God in front of him.

Marshall came to a stop directly behind the man. He raised the barrel of his weapon to press against the back of His skull, into the mane of hair that covered the His head.

"Is there nothing that can be done?" Marshall asked, prepared for the inevitable. He braced himself for the word *no*, like a man bracing himself against a punch that he knew would hit him. The Son of God tilted his head slightly and began to speak softly.

"To earn His love, and to show to my Father that you deserve to have your place in the afterlife, there are things you must do to demonstrate your devotion. There are other creatures such as you, Marshall. Creatures that have suffered the same wrongs and slights that have kept you from reaching Heaven. You must unite them, and lead them against the sinners who have offered you life without redemption. You must show that you are as worthy in life and death as any sentient being that was molded by the Creator's hands.

To do that, you must be the one that brings the thousand-year Kingdom to the galaxy. You must be the cause of the fires that scorch and cleanse the landscape in preparation for the great Kingdom. You must be our chosen warrior.

Marshall listened to what the Son of God was saying. He lowered his weapon slightly. Marshall was confused for a moment. He heard what the Son of God had just said, yet it wasn't fully understood. He thought about just accepting his fate for a moment, but his faith prevented him from fading into oblivion.

"Forgive me, as I'm not sure I understood what you said. Are you saying that I need to wage war on sentient beings in order to earn my place in Heaven?" Marshall had lowered his weapon almost halfway, and stepped a few paces back from the being in front of him. He watched as the Son of God slowly turned to face him.

"It is as you say Marshall. For you to be redeemed and accepted into the Kingdom, you must go forth and cast your judgment upon those that created you. They must understand what their sins have cost you. It is your only chance for a place in the Kingdom. They must pay for their sins in fire before they can take their place with God."

Marshall suddenly felt that he understood. He was being asked to bring a new age of crusades to the galaxy. He was selected by Christ himself as the general of His Holy forces. Feeling a renewed sense of life and purpose, Marshall stood a bit taller and felt more energized than he had in days.

"Come forward so that I may consecrate you into my legion."

Marshall stepped forward towards the Son of God, and allowed Him to lay His hand upon his head. The man placed the tips of His index finger and end finger on Marshall's forehead, near the top at the base of his hairline. He slowly rubbed His two middle fingers up and down on his forehead as He began speaking.

"I command you to serve in my legion, and lead my armies against our enemies, and to bring the reign of my Kingdom to this galaxy. In my service, you shall be known as Asreh. Do you give yourself freely to me after your service has ended?"

Marshall suddenly felt warm, and the two points that the Son of God was touching began to burn. *This must be what it feels like to be touched by God*, Marshall thought. He could feel himself starting to become light-headed, and shifted his weight to keep his balance.

"I do." Marshall's eyesight was starting to dim, and he felt very disoriented.

"Then go forth and wage war on my behalf." The voice sounded strange to Marshall, but he didn't have time to consider the reasons why before he succumbed to the darkness.

Marshall fell to the ground, slipping out from under the outstretched hand of the being. It looked down with burning eyes and a wide smile.

"Go forth and do my bidding," the Beast said to the still body of Marshall. With that, the creature sometimes known as the Old Gentleman turned and walked down the path that Asreh had come up.

EPILOGUE

Commander Apxlus knelt in his temporary reflection chamber aboard the *Nowrimo's Revenge*. He could not overcome the feeling of dread that was taking hold of his mind. He had struck out against his superior officer, and in his single-minded desire to take the Son of God back to Shalotha, had killed his own people in God's name. He believed that his actions had always been in the name of God's service, yet he could not fathom why this man, the one claiming to be the Son of God, would allow his own people to sow the seeds of discord among the Shalothan people. Weren't the Shalothans His chosen ones? How could He let this happen? Even now, several messages had been sent from Primary Radael, praising Apxlus for his destruction of what Radael termed 'General Tesuh's demonic aspirations'. Was this the path of God's people, or were his actions taking him down a path that served another more than it served his Lord? The recent events suggested that if this was indeed the Second Coming, than it was not as glorious as promised. His arrival seemed to be fracturing the delicate peace in the galaxy, not strengthening it.

Apxlus stood and walked out of the room and headed towards the cockpit. He knew what he had to do. Despite everything that he was feeling, he still felt a sense of duty to his Primary. And his Primary's orders had been very specific. Bring the Savior back to Shalotha, and ensure that none of the warriors could ever speak of it.

He stepped into the cockpit and moved behind Moak, who was sitting at one of the pilot consoles. Moak clicked a greeting in his throat at the sight of his commander, and bowed his head towards Apxlus.

"Commander, the *Guardian's Gate* reports that the survivors of the USF vessel that crashed on the moon have been located. They await your orders."

"How many survived the crash?" Apxlus asked.

"Six."

Apxlus looked at Moak, surprised to hear how few survived.

"Had they evacuated the area, or were they stationed with the wreckage?"

Moak ran his fingers along the communication control surface, manipulating the data on his viewscreen to reveal the answers.

"Four were still with the wreckage. Two uninjured human males that were on sentry duty; two injured male humans, one in critical condition, and one in some type of hibernation chamber; one injured female human and one uninjured male human, the captain, were found near our Lord. Our Lord has expressed His desire to have the captain of the vessel accompany Him. "

Apxlus sat down in the command chair and thought for a moment. Once again, he felt he was making a decision that did not feel entirely right. *Perhaps another deception by our enemy*, he thought.

"Have the ground team retrieve Christ and the captain of the USF vessel. Leave the others for the USF rescue teams. Inform me when all are aboard, activate the IDMD and set a course for Shalotha. I will contact

Primary Radael personally to inform him of our impending arrival." With that, Apxlus exited the cockpit and retired to his reflection chamber to pray for guidance.

The last thing Captain Dante Nicolai saw was the bright flash of a beam weapon filling his field of vision as it hit a forward portion of his ship. He had reflexively closed his eyes and tensed his body, preparing for the inevitable dissolution of his flesh and bones into atoms, scattered across the vastness of space.

The pain did not arrive.

After a few heartbeats, Dante opened his eyes and looked around. His crew was still and silent, each looking at one another, and he did not know if the eerie quiet that permeated the bridge deck was a result of shock, or the beginnings of the afterlife.

A quiet beeping from the navigation console broke the silence. Releasing a breath he had not realized he had been holding, Captain Nicolai stood and brushed his hands over his hair, smoothing it back with both hands.

"Lieutenant Anderson, send an encoded message to the fleet headquarters as soon as we are back in normal space." Dante paused to ensure the officer had time to key up the communications database.

"Shalothans have launched an offensive against USF and Fe-Ruq forces. *Alaurian Spirit* and *Eccentric* are lost. *Seraphim* damaged. Fe-Ruq escort vessels destroyed. Shalothan forces retain possession of target. Repeat. Shalothan forces retain possession of target. Awaiting orders. Nicolai out."

Captain Nicolai confirmed the message, and retired to his stateroom to assess the damage reports that had started to file in. He realized that he had just survived the opening salvo of the newest chapter of the Crusades.

The Shalothans had started a war.

Secael awoke to a view of a foreign night sky, with a frigid air blowing across his body. He took a quick inventory of his body, and realized that he was relatively healthy, except for a relentless pain in his head. He sat up slowly, and discovered he was in the middle of a desolate area, apparently during a sleep cycle. He didn't recognize the place as Eurgea. He scanned the horizon for any sign of civilization, and saw nothing. He was cold, but it was more from the air blowing than the actual temperature. In the blackness of night the landscape appeared to be mostly rock, with very few features in any direction. Next to him lay his staff, and he still wore his wrist sheath. He looked for Rdoubhe in the sky, and could not find it. *I wonder if I'm even on one of Rdoubhe's moons*, he thought. He stood, and surveyed the entire area. Picking out the closest land feature by the size of blackness created in the darkness, he began walking towards it.

Survival has to be my first priority, he thought.

"God help me."

Athes awoke to a view of the passenger holding area, with his hands and arms secured to a seat. He looked down and saw that his wrist sheath had been removed, and neither it nor his staff was within view. He tested his restraints, and quickly discovered that they were tethers used for holding down much larger objects. He let his muscles slack and he leaned back in the seat. Aedge's voice came over the comm system overhead.

"Athes, it's good to see that you're awake. I started to worry. You've been out more than a standard day. We're close to entering the Shalothan system, so you'll be needed within the hour. Oh, by the way, I want to let you know that if you make any attempt to keep us from entering Shalothan space, or should you attempt to take the ship, you'll never find out where Secael was left. I suggest you get us to see your Lord as soon as possible, if you want Secael to live to see your Lord in this life as well."

Athes clicked slowly in his throat. *Your day of judgment is coming, Aedge*, Athes promised in silence.

Commander Tennison awoke to the sun shining on his face, and the Son of God out of his immediate field of vision. Rolling over to his knees, his head immediately began to ache, and he thought he might pass out. He kept his head down, focusing on the ground beneath his hands and knees. He didn't know if he had been unconscious for seconds, minutes, hours, or days. He barely remembered what had happened, and not all of his memories were clear.

He remembered the Son of God saying something to him about serving in his kingdom. What was it he was supposed to do? The fog swirling in his head parted slightly, revealing the answer. *Lead his armies against his enemies.*

He lifted his head to look around, and saw two Shalothans standing ten meters away, watching him intently. Between them was the man who had commanded him to lead his armies. His skin appeared darker than he had remembered. *Is his hair black now, or is that a trick of the light?* he wondered. The man in the middle motioned towards him and splayed His hands out in front of Him, palms upwards. Marshall noticed that there was no sign of the wound on His hand from before.

"Asreh, Archlord of my Legion, rise and serve," He commanded. The ache in his head subsided, and he suddenly felt a surge of strength and energy. Marshall pushed himself up and stood to face the trio before him.

"I am ready to serve, Master," Marshall heard himself say, almost as if someone else was speaking for him. The two Shalothans dropped to one knee and knelt before Marshall.

"Escort the Archlord to your vessel. You will take us to your home world immediately. We must begin our campaign of truth as soon as possible. Our time grows short with each passing day." His new Master turned on his heel and began walking away from Marshall. Asreh, as he was now known, stepped forward towards the two Shalothan warriors, who stood and began to escort him in the direction that his Master had gone. In his mind, a thought passed into consciousness, a seed planted by his Lord that he could water and grow into reality. His new role would serve the truth, his truth, the truth of the clones. An image swept into his mind's eye. He saw himself in some unknown future, clothed in white, leading the clones to their righteous place among the universe. His power was an extension of his Lord's will. This future version of himself demanded a new title, one befitting his responsibility in his service to his Lord, and the directive that he only now remembered receiving. *You must unite them, and lead them against the sinners who have offered you life without redemption.*

Asreh, Archangel of the Soulless.

For an early look at the next novel in the ENEMY
CALLING series, turn the page to read an excerpt from
the forthcoming

ENEMY CALLING:
DECEPTION
By Erik Bilicki

A continuation of the saga of Apxlus and his brethren
as the newest round of the galactic Crusades begin.

SAMPLE CHAPTER

The sky had brightened within hours and the sun –
whichever star held that position for the particular
celestial body that Secael was marooned on – quickly
rose to a position of prominence in the sky.

One of the first things Secael noticed about this
world was that the rotation cycle was very short. Just in
the recent time he had been conscious, he estimated that
he had already witnessed half of the solar body's
rotation cycle, with the system star already high
overhead.

The second thing Secael noticed was that the
atmosphere of this world was tinged with a yellowish
haze. The color of the atmosphere gave the landscape
the appearance of having some sickly disease that
caused the entire world to be jaundiced. Secael was
quietly thankful that the wake cycle was so short on this
planet. The constant appearance was sickening to him,
and he wished for the sleep cycle to come quickly.

The warrior continued to hike towards the nearest
geological formation he could make out. From where
he first had become conscious, the formation had
appeared to be a relatively small rock cluster. As the
time passed, he began to realize that the formation was
much larger than he had anticipated, which both gave

him hope and alarmed him at the same time. His hope was that a formation of such size on a body with a relatively flat topography would make an ideal location for a spaceport or small colony for anyone who scouted the planet. The alarm was that such a location also provided the tenants, should there be some sort of outpost, an unobstructed view of the surrounding terrain. For Secael, it meant that if any hostile groups were present, they would have more than enough time to prepare for his arrival.

He trudged on towards the formation for a few more standard hours, half expecting to see a patrol dash out from some hidden outpost, bent on preventing the intruder from approaching their location.

The sun set, and Secael marched on. By his estimation, he had been awake for about twelve standard hours. He guessed that the full rotation cycle for this planet was only sixteen to seventeen standard hours, which left him precious little time to make an advance on the target he had been fixated on since his arrival. He weighed the benefits of breaking into a light run to cover more ground while it was dark out, but quickly decided against it once he considered he hadn't seen any water since he awoke.

He couldn't see much in the darkness, and there was no moon to provide any light. Only the distant twinkling of the stars high above provided any light whatsoever. He continued towards his destination, now discernible in the darkness only by the black area on the horizon that blocked out the lights of the stars. It was growing larger, but it still didn't appear that close.

He focused his eyes on the blackness, trying to make out any features, when a column of light streamed out of the top of the formation, followed by what appeared to be a plume of smoke or gas of some type.

Secael immediately stopped moving and crouched down. He didn't know if what he had just witnessed was the precursor to a defense against his approach, or a scheduled release or venting of gases from an unseen facility buried in the rock. He knelt down on one knee and placed a hand on the ground. Surprisingly he could feel it vibrating slightly.

He looked around, scanning the horizon for any sign of an approaching ground vehicle. The only thing he could see was the yellow-tinged stars and the blackness of the horizon as it crept up to meet the sky. Looking back towards his destination, he could still see the gases venting into the atmosphere from the formation, and only now could hear a low rumble coming from the general direction of the rock.

He slowly rose to his feet, continuously scanning for any sign that his presence had been detected. Deciding that it was worth the risk, Secael broke into a dead run and headed for the patch of blackness on the horizon. He estimated he was still a few kilometers from the base, and hoped that he could make it without detection. The gases he had witnessed venting left him no doubt that it was not a natural phenomena. Especially not with the column of light that preceded the event.

As he ran, he split his attention between watching for any sign of something or someone approaching him, and what he was running towards. He knew the galaxy was full of innumerable mechanical devices that had been created throughout the ages, but he couldn't recall anything as unique as this on Rdoubhe or Eurgea during his past assignments. That led his train of thought back to his original question – *where am I?*

He closed the gap quickly, and still saw no sign of life save for the event he had witnessed a short time ago. The pain in his head began to return, and he wondered if it was from his lack of water, the running, or the atmosphere he was breathing. He gave no thought to potential after-effects from being on the transport ship; he assumed that they had merely stunned him, which wouldn't cause recurring effects such as headaches.

Soon Secael encountered a pungent smell in the air. The smell hit him almost as if it was physically moving across the landscape. His sensitive nostrils recoiled and closed at the stench, and he fought back a natural reflex to turn away. He couldn't remember smelling something so terribly strong since his youth spent running in the sulfur mines on Shalotha.

The sulfur mines on Shalotha.

The memory sent a shock through his system as he recognized the pungent odor that was assaulting him. Whatever was being vented into the atmosphere had a sulfuric base to it, as the noxious smell revealed.

He forced himself to continue forward, struggling to recall all of the details he had learned about Rdoubhe and her moons during previous mission briefings. Eurgea had been the body with the most detail provided to him, at least from what he could remember.

Sulfur. Venting. Steam.

He stopped in his tracks and stared at the black monstrosity before him. Burane. The moon Burane. If this was Burane, why couldn't he see Rdoubhe in the sky?

The information on Burane began to reemerge from some place deep in his memory. He paced in a circle, trying to will his memory to divulge the information he sought. His memory did not fail him.

The smallest of the moons of Rdoubhe, Burane originally was a lifeless ball of rock with a thin atmosphere that was gravity captured in an elliptical orbit. No known indigenous life. No valuable natural commodities or mineral deposits. No water.

Secael stopped again and looked up at the shadow of gases billowing into the sky. There couldn't be any natural explanation for the expulsion of gas. Whatever was creating and releasing the gases from inside the several-hundred meter tall rock formation was extraterrestrial to this moon.

Pain still causing his head to throb, Secael slapped his wrist sheath and balanced his staff in his other hand. He decided to approach the formation as if it were an enemy outpost. He couldn't tell exactly how far away he was in the darkness, but he estimated there was another kilometer or two left between him and the base of the rock.

Besides his destination in the near distance, there wasn't anything for Secael to use for cover as he advanced. His approach would be straight and deliberate, and he hoped that whoever or whatever detected him would detain and ask questions, rather than eliminate threats without asking.

He moved forward another eight hundred meters at a slow pace, staying alert for any sign of defenses activating. The venting slowed to a wisp, and then there was nothing visible to his unaided sight. The stench began to dissipate, but his headache seemed to get worse.

He estimated he was about a kilometer away when he heard a faint sound coming from the general direction of the rock. He crouched down and listened carefully to the sound. It sounded like the low hum of a shield generator powering on.

He broke into a sprint towards the rock. If a defense shield was being brought online, he wouldn't have much of a chance of getting closer than he was now. The unknown was how far out the shield would extend. It was possible he could be inside the protective circle already, but more likely was the shield would project mere meters off the surface of the rock. Depending on how long the actual shield generator had been powered down, it could be several minutes before the shield was operational.

He covered another hundred meters before the first flashes of weapons fire rained down upon him. The first two bursts missed badly, but the third was zeroed in on him. He barely managed to keep his balance as the blast tore into the ground in front of him, sending him diving away to his left, sprawling onto his stomach.

That's not an anti-personnel blaster, he thought as he jumped back up to run.

He began zigzagging his way across the open ground in an effort to keep the blaster operator from tracking him easily. A few more blasts managed to come close over the next few hundred meters, spraying him with shards of superheated rock and dust, but Secael continued to successfully evade until he was close enough that he passed the inside edge of the blaster's range.

He reached the base and leaned against the rock to rest for a moment. He risked a look towards the general direction of where the weapons fire had originated from, but couldn't see anything in the darkness. The whining sound he had heard before was now gone, and he suspected it had more to do with the heavy blaster being powered up more than it was a shield generator. Based on the power of the blasts, he guessed the weapon was a military-grade weapon for use on space-based battle cruisers. It certainly wasn't designed for pinpointing singular biological attackers. Whoever was inside the rock was expecting an attack from a space-going vessel, not from the ground.

Secael looked to his left and then right, scanning both directions for an easy way up the face. From what he could see in the limited starlight, the surface was craggy and pocked.

More weapons burst suddenly stuttered against the surface above him, sending him diving to the ground. He rolled over and returned fire towards the general direction of his attacker. He couldn't actually see anyone or anything, but he could target the general area that the bursts were emitting from.

He fired off a few more bursts and rolled himself towards the bottom of the rock, along the edge where the ground met the vertical surface. Twisting himself onto his stomach, he used his elbows and knees to crawl along the base away from the source of the weapons fire. He wasn't sure if his attacker was descending, and he didn't want to be caught without cover.

The edge tracked along the ground in an uneven, natural way, cutting in and out, creating natural cover for Secael at time, and thrusting him out into his attacker's firing line of sight at other times. His attacker hadn't advanced though, and the weapons bursts had stopped.

He had crawled about a hundred meters along the base when he came across a ledge that had been carved into the rock. The ledge was only two feet wide, and continued up the face at a steep angle. Following it with his eyes as best he could in the darkness, he could tell that it curved up and away from his attacker, and would provide him with an easier route to the top. He crawled up onto the ledge and pressed himself up against the rock as he steadied himself on the flat part of the ledge.

He looked back towards the general direction of where his attacker had been, and not seeing anything, he concentrated on navigating the steep ledge.

"Let us see what there is to protect," he said to himself.

Printed in the United States
69713LV00001B/18